Cheating Like Breathing

Cheating Like Breathing

M M Ryan

MaRyn Enterprises LLC

PART ONE

"I don't need *you*," the old woman snarled. Her body twisted, hanging on and off the bed. She'd dragged herself to the restroom, refusing to use the walker that rested against the wall, and was now struggling to pull the lower half of her heavy frame back onto the bed. "Go away —get on about your business, and I'll tend to mine."

"Just what business do you have, Aunt Sarah?" Brenda, the younger woman who was also her caregiver, said. With a hand on her hip, she peered down at the older woman, whose legs were stiff and weak from lack of use. It would have been easy for her to lean over and help her into a sitting position, but she held back, never knowing when her feisty aunt would decide to throw a punch.

Watching the woman struggle, Brenda shook her head—*wisdom comes with age, huh? The old woman was a fool when she was young and is...*

"Get out of here now!" Sarah yelled, then grabbed a plate from the tray near her bed. It contained the remnants of that morning's breakfast. Awkwardly she launched it at Brenda, who jumped aside in time. The plate smacked the wall then broke as it hit the floor, leaving on the powder blue surface a lumpy, yellow, and white mélange of cold grits and scrambled eggs.

Brenda's eyes popped open. The old woman was stronger than she looked. "You ornery old bat! You're going to clean this up."

"That's what I pay you for. Now I said get out of here." Sarah laughed, and though she was still in a gangly position on the bed, her mood had brightened, nothing like giving Brenda a little hell to get her day started off right.

Brenda stomped from the room, slammed the door then took a deep breath as she leaned against it. *LORD, I know I shouldn't have said that... I'll apologize to her later when she's in a better mood—once her pain medication kicks in.* She then slapped her forehead and muttered, "I forgot to give her the pain pill." She loathed to go back into that room, but if Aunt Sarah missed her morning pain medication, she'd be more unbearable the rest of the day. There was also that mess to clean up. She took a moment, then turned the knob and re-entered.

"What do you want now? Didn't I tell you to stay the heck out of here and keep that mess you call food...probably why I can't get around so good—you're putting something in it."

"You can't move because you have arthritis, and you're eighty years old. That mean spirit of yours doesn't help either," Brenda said as she retrieved the pill bottle from the top drawer of the bureau beside the bed. "Take your pill now while I'm standing here." She placed it in front of Sarah, observing her. Her aunt liked to create a diversion, then hide the pill under her pillow, to be discarded later. She'd fooled Brenda before.

"I ain't takin' that. How do I know what it is? And as for my spirit, who are you supposed to be. You ain't foolin' nobody—you church people are all alike. A buncha devils—startin' with that double talkin, money grubbin preacher of yours...." Sarah ranted until she ran out of insults then swallowed the pill, chasing it down with water from the glass Brenda handed her.

Brenda moved on to cleaning the mess Sarah had made with the plate, sighing as she worked. It was Sunday morning, and she was on her way to church, but Sarah knew that. It was the reason for her antics.

She cleaned the area, then, being reasonably sure Aunt Sarah had swallowed the pill, poured her another glass of water. "Aunt Sarah, you know good, and well, if it wasn't for your medicine, you'd be hurting all day. Then I can't do anything for you."

"You're worthless anyway," Sarah growled, "think you can just tell me anything, but wait till my son gets here. He'll straighten you out." She glared at Brenda, a triumphant smile curling her aged lips, "yes indeed, when Russell gets here, he's gonna take me away from here, and I'll be in a nice place, with nice people taking care of me; people who know what they're doing. Then I'll get better."

"Yes, ma'am," Brenda said, leaving the room, the drug's euphoric effect starting to kick in. Further conversation with the old woman, reminding her that precious Russell, a thief, and con artist, had been dead for years, would be a waste of time.

In the hallway, Brenda checked her watch, alarmed at how the morning was flying by. She needed to hurry to arrive at church by her usual time, thirty minutes before the start of service. In her twenty-two years as the head usher of the Mount Hebron Baptist Church, she'd rarely been late, and God willing, she wouldn't be today.

Walking briskly down the short hallway, mind on her Sunday morning task list, she heard a car in the driveway. As she moved toward the window, a key turned in the lock. Gia, Brenda's 28-year-old daughter, entered the house colliding with her mother's stony glare.

"Hey, momma," Gia said, with a rigid smile, as her mother conducted a head-to-toe inspection. Her ensemble: a curve-hugging, red spandex mini-dress and matching stilettos, was befitting the cover of Vogue magazine but failed Brenda's scrutiny.

"Hey yourself," her mother said with folded arms.

"Running late, aren't you?" Gia tipped toward the stairway leading to her second-floor bedroom, ignoring her mother's sour look. She could've waited another hour until the coast was clear, but having been out all night, she was ready to climb into her bed. So, what if her mother disapproved, she was moving out soon anyway.

"I guess you won't be joining us for church today," Brenda sniffed.

Confident her expression was hidden, she scowled and cursed under her breath, then pulled off her heels and ascended the stairs.

"Since you're gonna be here, keep an ear open for Aunt Sarah in case she needs something," Brenda said. Gia paused but didn't turn around.

"I'll try, momma, but it'll be hard to hear her since I plan to be fast asleep in the next five minutes." She resumed walking faster.

"Stop running the streets all night, and you wouldn't have to try so hard!" Brenda managed to get out before she heard the bedroom door close.

She stood tapping her foot, reminding herself Gia, her only child, was an exceptional daughter, a college graduate with a promising career, and head on her shoulders. *Why do I always have to start in on her?*

Heading again toward her bedroom to dress for church, she emerged a few minutes later, in her navy-blue usher's uniform, a plain white blouse, and matching low-heeled, navy-blue pumps.

Stacked on the floor beside the door were church supplies she needed to load into her car. Canned goods for the food bank ministry, freshly laundered aprons and tablecloths for the hospitality ministry, arts and crafts supplies for the children's ministry, and other odds and ends she'd picked up during the week. Once that task was finished, she'd be ready to go.

She then noticed movement outside and, peering through the window, spied a man jauntily striding toward her door. *Not him again,* she grimaced.

Yet here he was. Lawrence Foster, a dapperly attired widower, and fellow church member, who'd recently become her neighbor, was headed to her door. He'd been dropping by the last few Sunday mornings, catching her as she was leaving, inviting himself to ride with her. Lawrence was good company when minding his own business. Last week, however, he got on her nerves.

"Ms. Brenda, why are you doing all of this, don't they have anybody else?" He'd said while helping complete her before church errands. "Seems to me, you're so busy, you have no time to enjoy the service. That can't be what God wants, can it?"

"Mr. Lawrence, things don't get done unless somebody does them. I'm not one to sit around and wait until others get a revelation from God to get moving. If I see something that needs to be done, I do it. Not like some of them, waiting around, praying for inspiration and won't stop to help people when they need it..." she gave him an earful while he held the driver's side door open for her. She was still frowning as she slid behind the wheel of her Buick.

"Okay, Ms. Brenda," he said, fastening his seatbelt, only to start in on her a few minutes later. Then he dared to suggest she arrange for someone else to be the head usher the following Sunday so she could sit in the service, even offered to save her a seat next to him.

"I could never do that, Mr. Lawrence," she said, gawking at the suggestion. "I'm not in the habit of shirking my responsibilities. Besides, there's nobody else."

"Of course, there's somebody else; you're just showing people to their seats. I mean, how hard can that be?" He watched her bristle.

That was the culmination of weeks of comments, remarks, and suggestions. Each week Lawrence would go a bit further and pick with her a little more. Today she didn't want to be bothered; she didn't feel like defending herself. She snatched the door open before he had a chance to ring the bell, planning to get rid of him quickly and be on her way.

"Good morning Ms. Brenda," Lawrence smiled brightly.

His cheerfulness always disrupted her, but she fought through it. "Good morning..." she said, unsmiling. When she tried, she could look so mean those who approached her took a step backward, seeking a safe distance. Lawrence, however, was impervious.

"Why don't you give me the car keys, and I'll load your supplies into the trunk for you," he said, without even asking if he could ride with her that morning, "You can go get your purse."

Who does he think he is? She was caught between a choice of going along politely or being rude and un-Christian on a Sunday morning by telling him to get lost.

"Well I...," she started, then sighed and stepped aside, handing him her car keys. Standing by awkwardly, arms folded, she observed him gathering up the supplies merrily, and marching out to the car. While his back was turned, a smirk formed on her lips. She wasn't in the habit of requesting, nor accepting help or company; there weren't many brave enough to offer her either.

She grabbed her purse then stopped to check her reflection in the hall mirror, something she rarely did. Disappointed by the drabness looking back at her, she wondered why she didn't try harder and when she'd stopped caring...

"Sarah, I'm leaving," she called as she stepped out the front door.

"Good, don't come back," Sarah said. Such was a running dialog between the two of them.

Brenda locked the door, and as she walked the few steps to the driveway, she told herself to relax. She refused to become accustomed to Lawrence hanging around but resigned herself to accept his help, one more time. The stress of her morning eased as she walked to her six-year-old Buick, parked beside Gia's flashy red sports car.

Lawrence walked around to the driver's side and held the door for her like she was royalty. *Something about a man with good manners,* she allowed the corners of her mouth to turn up ever so slightly as she nodded a thank you to him. There was nothing to gain being mean to him; he paid no attention anyway.

As the two of them completed her errands, Brenda admitted, his company was a nice change from complaining Aunt Sarah at home, and the other two elderly ladies, Miss Logan, and Miss Evans, in the back seat who often rode with her to church. Lawrence made easy conversation, didn't talk just to hear himself, and was unpretentious. Her only irritation with him was he wouldn't stay out of her business.

On the final leg of their trip, Lawrence turned to her, "You haven't given me an answer yet, Ms. Brenda."

She wished he'd stop making statements and asking questions as if they were in the middle of one continuous conversation. "An answer to what, Mr. Lawrence?" Her jaw constricted.

He saw her tense up and was tempted to leave her alone, but in his opinion, everyone needed a shakeup from time to time.

"You know the last time we talked, I asked you when you were gonna take a Sunday off. I was wondering, did you have an answer yet. I'm sure the rest of the congregation of Mount Hebron would appreciate the much-needed break."

2

"BEEEP BEEP BEEP BEEEEEEEEEEEEEP!!!!"

Gia had been sleeping soundly until Aunt Sarah started laying on the house intercom button.

"BEEEEEEP!!!"

How does she know when I'm here? Gia pulled the blanket over her head to block out the noise. Her mother always made ample provision for Sarah on Sundays and called or came home to check on her, but the old woman was determined to force Gia to wait on her. *'See, you should have come to church...* is what her mother would say.

"BEEEEEEEEEEEEEEEEEEEEEP!!! BEEP BEEEP!"

After ten minutes, unable to take anymore, she dragged herself into the hallway and pressed the answer button. "Yes, Aunt Sarah?"

"Who's that?" Aunt Sarah said, then pressed the call button while Gia attempted to answer.

"BEEEEEEEP!! BEEEEEEEEEEEEEEEEEEEEP!!"

Gia closed her eyes and bowed her head. *Lord, I guess you're punishing me for not being in church today.* She shuffled down the stairs while Sarah kept pressing the button.

"Yes, Aunt Sarah, what do you need?" She said, entering the room.

"Oh, it is you. Why didn't you say something, little girl? How did I know somebody didn't come breakin' in here?"

"Now, you know. Did you need something, or were you just trying to catch a burglar?"

"I need some food to eat."

Gia spied the sandwich and fruit wrapped in plastic Brenda had left for her. Sarah followed her eyes.

"I don't want that. Can't you get me somethin' good?"

"You know I don't cook."

"Cook—who asked *you* to cook? Can you get me some of that fried catfish you got the last time?"

"Who's paying?" Gia said, her head cocked to the side.

"Your momma."

"Right," Gia said, leaving the room without giving Sarah an answer. The old woman was more interested in attention than catfish. Whether Gia went to get the food or not, she'd have no peace until Brenda returned home.

"BEEEEEEEP!! BEEEEEEEEEEEEEEEEEEEP!!" was all she heard while heading back up the stairs.

Mr. Lawrence," Brenda said, keeping her voice low so the two ladies, engaged in conversation in the backseat, wouldn't detect friction and tune in to overhear. "I realize some don't consider the office of an usher to be an important one, but as I tell our recruits, *we* are the face of Mount Hebron. The very first contact many visitors have with our ministry; we must perform our duties in an orderly, efficient, and—"

"Joyful, friendly manner," Lawrence said.

Brenda felt the blood rush to her face and was grateful her brown complexion hid her agitation.

Lawrence watched Brenda's body language as she pulled the car into the Mt. Hebron Baptist Church lot, parking in silence. She appeared flushed; her lips were tightly pressed together, and she avoided looking in his direction.

"You know, Ms. Brenda," he said, breaking the silence as they unloaded the supplies from her trunk. "Why don't I drive us to church next week? I'll come over a little earlier so we can get all of your gear loaded up."

Brenda swung around to face him, to give him the full impact of her answer; a simple 'no' wasn't strong enough to get the message across to Lawrence Foster. Before she could get it out, however, he'd walked away, greeting one of his friends.

"That was a wonderful service, wasn't it, Miss Brenda?" Miss Logan said from the back of the car. Miss Evans, seated beside her, nodded. "I see we don't have the pleasure of the company of your gentleman friend this afternoon."

"Deacon Lawrence is riding with his daughter," Brenda said while starting the ignition, "and he's not my gentleman friend. He's just my neighbor."

The two women exchanged a smirk as they buckled in for the ride.

"She laid on that intercom all afternoon, claiming she wanted some fish, but when I finally agreed to go and get it, she changed her mind," Gia said, seated at the dining room table as Brenda placed a steaming plate in front of her.

"She gets bored, and you know how fond she is of you," Brenda said, taking her seat and watching Gia attack her plate. "How's your food?"

"Nobody cooks pot roast like you do, momma. I'll take your food over a restaurant any day." Gia devoured a mouthful of mashed potatoes, dripping with Brenda's onion mushroom gravy.

"I'm glad you're home to enjoy it. The church service was wonderful today; I wish you'd been there to enjoy that too. I'm not trying to preach Gia, but why don't you come more often?" Brenda filled Gia's glass with her favorite mint, lemon iced tea.

"For one, I'm tired of how people treat you. You work so hard for that church all the time, and what does anybody do for you? Where's their appreciation? Even the pastor takes you for granted," she said, slamming her glass down on the table harder than intended.

"That's an excuse, and you know it. I'm fully capable of taking care of myself. I don't serve the Lord for people. I work to please Him. I don't impress God one bit, and He owes me nothing."

"Maybe God doesn't owe you, but Mount Hebron does, and I'm sick of seeing you being denied the respect you deserve."

"I'd be flattered if I thought you were being straight with me. You're making excuses, but one of these days, you'll run out of them."

On cue, Gia became engrossed in her social media feed on her phone, bringing their dinner conversation to an end.

"You ain't no good, you liar you!" Aunt Sarah screamed. "You're puttin' something in my food; I know it. You and my so-called daughter got your heads together, think you're gonna get rid of me. You don't fool nobody. I'm gonna call Russell tonight; wait till he hears about this..."

Brenda took a deep breath while standing beside the bed and allowing her mind to drift, again asking herself the question; *is this worth it?* Working in her home had its advantages, but in all the years she'd worked in nursing facilities, she couldn't recall one patient as obstinate as this old woman, who also happened to be her late grandfather's sister. *Come to think of it; he was a pretty mean somebody in his own right.* She smiled fondly at his memory but was rudely jolted back to the present. Sarah had picked up the full glass of orange juice Brenda had given her and threatened to throw it.

"Now, you hold on one minute!" If you do it, I'll drag you out of that bed, give you a bucket and a scrub brush, and you'll crawl on your belly and clean the wall and the carpet," Brenda said through clenched teeth.

Sarah slammed the glass back down on the tray so hard the juice spilled all over it.

Brenda stood up straight and took several deep breaths before speaking. "Sarah, dear, it's time for you to get dressed."

"For what?"

"It's Monday. The bus to the Senior Center will be here in less than an hour."

"I've told you. I ain't goin' back there. Sittin' all day with all those sick, old people. Some of em' half crazy. I'll stay right here, and you can't make me do otherwise."

Brenda pointed her finger, "It's Monday, and you're going to the Senior Center. You might as well make up your mind to enjoy it instead of being miserable. They're nice to you, and you take great day trips. I get a break and a chance to give your room a good cleaning."

"Hmph, so that's the way it is—is it?" Sarah said. "You get old, and your rights are taken away." She made a sweeping gesture with her arm, knocking over the glass of orange juice she'd threatened to throw, spilling its contents over the bed and carpet. "Oh, I'm so sorry," she smirked. "I just gave you more work to do. I hope it don't take you the whole day to clean this room."

"That's okay, Sarah dear," Brenda said, giving her a tight-lipped grin.

Sarah's smile vanished. "Gimme my clothes so I can get out of here."

3

"I want to congratulate you all on a well-earned accomplishment," Chase Weller, the Director of Brokerage Services, announced late Friday afternoon at their quarterly status meeting. The entire sales team was assembled in the boardroom of Titan Investments and Capital Inc.

To Gia, the room, with its massive mahogany table surrounded by high-backed, black leather chairs, and classic artwork adorning the walls, radiated wealth. Nothing in that chamber spoke of the late nights and marathon meetings during that last quarter, or the times a team member was verbally dismantled by a boss or client within the glass and wood enclosure. All was forgotten because they'd made their numbers and had survived to start it all over again on Monday (or Tuesday if Chase gave them Monday off), which seemed to be a lifetime away.

"We've had another excellent quarter; the numbers are up in all of our operating divisions. I'd also like you to join me in giving special thanks to Gia Collier," he stretched his hand toward where she was seated to his right. "Her contribution has been tremendous, and I'd like you to know that effective immediately, she's been promoted to Division Supervisor. I'm sure she'll do a fantastic job in her new role." Gia smiled and accepted the applause, cheers, big smiles, and high fives from her colleagues.

Chase's secretary Holly then wheeled in a tray with iced champagne, sparkling cider, and hors d'oeuvres. A bad sign: it meant the workday was over early, but they could forget about having Monday off.

"Here's to all of you." He raised a crystal flute filled with cider. "Enjoy this celebration, and I'll see you bright and early...." The room became so quiet he wondered if they were breathing, "Monday." Their groans made him giddy with laughter. It was the same thing every quarter. He'd given them Monday off once in three years, but they clung to the same hope each time. As the team basked in their success, he slipped out of the conference room to clear up some details so he could leave the office early also.

"Gia, you're our new supervisor; that's no big surprise," Kyle, her coworker, said.

"No surprise at all," Melody chimed in, "She's the classic over-achiever, type-A workaholic. Chase will have to look out for his job in a couple years." Everyone laughed and nodded in agreement.

Gia slammed her glass down on the table. "I resent that! The workaholic part anyway," she grinned. "Don't be jealous because I believe in being ultra-productive while I'm working, so I can enjoy my time off. When's the last time you've seen me in the office on the weekend?"

"You're a maniac during the week; even crazy people need a break," Melody said, drawing more chuckles.

Gia knew that although they were teasing, there was truth behind their words. Her pace, ambition, and intensity drove them insane, all except Chase, who treasured it. If he could find a way to clone her, the rest of them would be out of a job. She'd joined the firm right out of college and had moved up quickly. After six years, she'd surpassed many of her peers who'd been there longer. So far, no one had been resentful, but starting Monday, four of the seven in that boardroom would report to her. They were smiling now; she wondered how long that would last.

The meeting moved around the corner to the Diamond Life Bistro, transitioning to happy hour, where Gia and her co-workers toasted her promotion a couple more times before she slipped out and into her red convertible.

At five o'clock, Gia's cell phone came alive with the promise of Friday night festivities. She had yet to decide what she was in the mood for. Another happy hour was a bad idea; she'd consumed her alcohol limit for the night. It looked like a date; maybe with the new guy, Nathan, she'd met during that week. Not the corporate type she preferred, but he was cute. First dates were unpredictable, however, and she questioned if she was in the mood for the drama. As she drove, she mentally went through her list of regulars then a call came in.

The name Keith Greyson displayed on the dashboard screen. He was what she was in the mood for: a suite at a classy hotel, a room service dinner, and a soak in the Jacuzzi, all private and discreet. The wife frequently traveled, leaving him behind to take full advantage of her absences.

Instead of picking up, however, she decided to wait and listen to his voicemail. He didn't leave one. *Just moved on down the list.* She considered calling him back then had another idea.

"Monique," she said to Siri, and her cellphone dialed the number. She decided to forget about men and hang out with her girl. Wild, fun, Monique was always the right choice for Friday night.

"Hey, Gee, where you at?" Monique wasted no time with hello. "Hurry up, get dressed, and meet me at the shop; we got a couple hot stops for tonight. Get here soon as you can if you want me to tighten up that weave before we go."

"Why, what's up?" Monique always had a line on the hottest events. As a hairstylist at one of the most upscale salons in St. Louis, she usually had a foot in the door and name on the list, often scoring free tickets and backstage passes.

"All you need to know is a football player, a private party, and I got the hookup. It's gonna be you and me, dressed to kill, steppin' out of your ride."

"You don't have to tell me twice; I'm there. Gotta stop to make, though. There's an outfit I've been eyeing at Raphael's I'm going to treat myself to. Don't hate on me when you see me, okay."

"Is that so? If you're banking like that, pick me up a little somethin' too. There's this blouse—" Monique said.

"See what I can do," Gia laughed and pressed the button to hang up, knowing her friend would keep pushing until she agreed to buy her something.

They made it to the party, held at a posh private club on Delmar Boulevard, and though it didn't live up to Monique's hype, the host was a retired football player, and there weren't many celebrities in attendance, it was a good time. There was plenty of food, and men kept the free drinks flowing. To Gia, it meant phone numbers and potential dates. As was their norm, they never stayed any one place too long and were soon off to another affair, a charity event in Soulard hosted by a local radio station. From there, they split up. Gia met a guy who offered to buy her breakfast, while Monique met up with a friend and flew off to another party.

She arrived home at five a.m., which was before Brenda was usually awake, but decided to enter through the back door anyway, just in case. No point spoiling the pleasantness between them; her mother had been thrilled to hear about the promotion.

Upon entering the house, she tipped into the kitchen to get a drink of water before going upstairs.

"Who's that...Who's out there? I hear somebody!" Sarah called out from her room on the other side of the house. Gia cursed under her breath. That old woman could hear a pin drop a mile away. If she didn't go in and let Sarah know it was her, there'd be a ruckus; she'd been known to dial 9 1 1.

She hurried into Sarah's room quietly so as not to awaken Brenda.

"It's me, Aunt Sarah," she said, whispering.

"Who are you, and what you whisperin' for?" She calmed down when Gia came into view.

"Oh, it's you, little girl. What you doin' walking around this early. I forget, your momma says you don't know how to bring yourself home."

"Is that what she says?" Gia said, crossing her arms.

"And what's that outfit you have on," the old woman said, squinting, then grabbed her glasses to get a better look. "My, my, you girls don't wear any clothes, do you?" She referred to Gia's green silk halter top that ended at her rib cage. The matching mini skirt hung low on her hips, highlighting her tiny waist, complete with a waist chain and diamond belly button ring. Matching green stiletto pumps showed off her long legs. Naomi Campbell couldn't do any better, but Aunt Sarah was unimpressed.

"While I'm here, do you need anything?" Gia said through clenched teeth.

"No, child, but why you gotta rush off? You feelin' a chill since you don't have any clothes on?"

She turned and let out a breath, "I'm going upstairs; I'll see you later."

"You young people don't have time for nothin' and nobody. That's what I tell her all the time. When she gets old, she's gonna be all alone too. You ain't gonna have time for her."

No way, Gia thought, as she yawned and climbed the stairs to her bedroom, was her mother going to end up like Aunt Sarah.

4

"Marvin, please talk to Momma about bringing in someone to help her care for daddy. It won't be cheap, but she needs the help and won't admit it," Brenda said to her older brother Marvin Jr. He coughed and cleared his throat. Otherwise, the phone line was silent. "I'm not sure you, Darwin, and Chris realize the seriousness of the situation. Alzheimer's is a terminal diagnosis." She'd been prodding her three siblings for six months, since receiving the news from their father's physician. So far, they'd been sluggish.

He'd called to speak to their mother, but Brenda answered the phone and hijacked the call.

"Are you sure that's the correct diagnosis? I mean, have you gotten a second opinion? And why are you trying to bring somebody in Brenda, you're a nurse, isn't that what you do? We don't need to pay anybody; just tell me what you need, and I'll make sure you get it."

She took a deep breath to keep from throwing the phone across the room. All the conversations she'd had with her siblings took the same turn when she brought up their father's care.

"Don't ask me for any money," her sister Christine said the last time they'd spoken. "You're there, and you don't have to go out and work. Momma's house is big enough for all of you; sell yours and move in with them. The money from the sale and free roof over your head should be plenty of compensation for you to care for Daddy. What do you need money for anyway? It's not like you go anywhere."

Her most recent conversation with Darwin, her younger brother, was more of the same. "What do you mean, being dad's caregiver isn't what you want to do? That's selfish, Bren', our father needs you. It's the least you can do. Besides, Gia is an adult now, and you don't have a man. What else are you gonna do with your life?" He then added. "Aren't you Christians supposed to live a life of sacrifice?"

Her two brothers had successful high-profile careers, Marvin owned a successful real-estate firm, and Darwin was an attorney. Her sister Christine, unlike herself, had a successful marriage. Their lives were significant and couldn't be disrupted for their dad. She was expected to take the burden. Marvin's statement *it's what you do* echoed in her ears. When did she lose the right to decide *what she did*? They called her selfish, but they were the selfish ones. According to them, she was supposed to sacrifice and leave them alone. After all, what else did she have to do?

Of course, their mother could bring an immediate halt to the burden-shifting. They'd take notice because Corene never asked for anything unless forced to.

"No need to bother them, they have their own lives. We're doin' okay for now," was Brenda's mother's response every time Brenda asked her to call—just call.

"You don't have to ask them for anything, Ma, but they have a right to know you're struggling. They need to hear it from you. They won't listen to me." Her mother would nod, say she'd think about it, and that would be the end until Brenda brought it up again.

It was Monday afternoon, and Sarah was returning from her day at the senior center. Brenda stood at the door and watched as the bus driver helped the elderly woman up the concrete walk; she took a few deep breaths to get her mind ready for what was to come. It was challenging dealing with the aged who often didn't feel well and sometimes didn't remember who you are. She'd done it for a long time, but perhaps she'd stayed in the same place too long. Maybe God was shifting her into a new direction. If God were giving her a chance for a brand-new path, nobody had the right to say she couldn't go.

Once Sarah returned from her Monday outings, Brenda's hectic week began, and there'd be no breaks until that following Monday. In addition to caring for Sarah and driving her to various medical appointments, she made frequent checks on her parents, who lived nearby. Gia helped during the week when she could, but on the weekends, Brenda was on her own.

Gia's social life kept her mostly out of the house from Friday after work through Sunday afternoon. She spent her Sundays catching up on sleep and getting ready for the workweek. Brenda wished there was a boyfriend's house where she could track her daughter's weekend whereabouts. The way Gia lived her life, she was liable to be across town, or out of the country, at the drop of a hat, always with some unnamed male companion. She called her mother to check-in, no matter how far away she was, but never said much about the playmate of that week; Brenda rarely met any of them.

"When are you gonna spend a weekend with me, Gia? Just tell me when and I'll make all the arrangements. You won't even have to pack a toothbrush, I'll supply everything. Just bring your sexy self."

Gia had the impulse to yawn in Max's face but held it in. It was Saturday night, and after a brutal week of work, she'd decided to step out with this guy she'd met online, big mistake.

Men who thought they could impress by talking about how much they were going to spend on her were a red flag. *Probably lying anyway.* Judging by the cheap restaurant he'd chosen and the cheesy way he was dressed, she doubted if he could afford to take himself away for the weekend.

"Maybe someday, if and when we know each other a little better," she said, smiling and taking a sip of her drink. She'd filed Max away as a loser and was ready to ditch him and go meet up with her girls.

Her opinion of him was confirmed when the check came, and he coughed awkwardly. Gia thought about giving him a hard time about his half but decided if she paid, she was free to leave and didn't have to play nice anymore.

"Thank you, baby," he whispered and was about to pat her thigh after she'd handed the waiter her gold card.

"No problem," she said, sliding out of his reach while looking away.

Once she'd signed the credit card slip, she rose from the table. "Max, it was nice. I'll give you a call sometime."

He nodded without speaking, a crooked smile forming on his lips. He held that smile as he watched Gia's long legs strut out of the restaurant.

"Ronnie," she said, into the air as she started the engine of her bright red BMW convertible. The dashboard came alive, *Dialing Ronnie,* Siri said.

"Gia? I didn't expect to hear from you tonight. Didn't you tell me you had a date?"

Gia could hear crowd noise in the background as she sat in her idling car. She then caught sight of Max, exiting the restaurant.

"Yeah, I had a date, where are you?"

"The Pyramid Club. What happened with Mr. Wonderful?"

When she looked up to see Max hopping into an Uber, she giggled.

"Nothing at all. We ate, then I left. He wasn't my type," Gia said.

"You mean the date is over already; you just walked out. Girl, you're crazy," Ronnie laughed.

"I ain't crazy. When I see time's being wasted, I roll. Got other fish to fry."

"If you say so, Gee. We're getting ready to leave here, head over to The Plum Room. Seems Curtis is having a birthday bash."

"Curtis, who?" She sat up straight.

"The Curtis, your high school love," Ronnie said. "He asks me about you every time I see him. So why don't you—"

"Meet you there," she said, then put the car in gear. She never missed an opportunity to run into Curtis.

"I never know when you're going to pop up," Curtis said to Gia, on that chilly night in late April, "but I guess you like it that way." They were standing on the outdoor patio of the Plum Room, a Chinese restaurant that was a familiar neighborhood venue and party spot. It had been a while since the old lovers had crossed paths.

To Gia, he was as attractive as ever: tall and slim in a light grey suit paired with a black t-shirt. The question popped into her head as to why they never made it work. She remembered the answer: he'd let her run over him, she'd get bored then dump him.

Several high school classmates were attending the party, giving it the feel of a mini class reunion. She pursed her lips at Curtis, basking in the way he gazed at her; it was that affirmation she'd come looking for.

Suddenly a petite light brown-skinned woman appeared at his side, overshadowing her moment. She cut her eyes at Gia before turning to Curtis. "Baby, they're waiting for us."

"I'll be right there. First, let me introduce you. Felice, this is Gia, an old friend.

Gia, Felice is my fiancée, this isn't just my birthday party, we're celebrating our engagement."

Felice smiled brightly at Gia now that Curtis had established who was who. Gia blinked at the woman, then nodded slightly, concealing her fury at Ronnie for leaving out the details of the gathering. She would've come anyway if only to size up the chick, another one who thought she was going to have her Curtis. Her assessment was concluded in those brief seconds: *he can't marry that troll!* She looked on as they locked arms and strolled away, then searched for the bar; she needed a drink.

Sticking around long enough so her early departure wouldn't be attributed to jealousy, Gia made her way around the room mingling, then slipped out quietly. In her car and on the road, she felt confused by her feelings and started to head home for solitude. She checked the clock and saw it was only five past midnight, which was early for her. Her phone then buzzed, and the name Jamal flashed on her dashboard. She smiled.

"Hey baby, you must've been reading my mind," she said. "What do you mean what's wrong, I miss you, that's all." At the red light, she checked her makeup in the mirror, then grabbed a lipstick she kept in the console.

"Sure, whatever you want, baby. Tell me where you are, and I'll be there."

"No, you don't have the wrong number; quit playing," Gia giggled. "Where are you? Great, I'm on my way."

Seated on a stool at a neighborhood bar, Jamal turned off his cell phone and stared at it. He and Gia saw each other occasionally; they had a good time, but she never seemed to be that interested. Tonight, she was acting like they were long lost, lovers." *She hasn't seen me for a while, maybe she finally realizes what she's missing...*

Why don't you stay awhile, relax? We can go to lunch downtown and—" Jamal was speaking to Gia the following morning after they'd had breakfast. They were seated around the table in his kitchen. He wore his bathrobe, but she was fully dressed.

"Sounds nice, Jamal; maybe another time," she said, engrossed in her phone.

The real Gia was back, leaving him longing for the woman who'd been all over him the night before. He should've known she'd been play-acting again, and now the show was over.

"Gotta go; promised my Mom, I'd go somewhere with her today," she said, standing and avoiding Jamal's eyes. She couldn't bear his sad puppy dog look, having used him to make herself feel better after hearing Curtis was engaged. He did the same thing to some woman every night of his life and would do it to her if allowed. "Bye, baby, see you next time," she whispered and leaned over to kiss him.

"Yeah, right," he pulled away. "Who said there's going to be a next time?"

She laughed out loud while gliding to the door, leaving him sulking in the kitchen of the small apartment. "You can't resist me," she said, opening the door, then turned, winked, blew him a kiss, and made her escape.

Driving home, she knew there'd be no running into her mother that Sunday, as it was after 11 a.m. Brenda was well into the pastor's sermon.

5

"I was noticing your yard could use a little work; your grass is dead in spots, and the hedges need pruning, Lawrence said, standing on Brenda's front porch. It was a St. Louis, Saturday afternoon, and while out for a walk, he'd caught her coming in from the store.

"Thank you for noticing Mr. Lawrence, but I hire someone to take care of that for me," she said, walking past him to the door. She put down her bag to fish her keys from her purse, intending to enter the house and ignore him.

"They're not doing a very good job."

She exhaled, "It's early in the season; I haven't called him yet. Now if you—"

"This is the perfect time of year. What do you say we do it ourselves, then you can keep your money?"

She stopped and frowned. "We?"

"Yeah, we. It'll be fun. We can go to the garden center and pick out flowers, maybe new shrubs, or grasses..."

With her door open, Brenda turned and watched as Lawrence talked on, becoming more animated with every word. She wanted to scream. First, he invites himself to ride with her to church on Sundays, then begs her to ride with him to Tuesday night bible study, now he wants to drag her out into the yard to plant flowers!

"Mr. Lawrence," she said, shouting; he was now at the other end of the yard, pointing out possible locations for a rose bush.

"What do you think about here in this corner, a little mulch, maybe a tree?"

"I don't think anything!" she said, balling her fists.

"What?" Sarah said, from the rear of the house.

"I'm not talking to you," Brenda said, as Lawrence strode back towards her.

"Then who are you talking to? I thought I was the only one you used that nasty tone with."

Brenda swung her head around and scowled. When she turned back, Lawrence was peering at her, his eyebrows raised.

"Have I done something wrong?" He said.

She exhaled then looked up at the sky, "I didn't ask for help with my yard, and I didn't ask for help or company on Sunday mornings nor did I ask for a ride to church on Tuesday evenings."

"Oh," he said, nodding slowly and stepping back.

"Don't get me wrong," she said. "I know you mean well. It's just that I'm used to being on my own and—"

"You want to keep it that way?" His eyes widened.

She blinked and peered at him blankly. *Is that what I want?*

He cocked his head to the side and waited.

Her shoulders slackened, and she sighed. "It's just that—"

"How long am I going to have to wait to eat in this dump?" Sarah yelled. Brenda looked at her watch, then cleared her throat.

"Have you eaten—you want some lunch?" She said. He didn't have a chance to answer either question. She waved him in and closed the door. "Mind coming in to speak with Sarah for a minute so she can connect a face to your voice? She keeps tabs on everything that goes on in here, even if she rarely leaves her room."

He followed Brenda to Sarah's room in the rear of the house. After a quick introduction, Brenda ducked out, leaving him alone to listen to the older woman's list of grievances.

"It's about time," Sarah said when Brenda appeared with her lunch tray.

"You're welcome," Brenda said, placing the tray in front of her, then went about positioning her and arranging her napkin and silverware.

Once Sarah was situated, she shot Lawrence a look and motioned him toward the hallway.

"It's been a pleasure talking with you," he said, following Brenda's cue. Sarah, immersed in her meal, made no response. When he got to the dining room, he found the table set for two; a tossed salad, rolls, and two steaming bowls of chicken and dumplings.

"Miss Brenda, you didn't have to go to all this trouble, or is this your way of getting rid of me for good?"

She pointed to a place at the table. "Sit down, Mr. Lawrence, before the food gets cold."

He complied and dug in. The chicken was tender, the dumplings light and airy, swimming in the savory gravy. All was quiet; Brenda's cuisine often halted meal conversation. "What were you about to tell me earlier," he said after he'd finished eating and leaned back from the table.

"Would you like some coffee and maybe a slice of pineapple upside-down cake?"

"Homemade?"

"Homemade," she said, a shadow of a smile on her lips.

He smiled and nodded. Once Brenda set the dessert in front of him, he shook his head. "You cook like this all the time?"

"It's my passion, and Gia may not look like it, but that child loves to eat. We don't have many leftovers around here."

"Wow, how is Gigi? I haven't seen her in a while."

"She's doing great," Brenda brightened, then turned somber. "I owe you an apology."

He studied her a moment then shrugged, "Not if you were being honest," he sipped his coffee.

"Honesty is no excuse for rudeness. I don't want you to think I'm unappreciative."

"But?"

She bit her lower lip. "I've been around you and your family long enough to know you're a nice man, and I don't want you getting the wrong impression, being a widower and all. I'm probably not one you should be wasting your time on."

"Why not?" He leaned forward. "You're as single as I am, aren't you?"

"That's not the point. I'm...I don't know. It's been a long time since my divorce and..."

"Just because you've gotten used to being alone, doesn't mean you resign yourself to it." Brenda's mouth twisted, and she looked away.

"I miss my wife, terribly," he said, and Brenda nodded. "We were married for 25 years, and I don't know if I can ever get married again, but I admit, I find you an interesting person."

"See, that's what I mean," she shook her head. "I'm not sure what you're expecting, but nothing is interesting about me."

He leaned across the table, "Why don't you let me decide that, and as far as my expectations go, I want to be your friend – first, foremost, and forever. I need a friend, and something tells me, you do too. If my feelings go beyond that and yours don't, we'll deal with that when the time comes."

Brenda sat back and exhaled, releasing the tension that was always in her face when she spoke with him. She chuckled and looked up at the ceiling. "That was well said."

"Is it a deal; do we understand each other? If you don't want to be bothered with me, say so at any time. I can take it."

She'd been trying to do just that for weeks, but now waved her hand. "I think you've shown me, I need to lighten up."

They sat awhile, drinking coffee and talking. Brenda allowed herself to forget, for the moment, her long list of tasks lined up for that afternoon. The more they chatted, the more they found to talk about, mostly sharing about their adult kids, who'd grown up in the church together.

"They're doing well. I'm sure you see Margot all the time at church. Kevin's doing okay. Stephanie, let's just say she needs much prayer," Lawrence said.

"She's always had a bit of a wild streak, like Gia. The only thing stable in my child's life is her job. Her personal life is like a high-speed racetrack."

She has a beautiful smile and laugh; if only she'd do it more often, he thought, telling one funny story after another just to hear her laugh. Finally, he looked at his watch. "We never got to the yard work, but it doesn't seem like you were interested anyway."

"I'll think about it," she said, clearing the dishes.

"Thank you for the lunch and the company. Maybe we could do it again sometime?" Lawrence said.

Smiling as she walked him to the door, repeating his words in her head, *maybe we could do it again sometime,* she had a better idea. "Come over a little earlier tomorrow, and I'll make us breakfast."

"Thank you. That'll be wonderful, I'll be here," Lawrence said, beaming before heading down the driveway.

6

"Dad, what do you mean, you spent the afternoon at Miss Brenda's —the same Sister Brenda from the church; the lady who watches the door? I can't believe you survived to tell about it. She didn't give you the evil eye for chewing too loud?" Kevin, Lawrence's son, said. He'd stopped by that evening to help his father with a computer problem.

When Lawrence dropped that nugget, Kevin stood up from the kitchen table, wagging his finger. "I know I promised to stay out of your love life because you claimed you could find your own woman, but Miss Brenda, the head usher? She's ferocious. When we were kids, we used to call her the pit-bull."

"You're exaggerating, and it's unkind. You shouldn't say things about a person, just because they're a bit abrasive. Can you focus on my computer please; is it a virus or what?"

Kevin shook his head, then tapped the laptop keyboard a few times, and the screen came alive. "Well, you work with the prison population every day, so Miss Brenda must seem mild compared to them." He threw up his hands when his father glared at him, "Okay, Pops, you're right, I don't know her so I shouldn't judge."

He did know that, as a kid growing up at Mt Hebron church, everybody was afraid of Sister Brenda and wondered how her daughter, Gia, survived living with her. Sister Brenda missed nothing, mainly candy being smuggled into church service. It was a common belief among the kids that she had x-ray vision like Superman, demonstrated by her ability to detect the contraband bubble gum, even if it was hidden under your tongue. Getting caught too many times, meant she'd tell your parents, which would guarantee you were in trouble. If Sister Brenda said you were guilty, there was no such thing as reasonable doubt. Everybody knew she didn't lie or make a mistake.

"Don't get me wrong, she's pretty. I even thought so when I was a kid, and Gia is perfection. But—"

"We've been riding to church together, and she seems to be a nice lady.

"If you say so," Kevin shrugged. He and his two sisters had been trying to get their father to start dating for a year. Lawrence replied that their late mother, Yvonne, was all the woman he'd ever want; that part of his life was over. There'd been plenty of eligible women, some younger and others closer to his age, to cross his path, and he'd displayed no interest. *Has he lost his mind?* Kevin scratched his head. *Sister Brenda of all people.*

The next morning Brenda had potatoes with onions frying in one skillet, bacon, and sausage in another, biscuits were in the oven, and fresh coffee was brewing. She'd started early to get Sarah's breakfast out of the way first.

"Did you bump your head or something? Mother's Day ain't for another week, and it's not my birthday; not that you care," Sarah said as Brenda set the tray down in front of her. Despite her sarcasm, she was sitting up straight in her bed, mouthwatering; eyes focused on the feast placed in front of her.

Brenda couldn't make Mr. Lawrence such a breakfast and exclude Sarah, even though the snide remark made her wish she had.

Once back in the kitchen, she finished up, making sure there was extra for Gia, who'd also be surprised if she'd bothered to come home the night before. Just then, she appeared dragging herself half-awake into the kitchen. She was in her robe and pajamas, hair all over everywhere, which meant she'd been home a few hours anyway.

"Momma, is that fried potatoes with onions?" She yawned and stretched.

Brenda laughed; the smell of food could wake Gia out of a coma.

"If you wanted me to go to church with you, you could've just asked. You didn't have to make me breakfast." She quickly washed her hands and grabbed a plate.

"Keep dreaming; this ain't for you." Brenda laughed as she blocked her path to the stove.

"Who's it for then? You're usually too busy on Sunday mornings to make a big breakfast unless we have company." Just then, the doorbell rang. "Who's that?"

Brenda didn't respond as she left the kitchen to answer the door. When she opened it, there was Mr. Lawrence Foster, punctual, impeccably dressed, and grinning as usual. "Something sure smells good, Miss Brenda; I could smell it a block away. I hope you didn't go to too much trouble."

"Yes, you do. Just get in here and eat; we don't have all morning," Brenda said, pretending to frown.

"Why don't I load your supplies now, so I don't have to worry about it later." He grabbed a couple of piles, and her car keys then walked out to the car. When Brenda turned, Gia was staring at her from the kitchen entryway.

"Momma, why are you making breakfast for Mr. Lawrence?" From what she knew, they were only casual acquaintances.

Brenda walked around her into the kitchen and started placing food on the table.

"He's been riding with me and helping me out for the last few Sundays. I thought I'd make him breakfast today."

Gia stood and blinked as she processed her mother's answer. There was a knock on the door, as Lawrence had inadvertently locked himself out.

"Can you go let him in, please?" Brenda was taking the carton of eggs from the refrigerator.

She headed to the door, thinking she may get more information from him. When she opened it, the Mr. Lawrence, she remembered, smiled brightly at her.

"Is that you, Gigi? Girl, you sure have grown up," he said, hugging her.

"Hey, Mr. Lawrence," she said, feeling like a little girl when he used her childhood nickname. "You're here for?"

"Having breakfast, then driving to church with your mom."

"What are you waiting on Gia, show him to the dining room," Brenda said. "Lawrence, how do you like your eggs?"

"Scrambled, thank you," he said, taking a seat at the table. Brenda had a glass of orange juice and warm biscuits with butter and jelly waiting.

Gia was in the twilight zone. There was a man in the house, having breakfast at their table, visiting with her mother. That didn't happen every day; it didn't happen ever. She watched as Brenda fussed about from the kitchen to the dining room, and Mr. Lawrence made small talk, enjoying the fuss. She was unsure if she was supposed to join in or make herself scarce, but the scene was too weird for her to just turn around and leave. They took no notice.

"How'd you know I love fried potatoes? This is what I call breakfast." He ate like a man who hadn't had the pleasure of a woman to cook for him in a long time.

"Glad you're enjoying it." Brenda placed two steaming cups of coffee on the table, then sat down opposite him checking her watch. "You better eat up, you know how I am," she said, then, out of the corner of her eye, caught Gia, in the hallway, staring at them. "Girl, what are you doing standing there, haven't you seen people eat before?"

Her brain was struggling to put the facts together but knew she needed to move on. She shrugged, then went into the kitchen and finished making her plate. While eating at the kitchen table, she listened in on their conversation.

"Gia, can you—" Brenda called out while removing her apron.

"Yeah, Momma, I'll clean up when I'm finished," she reappeared in the entryway. "You two kids just run along," she waved.

"That'll give you enough time to make it to the service," Lawrence winked as he followed Brenda to the door.

"You have been spending too much time around my mother," Gia said, smirking, "but I might just do that." It'd been a while since she'd been to church; it was time she popped in to get a reminder about everything in her life that wasn't right with God.

When they got to the nursing home, the two church mothers, who Brenda picked up every Sunday, were thrilled to once again ride in Lawrence's shiny cream-colored Cadillac with matching leather interior.

"We get to ride to church in style again this morning. You've become our chauffeur, haven't you, Mr. Lawrence?" Miss Logan said.

"Yes, ma'am, I guess I am."

"Miss Evans, nudged Brenda lightly, while Lawrence wasn't looking. "Girl you somethin' else," she half-whispered," got that man, driving you and us too. You gonna be draggin' him in front of the preacher soon," she chuckled.

Brenda looked back at her unsmiling. "Don't get the wrong idea, Miss Evans."

"I've got the right idea, but do you?" She shook her head and laughed at Brenda as she fastened her seat belt.

That day, Brenda was more laidback as she went about her duties as head usher of Mount Hebron church; long-time members noticed. She smiled and was pleasant to everyone at the door, even allowing congregants to select their own seats.

When Jason Fields got up to leave the sanctuary for a second cigarette break, instead of giving him the eye, she gave him a smile with a look that said, "*Let's make this the last time shall we...*"

She was enjoying being in church that day and recognized this was how it was supposed to feel when being in and serving in God's house. Somehow, she'd lost her joy and hadn't even realized it. When she turned around during praise and worship and saw Gia stroll in—late, but she was there, she knew it was her day.

After service, Brenda approached Miss Jackie, her assistant who'd served with her for years. "Jackie, I think I'm taking next Sunday off; do you think you can handle it?"

"You're going out of town?" Jackie said. That was the only time, Brenda left her post.

"No, I think I just want a day off; it's been a while." As she grabbed her purse and other belongings, she spotted Gia, on one side of the church, chatting with friends, and Lawrence on the other side waiting for her. She didn't see Jackie's jaw drop.

"This is a new day. What brought this on?" Jackie said as Lawrence approached.

"I'll go and help our passengers and meet you at the car," he said to Brenda. "Hey, Miss Jackie, good to see you." He shook her hand, then walked away.

"I see," Jackie smiled and with pursed lips, batted her eyes at Brenda.

"You don't see anything, girl; you need to stop." Brenda pushed her playfully and laughed.

Gia stepped up to the two of them and marveled. Seeing her mother joking and smiling was a nice change.

"Miss Jackie, you think my momma's got herself a boyfriend?" Gia whispered while placing an arm around her mother's shoulders.

"Could be Gigi, yes indeed," Jackie said, laughing as she exited the sanctuary.

Brenda and Gia strolled out after her.

"He seems like a nice man, momma," Gia said while opening the door for her.

"Don't make too much of it. We're just friends, and yes, he's nice."

When they got outside, Lawrence was standing by the car talking with Deacon Patterson. The two elderly ladies were seated patiently in the back seat. "I'm going home now. Are you coming?"

"No, I'll be home later; I have a date." Gia kissed her mother's cheek then strode to her car parked prominently and illegally in the fire lane of the church.

"Gia!" She'd told that girl about parking her car anywhere like she had the right to. She'd already racked up a fortune in parking tickets. The city of St. Louis sent bills every month.

"What Momma? I'm not parking my car down the block. Not in this neighborhood."

She was still shaking her head when she'd gotten to Lawrence's vehicle.

"Don't fuss, at least she came to church," he said as he opened the passenger side door for her.

He made light conversation on the drive to her house, then once in her driveway, walked her to the door. "Are we on for Tuesday bible study?" Before she could respond, he squeezed her hand. "Just think about it." He said goodbye, hopped in his car, and drove away.

7

"Underwriting, this is Curtis Morton speaking."

"Hey stranger, it's me," Gia said.

"Hey, you." There was a long pause

"How are you, Curtis?"

"Well, and you?"

"Doing alright." Another long pause.

"Are you still planning on getting married, or have you changed your mind?"

"September. Would you like me to ask my fiancée to send you an invite?"

"Ha-Ha."

"Look, Gia, I've to go."

"Let's have lunch. I'd like to talk."

"Can't."

"Dinner then. Meet me at—"

"No."

"I'll be waiting outside your building at noon. If you don't come out, I'll come in and get you," Gia said, then hung up the receiver smiling. *What is it about pursuing other women's men that's so much fun?*

Curtis slipped out of the office building, where he worked as an insurance underwriter, precisely at noon, and stepped up to the driver's side of Gia's waiting red BMW.

"I don't know what you think you—"

"Get in," she said, admiring her lipstick in the mirror.

"No, not this time. I'm done with this."

"Come on, baby. For old time's sake." She turned to him and pouted. "You're getting married, and you'll be out of my life forever. Indulge me this last time. I just want to talk."

He exhaled loudly then looked up at the sky. *Nobody begs like Gia; God, why me?* He turned and took a few steps toward the building, but when she reached over and pushed open the passenger door, he pivoted and slid into the seat. He'd barely closed the door before she sped off. He slunk down and put a hand over his eyes.

The ride was short. Gia had driven to an Italian restaurant near his job. Before he could object due to his short lunch break, she informed him she'd already ordered, and lunch was waiting.

Once seated, Gia dug into the plate of pasta while Curtis sat back in the chair opposite and watched her.

"Go ahead and eat. What are you waiting for, a formal invitation?" Gia said in between mouthfuls.

Eventually, hunger overcame his frustration, and he started in on the salad.

"You love her?" Gia said, munching on a breadstick.

"Wouldn't be marrying her if I didn't."

"More than me?" This time she put down the bread.

"I don't love you; I just thought I did. That was high school, Gia. We're grown now. You don't love me and never did."

"You love me. You did then, and you do now. Don't marry that woman. You won't be happy. She's not me."

Curtis threw his fork on the table. "Gia, you're beautiful, but you're not all that. You love you. I'm not going to spend my life trying to compete with that," he clenched his teeth and shook his head. "I must be crazy to be here. Take me back to work, and don't call me again."

She sucked her teeth. "Relax. Eat your lunch; why are you so touchy anyway? I'm just expressing my opinion. If you don't agree, then you don't. It does make me wonder if I hit a nerve."

He stood. "I'm leaving now. No, don't get up. I'll walk." Before she could settle the bill and follow him, he was gone.

"How are you doing, Mother?" Keith Banks said to Sarah. It was a warm, sunny Friday afternoon, and the two of them were seated, facing each other in Sarah's bedroom. He surveyed the brightly decorated room, breathed in the scent of fresh flowers, then smiled and patted her hand. She squinted back at him.

"Is the sunlight too bright for you; should I close the blinds?"

She waved him off. "Don't bother. I'm doin' the same; amazin', I'm still alive considering the way I'm treated here."

"It looks to me like Bren's done a good job," Keith frowned. Sarah's accommodation was comfortable, and she appeared healthy and well cared for. "By the way, why don't you open the presents Kathy and Jill sent you."

The gift bags were sitting at her feet, but she refused to look at them. "She knew you were comin', didn't she? Pop in here unannounced some time," Sarah sneered. "Then you'll see what goes on."

Keith sighed. "We've gone through this a hundred times, mom. If you want to leave here, it's your choice. We'll have to find you a facility, and it'll cost more, but if that will make you happier."

"How many times have I told you I don't want to be in a nursing home with a bunch of old, sick people. That place she ships me off to every Monday is bad enough. I want you to buy me a house and hire someone to look after things. Don't tell me you can't afford it. You think I don't know how you sold my house and pocketed the money. You owe me; you've left me homeless and took everything I had." Her fists were balled up; her face was contorted.

Keith rubbed his temples. Jill, his wife, had advised him to be patient with his mother, but then she backed out of the visit at the last minute. His sister Kathy rarely came. She just sent cash.

"Mom, you and I both know, the proceeds from the sale of that house were used up years ago, paying for your care. Kathy and I, with some help from Social security, are footing the bills. We can't afford what you're asking."

"Um-hum, what good have you ever been to me?"

Keith stood and looked at his watch, "Okay, mother, I'll see you the next time. Is there anything you need before I go?"

"Just go," Sarah said, turning her back to him.

"I love you, Mom. Jill sends her love, and we hope you like the gifts," he then patted her back; she shrugged off his touch. Keith left the room, forgoing the obligatory kiss on the cheek. When he entered the dining room, Brenda was setting the table and had dinner prepared.

"I know you like my fried pork chops, so I took the liberty. Figured you'd need a little pick-me-up after spending time with Sarah," she said.

"He slumped down in the chair. You're right. How do you do it?" Keith said, reaching for a dinner roll then the butter. The smell of boiled potatoes let him know there'd be creamy mashed potatoes dripping with Brenda's onion gravy to go along with the chops.

"I got Jesus on my side, " she sang while placing the delectable meal items on the table. "Honestly, Keith, some days I don't know. Especially when she throws things and deliberately messes up the place for me to clean up, and she's so mean. But somehow, God gives me the strength."

"I think it's too much, don't you?" Keith said absently, his mind fixated on the food he spooned onto his plate. He wondered if he came to town more for Cousin Brenda's cooking than to see his mother.

"It's hard, Keith. I won't lie to you, and I don't plan on doing it forever." Brenda felt the timing was perfect. "I'm not going to up and quit on you, but since we're having this conversation, I think its best if you and Kathy start looking for Sarah's next home. Take all the time you need, but you know my father's been diagnosed with Alzheimer's."

"I heard. I'm sorry. How's Cousin Marvin doing?"

"You know how it is, good some days bad others. The problem right now is we, my mother and I, aren't receiving much help."

"Are you planning to care for him when my mother leaves?"

"No, I'll help coordinate his care, but I'm done with nursing. I'm ready for a change." The words she'd spoken aloud for the first time felt good.

"I'm glad to hear that, Brenda. It's about time you lived a little. You're still a good-looking woman. Go get yourself a new husband." Keith grinned. "The way you cook, even if you were ugly, you'd have no problem. You know that old saying about a man's heart."

Brenda playfully threw a napkin at him, "You need to quit."

"What do you mean you want your hairstyle changed? You want it pinned up higher? Maybe to the side?" The hairstylist stood back, staring at Brenda as if she didn't recognize her.

"No, you're not listening. I want the braids gone, Cozy. I want to see my hair," Brenda said. She was eyeing her reflection in the large mirror while seated in the beautician's chair.

"You've worn braids since—"

"I know that, but now I want them out. I might change my mind next week. But today, I want these braids gone, so start cutting." Brenda took a pair of scissors she spotted on the counter and handed them to Cozy.

"It'll be my pleasure," the beautician said as she started chopping. She'd been trying to get Brenda to change her hairstyle for at least two years and had failed. She was curious as to what had brought the change about and considered there might be a man in the picture, dismissing that thought immediately, however. Everybody knew Miss Brenda had no time for that.

Once her hair was done, Brenda was so pleased with the look she had Cozy do her eyebrows and treated herself to a manicure.

That was all the proof Cozy needed. Miss Brenda or not, there was a man somewhere.

"So, you got someplace fancy to go tonight? That why you're gettin' all dolled up, Miss Brenda?" she said, eyeing her watchfully.

"No, I just decided to pamper myself for once," she said, knowing Cozy was fishing for information. She checked her watch and was surprised to see it was nearly one o'clock. She had to get home to feed Sarah her lunch.

When Brenda arrived home, she found Sarah napping, an empty lunch tray beside her bed. *Gia must've made her lunch. I don't believe it.*

"Gia, are you up there?" She called from the bottom of the staircase.

"There you are," Gia said, leaning over the railing. "I thought Sarah was gonna call the cops on you. She was having a fit about her lunch being late." She had to do a double-take when her mother came into view. The braids she always wore were gone, and her hair had been straightened and curled. The change had softened her features. "Momma?" she said, trotting down the stairs. She then broke out in a smile, closed her eyes, and threw up her hands, "Thank you, Jesus, my prayers have been answered. She finally changed her hair. Oh hallelujah, Lord, I will be at church tomorrow!"

"Girl—hush," Brenda tried to keep her expression sober. "Does it look okay? I had her take care of my gray while she was at it."

"Momma, it looks nice. You could have gotten some color and extensions, but this is a start."

Brenda laughed, "Girl, what in the world do I need with extensions? I'm not trying to look your age."

"Why not? You look good for your age, might as well flaunt it."

Brenda shook her head, then glanced at the clock. "Thank you just the same. I'm going to do some shopping, want to come with me?" She wanted Gia to help her pick out an outfit for church the following day but didn't want her making a big deal of it.

"I can't. I have a bridal shower to attend, and then I've got a date tonight. What about you—do you have a date tonight or something? Maybe with Mr. Laaaaawrence," she giggled as she repeated his name a couple more times.

"Just because I changed my hair doesn't mean I'm dating all of a sudden."

"Doesn't it?" Gia said, winking, then waltzing into the kitchen.

8

I look rather nice...I think... Brenda was checking her reflection in the mirror the next morning. It was the first time she'd dressed for Sunday service in anything other than an usher's uniform in some time. Today she was sporting a fuchsia suit, tapered at the waist, with delicate floral beading around the collar and the lapel. Her matching fuchsia slingbacks were also beaded, as was her clutch bag. She fluffed her hair while admiring the gold and fuchsia earrings she'd splurged on, then the doorbell rang. She sauntered to answer it, hoping Lawrence wouldn't make a fuss over her new look.

"My!" Lawrence said, standing in the doorway. "You're a beautiful vision. Did you get dressed up for me?"

"You stop it. Come in here and have your breakfast, so we're not late," Brenda said with the glimmer of a smile on her lips.

"Good looking and a good cook," he tailed her into the dining room. "Good thing I'm not looking for a wife, or I might just snap you up."

"No one asked what you're looking for Lawrence Foster, just eat." When she turned to go back into the kitchen, he thought he detected more sway in her hips than usual.

He smiled admiring her; she had a sense of humor and kept him on his toes.

As he finished the last of his pancakes and coffee, he glanced around the quiet house. "Gia's not seeing us off this morning?"

She stiffened. "She's not here; never came home last night."

He nodded. None of his three kids lived at home anymore, and although he sometimes missed them, he didn't miss that part—especially with the girls. So many bad things can happen.

Checking his watch, he took a final gulp of coffee, then stood to put on his suit jacket. Brenda remained seated, sighing.

"I can't help but worry, but she's usually here by the time I get home from church. I just wish I understood why she can't go out and come home at a decent hour." She stood and cleared the table; Lawrence helped her before starting towards the door.

"Come back and say a little something to Sarah. She was offended last week, hearing your voice, and nobody came to speak to her."

"Hello, Sister Sa—" Lawrence started, with his hand outstretched to take hers.

"Hello, yourself, and I ain't your sister."

*What's wrong with my church family? They should be listening to the sermon, not watching me...*Brenda's elegant appearance and break from the Sunday norm of patrolling the aisles seemed to have sent a few members of Mount Hebron Baptist into a tailspin; they couldn't recover themselves. Yes, God was still on the throne; however, Miss Brenda wasn't guarding the door.

"Jesus is coming back today, for sure," she heard Mr. Lester murmur to his wife as she and Lawrence walked past them.

For Brenda, breaking her routine had been hard, but judging by the reaction, it'd been overdue. There'd been nothing wrong with her faithful service, but maybe she'd been too visible patrolling the church like God's policewoman.

She cringed as the pastor titled his sermon, "God doesn't need our help." It stung. When was the last time she'd asked God what He wanted from her, instead of plowing ahead, assuming she knew?

"Thank you for the pleasure of your company during service today. I know how important your duties are to you, and I don't take it lightly that you changed your routine because I asked," Lawrence said during the ride home from church.

Brenda was silent until he'd pulled into her driveway and cut the engine. "I think I'm the one who should be thanking you. Maybe God had some things to say to me for a while, and it was time I sat still so I could listen."

He smiled while holding the car door open for her. "Sure you want to end the day so early? You look so lovely; I'd love to escort you to a restaurant so I can show you off."

The automatic 'no thank you' was headed to her lips, but she willed herself to suppress it. She'd come this far, no point crawling back into her old life so soon.

She checked her watch, more to hide her nerves. "I have to make sure Sarah's taken care of first," she said. Even though Gia's car was in the driveway, her daughter may not have been home.

"You're going to dinner with Mr. Lawrence?" Gia, who was in the family room, working on her laptop, smirked. "You'd better bring yourself in this house at a decent hour, young lady." She joked, but the irony that her mother had a date and she didn't, felt weird.

"We won't be long, I promise."

"Loosen up, momma. Go out and enjoy yourself. I'll hit the liquor store and get a little something to take care of Aunt Sarah in there."

"I know that's right!" Sarah shouted from her bedroom on the other side of the wall. Brenda and Gia looked at each other, then stifled their laughter.

"She doesn't miss anything," Gia said.

Once they were gone, Gia picked up her phone, tempted to call Curtis. It was Sunday afternoon, and he and that fiancé of his were probably somewhere having dinner also.

She'd been chasing him hard, for two weeks trying to get him to dump that troll, to no avail. He presumed to question her motives, asserting she was insincere; just didn't want anyone else to have him. What did he know? Sure, she hadn't slowed down her dating life, while attempting to force her way into his. Curtis had always moved too slow for her. She didn't have time to wait around for him, but she did want him, and more importantly, knew he wanted her. She dialed his number, and it went to voicemail. *On to plan B...*

Lawrence was happy but guarded as he and Brenda took their seats for an early dinner at the elegant Ballentine Steakhouse. He wanted to talk—really talk about life, relationships, and love. He wanted to know so much about her but was dubious as to how far he could go before violating her boundaries.

"Lawrence, why are you smiling at me like you won the lottery?" Brenda said as the waitress placed salads and hot bread on the table.

He chuckled as he picked up his fork. "You underestimate yourself, Brenda. If you were me, you'd understand."

She smiled and fanned herself with her napkin, "You sure know how to say the right things, Mr. Foster. How is it you're still single?"

"Because, for the most part, I'm all talk. Flattery can be a useful smokescreen, like pretending to be mean."

Her mouth opened. "Are you calling me a pretender?"

Lawrence was pleased with the honest and comfortable start to their conversation. To him, it was apparent she wanted someone to talk to also. He was content to spend most of their dinner listening as she opened up to him about her life, family crisis, and dreams.

"Lawrence, it just seems like change is coming my way, whether I'm ready for it or not. At the same time, I know I'm ready; I've been yearning for it for a long time."

He nodded, "When my life changed three years ago, I was blindsided. I'd assumed our path was set; then my wife was gone. I don't want to be that blind again."

After dinner, they strolled arm in arm downtown along Market Street, enjoying the sunset. Brenda was home before dark.

9

"Brenda, your father said he was going into the backyard. I kept watching to make sure he was still there. But somehow, he got past me. He's been gone over an hour, and I don't know where he is."

Sarah had left for the senior center, and Brenda was looking forward to a few minutes of quiet; now this.

"Did you call the police?"

"No, I just thought you could..."

You just thought I could. Brenda thought on the drive to her mother's house. *They all assume Brenda could, but nobody asks. I'm supposed to fix it and keep it quiet, so the rest of them don't have to worry.* While stopped at a red light, she let out a growl resisting the compulsion to lay her head on the steering wheel. She wondered when her mother would admit the load was too much to bear even for the two of them.

"Daddy, what are you doing here?" Brenda found her father sitting on a park bench, staring at ducks splashing around in a pond. She'd startled him and could tell by the way he peered back at her he had no recognition of who she was.

"Come on, Deacon Marvin, you'll be late for service," Brenda said, knowing when he was disoriented, she needed to bring him back to a familiar place, or he'd refuse to leave. Her father was a big man; dragging him home was no option.

"Yes, okay," Marvin said, all his questions as to her identity answered as he sprang up from the bench and walked purposefully toward the car without asking which one was hers. He suddenly stopped. "I don't have my bible. Did I leave it on that bench?"

"No, sir. We'll stop by your house to get it."

In the few minutes it took for Brenda to drive her father home, his orientation returned.

"Brenda, why did Corene call you? I was okay; just took a walk, that's all. She needs to stop worrying and getting you upset. I'm still a grown man. Can't I leave the house sometimes?"

She didn't want to upset him by telling him he hadn't recognized her just a few minutes before. He'd only deny it and accuse her of lying. When he entered the house, he was so angry he walked past his wife, as she tried to question him, and locked himself in the den.

"You see how he is; what am I going to do with him?" Corene said.

"When's the last time you had his medication checked?"

"I can't get him to go to the doctor. If I make the appointment, do you think you can take him? He seems to listen to you, especially when I'm not around."

"Sure, Momma," Brenda said, inhaling deeply. There was no point lecturing her again about how things couldn't continue this way.

"You changed your hair; it looks nice...."

"You've got a gentleman friend, huh?" Sarah said to her later that evening. "He don't know what he's getting himself into, does he? Something's wrong with him anyway, always grinning. I wouldn't trust him if I were you. Next thing you know, he'll be chasing your daughter. No man wants nothing old as you."

Brenda was in Sarah's room, cleaning up a mess the old woman had made with her dinner. Food all over the floor was the older woman's method for expressing the anger of feeling she'd been neglected. "Do you want something to help you sleep tonight?" She hoped she'd say yes and felt like slipping her a double dose to shut her up.

"Don't drug me. I gotta keep my eyes open, now that some man is creeping around. If you try to slip him in here at all hours of the night, you know I'll hear it, and I *will* call your pastor."

"Who I choose to slip in or out of my house is neither your nor my pastor's business. Thank you for your concern."

"Just trying to keep you out of hell. Even though the way you've treated me, you're going there anyway."

"I don't know what to do, Lawrence. He's my dad, and I want to do the right thing, but I've taken care of the elderly all my life. How can I give him the care he needs if I do it out of obligation and not desire? Am I wrong; because my family sure makes me feel I am?" Brenda and Lawrence were in the coffee shop near the church. Coming there following Tuesday, bible study had become a routine.

"Our families mean well, sometimes. You know that, but there tends to be selfishness mixed in with those good intentions. After you've made the changes in your life that are right for you, they may not understand, but they'll get over it. Your dad's well-being is the most important consideration. Making your family feel comfortable by taking the burden for the rest of them is not."

A look of relief spread across Brenda's face, and she smiled. He could see her point so clearly, while her family behaved as if she were speaking in tongues or not at all when discussing the issue.

"I can see you're feeling better. Glad I could help." Lawrence said, squeezing her hand that had been resting on the table. She nodded and took a sip of coffee.

"I went through a similar situation ten years ago, when my mother was ill with cancer. Unfortunately, I was more like one of your siblings; my wife stepped in. She did that often over the years, wherever needed, doing her thing, never complaining, and not taking care of herself. Next thing you know, she has a massive heart attack and is gone. My big regret is that I let her take care of everything without making sure she was taken care of. Some things you can't do over."

It was the first time Brenda noticed him not smiling as she watched him look down into his coffee cup, stirring slowly.

"Speaking as a woman who tries to do everything. We don't listen to anybody anyway. God probably called her home because He knew it was the only way to slow her down."

Lawrence chuckled as he laid the spoon on the table and sat back in his chair.

"Why don't we go out on a date this weekend, like a couple of kids, maybe catch a movie? How about it?" Lawrence said, walking Brenda to her car.

"A movie. Lord, I haven't done that in—"

"Is that a yes?"

"Maybe," she rolled her eyes as she slid behind the wheel, and he closed the car door. After starting the engine, however, she called out to him. "We have to go early; I can't stay out too late. I never know if Gia will be around to help with Sarah."

Lawrence nodded and climbed into his car.

When Gia arrived home from work on Friday evening, she found Mr. Lawrence sitting in her living room reading the newspaper.

"Hey, Gigi," he said. "How was your day?"

"Fine," she furrowed her brow, wanting to ask him what he was doing there. Seeing Mr. Lawrence on a Sunday was becoming the norm, but it was Friday, and he wasn't even dressed in a suit; instead, he wore a pair of jeans and a button-down shirt. Her mother then appeared wearing a casual Capri outfit made from jean material with a matching jacket.

"We're, uh, going to the movies," Brenda said, looking down, picking at a loose string on her jacket.

"Going on another date, huh? Don't worry; I'll listen out for Sarah," Gia grinned.

Brenda's eyebrows raised. "Since when are you home on a Friday night?"

Her daughter shrugged, grabbed a soda and bag of potato chips, then headed up to her second-floor sanctuary. She stopped and turned to her mother. "I guess I'm moving out next week because you're getting a life."

"What was she doing there, Curtis?" Felice demanded. It was Sunday afternoon, and she and Curtis were sitting in his car, in the church parking lot, watching as Gia hopped into her convertible and sped off. The other woman had popped into the service late but made sure she was noticed.

"I told you I don't know," he said, rubbing his forehead. Gia made eyes at him during the service after taking a seat in the row in front of them.

"She acted as though you did. Like something is going on between the two of you. What's up?"

They were supposed to be headed to dinner, but Felice wouldn't budge. He was desperate to change the subject; he was in big trouble, having never gotten around to telling her about Gia's phone calls or the lunch date they'd almost had. Then Gia shows up in church, of all places, giving sultry looks and veiled innuendos. He was trapped.

Staring out of the car window, he heard himself say. "I hadn't told you about this, but she's been calling me...and she stopped by my job a few weeks ago...."

10

"Congratulations, Ms. Collier, you're a new homeowner. Here you are with our compliments," the closing agent handed Gia a set of house keys and a bottle of champagne.

She stood up from the table, where she'd been signing documents for over an hour, shook the woman's hand hastily, and headed for the door. She'd almost forgotten Brenda, who was still seated at the table laughing at her.

"Come on, Momma, why are you sitting there? We've got decorating to do."

Brenda tried to keep up with her, but Gia practically sprinted to her car. "Just remember," she said, sliding into the passenger seat of Gia's running vehicle. "I won't be cleaning or cooking for you."

"Cook—why should I cook? You do that every day. I'll stop by for my dinner on the way home. Just have it wrapped up and waiting."

Her mother laughed and braced herself as Gia raced her sports car down the road en route to the mall. "Did you call your father and thank him for the help he gave you with the down payment?"

"Daddy and I have an understanding," she said while stopped at a red light. "I ask him for what I'm due, nothing more. What do I need to thank him for?" Brenda shook her head, then turned and looked out the window.

It took Gia a week to get moved in, and once done, she couldn't wait to entertain. By the following Friday night, there was only one person in the world she wanted as her first guest. However, Curtis, who was having relationship problems—probably because of her, declined the invite.

"Why? It's not because of your fiancée. I heard the two of you broke up. Come on, baby. Can't we spend some time together, please?" She said while sitting outside on her patio, envisioning a candlelit dinner.

Brenda, who'd been in the kitchen helping with the dinner Gia was cooking overheard the call and wondered if she was talking to her old high school boyfriend. Her daughter had been too much for him to handle even back then.

Curtis, just home from work, disengaged the call, dropped down onto his sofa, and stared into space. All Gia ever wanted was to have her way at all costs. As a result, his engagement to Felice was hanging by a thread.

He was struggling to explain Gia's tactics to Felice, who didn't know their history. "This is more about you being in the picture than about me. If I were single and alone, Gia would have nothing to do with me, trust me," he'd tried to explain to her during their last argument.

"Then I'll talk to her," Felice said, and he winced. She took that to mean he had something to hide.

"She'd love that. It would prove to her she's coming between us. Look, she'll leave me alone when we move on with our lives. It's all about the chase with her."

"I can't just sit around and wait for that. You need to man up and do something about that woman, Curtis." Their engagement was on hold until he'd accomplished that undertaking.

His way of dealing with Gia had always been to wait until she got bored. It could happen in five minutes or five days; when it came to him, she had a short attention span.

"Daddy, you must get out of bed. Come on; you need to shower. Don't you want to go out later?" Brenda said, standing beside her father's bed. Her mother hadn't informed her, until that day, that he'd been in bed virtually the entire week. The only way he'd eat is if his wife brought his meals upstairs.

"Leave me alone. I'm tired. I'll get up when I feel like it."

"If you don't get up, I'm going to call the ambulance, and they'll take you to the hospital. Do you want that?"

"They're not taking me anywhere. Go away."

Brenda picked up the phone and pretended to dial and arrange for them to come. Marvin moved the blankets and set his feet on the floor.

"Get out of here so I can take my bath," he said.

"I think I need to stay and help."

"You get out of here now—Corene! Corene!"

"Alright, I'm going, but don't you lock that door. Do you hear me?"

"You've got to do something, Mama. I can't keep running over here every five minutes," Brenda, who was sitting in the kitchen having coffee, said to her mother who'd returned from helping her husband with his bath.

"He's just going through a phase. He does this every once and a while; it doesn't usually last long. This is the first time I've had to call you. Besides, this is a big house, you and Sarah can stay here for a while, just till he's over this."

Brenda exhaled, "Momma, you're in denial. He's not going to get over this. He may need a medication adjustment, but unless God steps in, Alzheimer's doesn't go away."

It was a good sign; her mother was admitted to needing help. The problem was she'd made the same assumption as the rest of her family, that Brenda was going to step in and be the answer.

"And secondly, about my moving in—we need to get something straight..."

"Where have you been? My lunch is late. Why didn't you call, how am I supposed to know you haven't had a car wreck or somethin'? What would happen to me? I guess I'd sit up here and starve to death."

"You know how to pick up the phone," Brenda said, placing the plate on Sarah's tray while ignoring her complaints. She had her parent's situation on her mind.

Her mother had finally heard her and knew she'd have to ask her other children for help. Brenda, though relieved, felt a heavy burden of guilt. She called the one person she could talk to. Lawrence came over for dinner that evening.

"You did the right thing," he said over the apple pie, she'd served him for dessert. "The only thing you owe anyone, except for love, is honesty. You were honest, now it's time to let things fall into place. I won't promise you things are going to turn out the way you want them to. If none of your siblings step up, you know you will; that's who you are, but God will give you the grace to do so."

Brenda smiled, "You're right. I'm here worrying about what they will or won't do, and that's not up to me. It's my job to step aside and let them do what's right, but I can't control that. If, in the end, the burden turns out to be mine anyway, I'll deal with it. I just have to pray; I don't become bitter."

"You're assuming you won't get any help. I bet you'll get some; some-times it takes people awhile. You'll have to pray for grace and patience. God will give it to you," Lawrence said, then sat back in his chair, patting his stomach. "Thank you for dinner, I'd better get home while I can still walk."

Brenda sat in church service beside Lawrence and realized three months had passed since she'd served as an usher at Mount Hebron Baptist; she wondered if she ever would again. Contrary to her thinking, chaos had not ensued because she wasn't at the door. Having trained the staff well, they kept order. The ship wasn't as tight as when she'd run it, but maybe it didn't need to be.

She and Lawrence had become friends, good friends, and she felt blessed to have him in her life, to the point she'd stopped thinking about her ex-husband Ray. Rumor had it, he was headed for another divorce. That news didn't faze her. Brenda was looking forward, not back, and God was doing good things in her life, despite her father's illness.

She turned and scanned the sanctuary to see if Gia might have sneaked in but didn't see her. Something was going on with her lately, which had Brenda concerned. Her daughter was drifting further from God, and after settling down into her new home, seemed unhappy.

"What's this all about, Brenda? Mom says we need to come to town for a family meeting about Dad. Did you put her up to this?" Marvin, her brother, said. Since their mother had called her siblings, Brenda's home and cell phone had been busy.

"Call Momma and ask her. It's her meeting, not mine."

"Are you still caring for Sarah?"

"It's none of your business what I'm doing. Do I ask you how you're making a living? Your parents need you. I hope you can make time for them."

"Don't give me that."

"Gotta go, Marvin. I'll give you a ride from the airport; call me when you get here."

Brenda had told her mother she'd support her wishes but wasn't going to take over; she meant it. Her role was to gather information on resources they may want to evaluate to keep Marvin at home. Bringing in the care he needed would be expensive, however.

She and her mother managed to get him to a doctor's appointment, and his medication was adjusted. He'd been less erratic since then, but the doctor told them Marvin's condition was degenerating. Any improvements would most likely be temporary. Brenda and Corene believed in divine healing and took the doctor's dire prognosis for what it was. They also knew they needed to plan for the worst.

"I don't like the idea of a stranger coming into my house. Are you sure you won't—"

"Momma. I'll do whatever I have to do, but this is too big for me, and I realize it. We need to do our best and leave the rest up to God. He'll send the right person our way."

The family meeting was arranged for Labor Day weekend. Marvin Jr. arrived in town first and was startled at how their father's condition had worsened in less than a year. The elder Marvin didn't recognize his son until the second day he was there.

Darwin flew in that Sunday, letting everyone know he had to turn around and leave the following day. Her sister Christine who complained of being broke and too busy avoided the trip entirely.

"Your father's not getting any better, and if God doesn't heal him, I won't be able to care for him much longer. I need a person in the house during the day, just to help with his medications and keep an eye on him. I should be able to handle the night's right now, but if it gets to the point where I can't, I'll need 24-hour home care, or he'll need to go into a facility." She let her words sink in before continuing. Marvin was frowning, and Darwin was checking his watch and fidgeting. Neither of them addressed Brenda.

They were assembled in Corene's living room, on that late Monday morning. Darwin had a plane to catch, so they sat down to talk immediately after having breakfast. Marvin Sr had gone to his room for a nap.

"Sorry, Momma," Darwin said. "I don't understand why you called us here. You and Brenda could've—"

"He's as much your father as he is Brenda's and expecting her to give up her life—" Corene paused, and Brenda turned to her and frowned. "is unfair. The bottom line is I need financial help, so our resources won't be exhausted. Brenda's looked into some agencies," she then passed out brochures. "She's also summarized the pricing involved. We've sent the same packet to Christine. I'll need you to look it over and get back with me with how much, if anything, you can commit. That will help determine where I go from here."

"I've got two kids in college, Mom. I'm strapped right now," Darwin said, speaking to his mother but looking at Brenda."

"I'll have to talk with my wife and see what we can do. She's just started her business," Marvin said.

"I've got a small sum put away, and after I pay off my mortgage—" Brenda started to say.

"It's just as I suggested in the first place Brenda," Darwin said, standing and throwing down the papers. "Sell your house, send Sarah packing, and move in here and help mom. It's the only option that makes any sense. Why are you putting us through this?"

"I don't want to sell my house now, and when I do decide to, I don't want to move in here."

"This isn't about you. It's about our parents," Marvin said. "None of us are in the position to make the kind of sacrifice necessary, but you are. Step up to the plate, and we'll do whatever we can to help."

"No," Brenda said, crossing her legs, and setting her jaw. "I'm not an only child. I'm tired of the rest of you behaving as if I am."

"I guess there's nothing more to say," Darwin stood. Just then, Marvin Sr. walked into the room.

"Darwin, when did you get here. Boy, it's been too long," their father said, walking toward him smiling, his arms extended.

"Hey pop," Darwin said, they'd seen and talked to each other twice that day. "Don't you remember we had breakfast?"

"Course I do, boy. Where'd Sheryl go?" The older man asked then, without waiting for an answer, followed his wife into the kitchen.

Darwin sat back down and covered his eyes. Sheryl was his ex-wife, and they'd been divorced for years.

"Maybe they can come and live with one of you," Brenda said, with their parents out of the room. "I'd be willing to do my best to help you with whatever accommodations you need to make."

"That's stupid, Brenda," Marvin Jr. said, shaking. "You don't move a man in his condition out of familiar surroundings. You know that."

Brenda shrugged and raised her hands in surrender.

The three sat in silence, not looking at one another.

"Mama is asking all of us to do what we can, and I think that's fair. No one's pointing fingers or asking for anything you don't have. One way or the other, Daddy will receive the care he needs. God will provide. You need to understand we're all part of this, and if you choose not to be involved, don't complain about the decisions that are made.

"Nobody's going to complain. Who are you to preach to us, anyway?" Darwin turned to her.

"Darwin, stop it. Brenda is who she is, she's not going to change," Marvin said, shaking his head.

She leaned forward, slammed her hand on the coffee table glaring at Marvin, ready to demand he elaborate on 'who Brenda is.'

"Brenda, can you help me, please?" Her mother called from the kitchen.

"Yes, Momma," she said, cutting her eyes at Marvin as she left the dining room.

He chuckled at her look of ferocity. It reminded him of when they fought as kids. She never backed down, even though he was older and stronger, she'd fight him until he got tired and apologized, even if he weren't wrong. She was ready to go a few rounds with him now.

"I'm sorry for that comment. It wasn't necessary," Marvin said when she returned.

"Why are you apologizing for telling the truth? I'm tired of her trying to run everyone else's life because she doesn't have one."

"Apparently, she hasn't told you about the new man in her life." They turned toward the kitchen, unaware their mother had entered the room.

"Is that so?" Darwin said. "Now it's making sense. You're putting your new man before family. You need to check yourself, Brenda."

Shaking her head, Brenda grabbed her purse and departed the house. It didn't matter what she did; if it didn't make life convenient for him, Darwin would have a problem with it.

"My mother then mentioned you, and my brother accused me of putting you before my family," Brenda told Lawrence over dinner the following weekend. "The bottom line is nothing was settled. I spoke my piece loud and clear, but they ignored me."

"I'm flattered," Lawrence said. "It's not every day a man makes it into a family argument. Things between us are clicking, huh?" He laughed.

Brenda sighed and put a hand over her eyes.

"So, are we—a couple?" He said, leaning across the table, in the dimly lit restaurant.

Brenda chuckled then shrugged. "I don't know if I want to be bothered with labels."

"Are we going to keep seeing each other?"

She cut then took a bite of her steak as if she were weighing what he was saying. "I don't have a whole lot going on right now."

"Not the answer I'm looking for."

Brenda smiled and put down her fork. "I've enjoyed the time we've spent together, and I don't know how I could get through what I'm dealing with between Sarah and my father if I didn't have you to talk to. You're a good friend, you love God, and you know how to pray. What woman would let that go? I've been called many things, Lawrence Foster, but I'm not a fool."

Lawrence laughed. "Now that's what I call an answer," he said, as they clicked their glasses together in a toast. "You know how to say the right things when you try, Brenda Collier. Keep talking like that and I might have to drag you before the judge and get some papers."

"Let's get this straight. If I go anywhere, you won't be dragging me," Brenda then sat back in her chair and winked. Lawrence's smile said he could've gone to heaven at that moment, a happy man.

"Get outta here right now. Bad enough I gotta put up with your bad treatment, but I'm not puttin' up with you when I don't feel like it. I was telling Russell about how I'm being forced to live, and he promised me—he said 'Momma if it's the last thing I do, I'm going to get you outta there, and they (referring to Keith and Kathy, her children) are going to have to pay you back every dime they stole from you.' That's what my son said to me. You just wait; you'll get yours."

"You have a doctor's appointment today. Get dressed so we won't be late. I'm tired of telling you the same thing," Brenda said, moving toward Sarah, with a comb in one hand, a jar of hair oil in the other.

"Keep your hands off me. Don't touch me!" Sarah said, in a high-pitched screech.

"Fine," Brenda said, throwing up her hands. "If you want to see the doctor with your hair all over the place, suit yourself. But you'd better have those clothes on when I get back in here."

She walked out on her grumbling aunt, then went into her room and stretched out on the bed. *I don't know how much longer I can do this.* She meant it. Between her father and Sarah, it was too much. Brenda had mailed out her final mortgage payment the week before, and something happened as soon as it left her hands. *It's time to make a change.*

"Gia, I hate to be the bearer of bad news, but your numbers are down month to date compared to this time last year. You need to prepare a proposal to present to the board on your strategy to remedy the situation."

She'd come into work that Monday morning and had been summoned to Chase's office before having time to boot up her computer. Nodding, she turned to leave.

"Also, Reid mentioned there was a problem with the Austin account. You haven't kept me in the loop. I'll need the details by this afternoon."

She stopped. "There's no problem."

He leaned back in his chair and frowned, tapping the end of his pencil on his armrest. "Something about a misplaced buy order?"

She shook her head. "That was a miscommunication. Nothing was misplaced."

He swerved away, shifting his attention to his computer screen. "Whatever you choose to call it, I'll need the details."

She left the office and found Reid, her subordinate, standing at the administrative assistant's desk, throwing side glances her way. Gia knew he was undermining her as he coveted her job. The problem was he was gaining favor with Chase; she had to put him in his place cautiously.

"Jessica, schedule a meeting for Reid and me as soon as possible; this morning if you can fit it in." She then marched past him into her cubicle and sat down, her plan already materializing. He would be assigned the proposal she was to present to the board. Usually, she'd distribute pieces to her team, but Reid was getting all of it. Then she'd make him revise it a few times, guaranteeing he'd be working late hours for the next three days. Crossing her legs, she grinned. *If you can't fire 'em-you make 'em miserable.*

"Can I come over? I'm going through some things at work, and I need to talk."

Curtis, who'd just gotten in from work, swallowed hard while holding the phone; it was hard to deny Gia when she asked him for something, which was rare. She usually demanded he complies with her every whim. "We're talking now."

"Come on, Curtis," she laughed. "You're acting like you're scared to be alone with me; is that what the problem is?"

He exhaled loudly into the phone. He had no reason to defend his manhood, but then again, he wasn't going to let Gia call him a wimp. "What's your address; maybe I'll try to stop by." He scribbled it down on a receipt.

"Don't bring anything but yourself, and don't keep me waiting," she said, ending the call quickly. Then, after ordering Curtis's favorite Thai food and pulling out a bottle of wine, she grabbed some candles and tidied up her place. Calling him was a lark, and she'd expected him to brush her off. This was her one shot at getting him back, and she was going to make it count.

"Nice place," Curtis said, stepping down into her sunken living room about an hour after they spoke. "We were planning on buying a house; even had a few narrowed down."

"Move in here with me. I've got room," Gia said, ignoring his woeful reference to his ex. She sat down on the sofa and crossed her bare legs, her short skirt exposing plenty of thigh. On the coffee table, she'd placed lit scented candles, and soft jazz was playing in the background. The living room lights were dimmed, but he refused to sit.

"This isn't a good idea. I should go," Curtis said, heading to the door.

"Why?" She jumped up after him.

"Candles, wine; I'm not sure what you have planned, but I don't want to disappoint you."

"Come on. Relax," Gia said, taking his hand and leading him back into the living room. "I appreciate you coming over. I wanted things to be nice; I'm not trying to seduce you. You're so uptight around me; even when we talk, I was hoping you'd let your guard down. That's all."

Believing he'd made himself clear, there'd be no romance that night, he sat down on the couch and relaxed. The food was delivered, and while they ate the fragrant Pad Thai, Gia poured out all her struggles at work and in her life.

"I'm not happy with my life. It's like from the time I saw you again at your party. It came to me. I've never met anyone even close to you in all these years, and I know you're what I need. I'll be honest, I'm sorry you're hurt about your engagement not working out, but I also believe it's our second chance."

"You've got to be kidding—a second chance? How about twentieth Gia!" He suddenly realized she'd slid close to him on the couch; he moved over to put space between them.

"It doesn't matter. We've grown up. It can work this time," Gia whispered in his ear, then wrapped her arms around him and rested her chin on his shoulder.

He removed her arms then stood, digging for his car keys.

"Don't act like this, Curtis. I have a lot of pressure on me right now. I need you. You're the only one who can help me get through it. Maybe you're feeling a loss right now, but I can fill that; you know I can." She started to reach for him, but he evaded her by walking around the coffee table.

"I'm not the man for you, Gia. I know myself well enough to understand that; I can't put myself in that position again. I'll try to make you happy; you'll be disappointed, then I'll get hurt. You're looking for a god, not a man, and God is the only person I can recommend to you.

You can't expect me or any human to meet your expectations because, when a brother doesn't measure up, you make him pay."

"Don't preach to me," she said, springing up. Curtis darted for the door, but she got there first.

"Look, I know I've been unfair to you in the past, but I'm telling you I've changed. You need to meet me halfway. Give me a chance."

He stepped back, then folded his arms. "You say you want to try again; let's try. Here and now."

She smiled and put an arm around his waist, leading him back to where they'd left their wine, untouched. While they stood, Gia grabbed hers and lifted it for a toast. "I don't drink anymore. I was starting to have a substance problem. After I committed my life to God, I gave it up."

She nodded, put her glass down, wrapped her arms around him, and moved to kiss him.

"I don't indulge in that either," he said. "I'm looking for a wife, not a hookup."

"Well, what do you do? I don't have any checkers," she said, snarling then picking up and draining her wine glass. *It won't hurt him to close his bible for one night. He could always pick it back up tomorrow...*"Really, what do you do in your spare time?"

"Play sports, go to concerts, and get together with a group of friends at my church, which is how I met Felice. It sounds dull, but it's my life. I'm happy," he said, then shoved his hands into his pockets.

"Even though your engagement didn't work out?"

He shrugged. "Things happen for a reason. Maybe we both need time to see if marriage is what we want."

Gia stared at him; he wasn't the same guy. He'd always been good-looking, dull, and in love with her. She'd thought by getting the fiancée out of the way, she could reclaim her place in his life. It was apparent now that woman wasn't the problem.

She drained another glass of wine, then leaned over the coffee table and blew out the candles.

He could tell by her movements and lack of eye contact, he was yesterday's news, which was okay with him.

"It was nice seeing your place," Curtis said and again headed to the door. "I hope you'll be happy here."

"I will be. Thanks for coming by." She followed him slowly then stood like a mannequin when he kissed her cheek.

Once he was gone, she took the wine bottle with her glass and plodded slowly to her bedroom, wondering where she'd go from there; having wasted six months pursuing a man, she now realized she didn't want and who didn't want her.

"What is wrong with you?" she asked herself out loud while looking at her reflection in the mirror. She worked hard to make herself happy, only to fall flat to where she was.

"Tomorrow is a new day, girlfriend, and it's all about you," she said, lifting the glass and toasting her reflection.

Suddenly Curtis's words floated back to her. *God is the one you need.* She knew that was true, ultimately, but before she turned her life over to Him, there were things she needed to prove to herself. She needed to fix her life so she could give God something He'd be proud to have.

12

"Daddy, did I hear right; you're dating Miss Brenda from the church? That mean lady who used to guard the door. Kevin was lying, wasn't he?" Stephanie, Lawrence's oldest daughter, asked him. She'd stopped by his house for a rare visit and had also brought dinner.

How much is this going to cost me? Lawrence forced a smile. He feigned enjoyment of the food she'd brought; greasy carry out fare she should've known he wouldn't like. *If she's going to act like she's doing something for me, she could try a little harder.*

"Don't go labeling people. She's a nice person, a bit misunderstood perhaps," he said, picking at the food with his fork.

"If you say so," Stephanie's voice trailed off. "Guess what happened to me this week Daddy."

Here it comes.

"I was offered an opportunity to become part-owner of a restaurant; this restaurant." She pointed to the tasteless plate of barbecued ribs. "The owner is a friend of mine, and he's just starting out. Anyway, we've been talking, and I've been giving him some ideas on what I think will help his business, and he's really been receptive and..."

Lawrence appeared to be listening but was really watching his daughter babble with excitement. He'd been here before.

He sighed deeply, unaware she'd stopped talking and was waiting for a response from him.

"I'm sorry, did you—?"

"Fifty thousand dollars, Daddy. To buy into the business. Then I'll be an entrepreneur. You've always told us we should aim high. This will be my break into the business world, and I know it'll succeed. I can feel it. I know you don't believe in astrology, but last week my horoscope told me not to pass up an opportunity when it comes my way. I can't pass this one up. What do you think?"

"It sounds great, Stephanie, if it's what you want. Go for it, commit yourself to it, and it will be a success. You're a talented young woman, you just need focus. Maybe this will provide that," Lawrence rose from the table and the meal he'd barely touched.

"Thank you for the encouragement Daddy, but you didn't say anything about the mon—the investment," Stephanie said, trailing him into the kitchen.

"What would I have to say about that?" He turned on the faucet. "If you have the money and believe in what you're doing, go for it."

Stephanie leaned her back against the kitchen counter, grabbed her head with both hands and grimaced while looking up at the ceiling, and howled. "Uhhh!!!"

Lawrence, unfazed, washed the few dishes in the sink while thinking for the hundredth time, her true calling had been in the theater. *Shame she won't ask for a one-way ticket to Hollywood. I might be tempted....*

"Daddy!" She shrieked. "I thought you'd support me in this."

"Baby, you know I support you in whatever direction you choose. I'm just not going to pay for it."

"What the he—" she paused and inhaled. "That's not an answer, Daddy, and you know it. You're playing games, and I'm serious," she said, pouting.

Lawrence scratched his head. It was going to take more than a pout for him to give her fifty-grand. Jesus was going to have to descend from heaven that moment and give him the word from His own mouth.

"I don't know what you want me to say. I don't have that kind of money."

"Yes, you do. Mom's life insurance alone, and then you sold the house," she blurted.

He frowned, and she fell silent as he continued. "—lying around. What resources I do and don't have is none of your business. I've worked hard and earned every dime, and I don't have anything to justify or apologize for."

"Yeah, yeah, yeah," Stephanie said, her eyes rolling up to the ceiling. She'd tried being nice, but with her dad, that never got her anywhere.

The anger churned in her chest, then moved to her mouth. As soon as she opened it, she knew what was coming. "You bible thumpers are all the same. You claim you want to help others, but you won't help your own flesh and blood. I'm sick of you. You and mean, Miss Brenda, can have each other. I bet she's even tighter with a dollar than you are."

"Sorry, you feel that way, sweetheart. Thanks for stopping by." *I've had enough of you, please leave.* "I wish you well in your new venture. If you want it bad enough, you'll find a way to make it happen. There isn't anything you can't do."

"Save it," Stephanie said through clenched teeth as she grabbed her keys and exited the house, slamming the door behind her.

Brenda doesn't appreciate what a blessing Gia is. Lawrence thought, shaking his head as he took the food Stephanie brought outside to the dumpster. *$50,000 for this?*

Stephanie cursed the world all the way home while driving the broken-down car she'd borrowed from her friend Brandon. Her own car wasn't running. She was late with the rent again, and her roommate was ready to evict her, plus she was on probation at the job for calling in sick too many times. She needed cash, and although fifty-grand was a bit ridiculous, she figured her dad would counter with something just to make her happy. What happened to a father wanting to make his daughter happy? But he hadn't cared. Didn't ask her how she was making out or if she needed help. He gave her one of his smiles, patronizing words, then watched her leave his house in utter distress.

Sure, she'd invented the story about the business; thought it would make him happy to invest money into her future instead of just giving it to her, but that had backfired also. The worst part: Stephanie wondered if he'd even detected the lie; she was skilled in that area. He wasn't giving her any money, whether the story was true or not. "This is all his fault," she said into the air, while stopped at a red light.

"How are you doing, Mother Sarah?" Keith said.

"How do you think? She's in here poisonin' me, and those doctors don't know nothin'".

"I've spoken with one of your doctors today mother, he assured me Brenda is—"

"What do you care anyway? You'll listen to anybody but me. I'm telling you; she's abusing me. You need to put a camera in here like you see on TV and that'll tell the story."

"Sarah," Brenda called from the kitchen. "What do you want for lunch?"

"Nothin' you cook."

An hour later, after lunch, when Brenda and Keith were in the dining room, having coffee, he said, "I've been thinking hard about our last conversation about how you're ready to do something else with your life besides caring for my mother. I want you to know, I've taken the next step and toured a few of the nursing homes in the area. I'm encouraged. There are no openings yet; however, I've placed her name on two waiting lists and started the paperwork for Medicaid and Medicare. By the time there is an opening, everything will be all set-up. I just wanted to give you that update. If you can hang in there with us, this can all work out."

"I'm glad to hear that Keith," Brenda said, setting down her coffee cup. "Take all the time you need. I'm not rushing you. I know first-hand how important it is to find the right care for a parent." He sipped his coffee and nodded.

"Sarah's going to be leaving soon," Brenda said to Gia as she placed the platter of meatloaf on the table.

Her daughter, who'd come over for dinner for the third time that week, smiled at the sight of savory meatloaf and the bowl of creamy mashed potatoes. "What are you going to do then, Momma?"

"Girl, I don't know, but you're going to have to learn how to cook for yourself. I'm not going to be sitting around here much longer."

Her eyebrows raised as she lifted a forkful of meatloaf to her mouth. *Where does she think she's going?* She also wondered where Mr. Lawrence fit in.

"By the way, I forgot to tell you the latest; I talked to daddy the other day. She's divorcing him and asking for a whole lot of child support. He started asking me about you."

"What's Ray asking about me for? I can't do nothing for him, never could," Brenda said, fanning herself even though it wasn't hot in the room. "When I think of all the time I wasted waiting for him to look my way, I could kick myself. He was a waste of my time when he was here." Gia put down her fork and cocked her head to the side. "Of course, you're the one good thing that came out of that union, sweetie," she smiled.

Gia nodded and went back to her plate. "What would you do if he showed up at the door, with a bouquet of flowers, a divorce decree, and a marriage proposal all on the same day?"

"No point in my answering that question because it won't happen." Brenda stood to clear the table.

"You know what I'm asking you, Momma."

She stopped moving and turned. "You're asking me am I still in love with your father. No, I'm not."

"What about Mr. Lawrence?"

She looked off into the distance, appearing to be reading her own thoughts. "I like Lawrence...he's a good friend. I didn't know how much I needed a friend until he pushed his way into my life, and I do mean pushed," she chuckled. "He's a good man, and he's a praying man. I don't let myself get too caught up in the whole romance thing; I've been on my own so long. I really don't know if I can be involved with a strong-willed man. Ray was a pushover, but don't let Mr. Smiling Lawrence Foster fool you; he knows how to stand his ground. It's hard not to respect a man like that, but I don't know if we could make it. Kind of like you and Curtis."

Gia, while drinking iced tea, nearly choked.

Brenda laughed. "I am right, aren't I? You two were seeing each other for a minute. What happened this time, the same old thing?"

She shrugged. "Yeah, I made a play for Curtis. I might have even broken up his engagement, but then it just wasn't right between us. I hear he's seeing someone else already. Goes to show life goes on." She was surprised at herself, as she rarely talked to her mother about her relationships, but then she'd opened the door by asking about hers.

"Nobody's right, are they? What do you want, Gia?"

She shrugged again, unable to put into words the man she was looking for. Knowing only she didn't want; every man she'd been acquainted with up to that point in her life. While Brenda took a plate to Aunt Sarah, Gia sat back in the chair, biting her lower lip, thinking about her latest romantic entanglement; she shook her head. *What the hell am I doing?*

13

Chase, Gia's boss, was the new flavor of the month; she hadn't seen it coming.

Things at work had been brutal, and in her new position of authority, she'd become everyone's target. Even Chase had become critical of her every move. When she did meet her objectives, he still found some reason to slam her. Having tried everything: working late, pushing her staff harder. She'd even fired an underperformer who'd been with the company for years; someone had to be sacrificed. None of it worked for long.

She felt the need to be in his good graces again. He'd always been her biggest supporter and defender, but she was losing ground with him.

One night, when they both happened to be working late, she invited him to have a drink. Maybe she'd smiled too much, flashed too much of the cleavage she was so proud of, tried too hard to be irresistible. Never anticipating he'd proposition her, never thinking she'd accept.

She'd gotten what she'd sought after, however. Chase eased up on her at work, but the affair was on. He didn't call often, but when he did, she felt obligated to be available, like it was part of the job. She tried to convince herself it was no big deal; a girl did what she had to do to succeed. She was in control and could end it at any time. That he behaved like it was a regular part of business caused her to wonder how many others he was involved with.

Gia knew they were unprofessional and unethical, but keeping him happy meant her work life was more relaxed. Her career was all she had.

"I want to get to a place where everything in my life is the way it's supposed to be, so I won't have to try so hard to be happy. I want a man who understands what it means to crave success, more than anything," Gia blurted when her mother returned.

Brenda stopped and folded her arms, "Uh-huh, that's what I thought. You don't have a clue," she said, then slipped into the kitchen to brew coffee.

Has she ever listened to me? Gia thought, then imagined marching into the kitchen and telling her mother she was sleeping with her boss. Would Brenda pretend she hadn't heard her, give her one of her famed looks of disgust, preach to her, or would she understand? She needed to talk to someone other than her mother. Brenda loved her unconditionally, but when unhappy with her choices, she never bit her tongue about it.

"Hi Curtis, how are you?"

Sitting in his living room, flipping through cable channels, he'd just seen a woman who'd reminded him of Gia, and then she calls. *Lord, what? ...*

"It's okay, you can speak to me. Last I heard, saying hello isn't a sin."

She'd called Curtis because she wanted to talk; he'd always been a good listener and gave sound advice. Whenever they'd had communication problems, it was because she'd been playing head games.

He let out a breath silently; it was a pleasure to hear the voice of the real Gia, the girl he liked. When she dropped her tricks and facades, she was a lovely person. Unfortunately, she couldn't be without the subterfuge for long.

"I just saw someone on television who reminded me of you. Funny, you called. Everything okay?"

Before saying a word, she was sobbing.

"Come on, Gia, it can't be that bad. What is it; something wrong with your mom?"

Her tears ceased almost instantly. Curtis had a knack for putting things into perspective in the subtlest of ways. *Something wrong with your mom*—now that was a problem. Compare it to another misstep, transgression, wrong turn, which had comprised her love life up to that point. What were the tears about?

"Gia?" she heard Curtis say and realized she'd gone silent.

"Sorry, I'm still here. I'm just thinking...about things. I didn't call to bother you; I just needed you to set me straight."

"Huh?"

"Nothing. I'm messing up again. I don't want to go into detail; just tell me what's wrong with me?"

He cleared his throat. He'd told Gia before and could tell her again, but it was a waste of time until she was ready to hear it. "Do you really want me—"

"No, I guess not. You know, not everything is for everybody. I know you've found church, and that's cool, but I'm—"

"Haven't found church, Gia. Doesn't take much effort to find church; church is everywhere. I found God, or rather He found me. He'll find you too and fix everything, but you've got to let Him."

"Is everything with you a mini-sermon?"

"I help the only way I know how."

She changed the subject, and they talked for a while. Curtis was seeing someone new and thought he liked her. "She seems to be more confident in who she is and what she wants. I now realize Felice wasn't the one, so I guess I have you to thank."

"I'm sorry for all the games I played. Sometimes I can't help myself. I've gotten myself into a fix, playing my games; it's my boss this time. I started playing with fire; now he's determined to hold me there."

"Walk away from it, Gia. You can't win."

"One word from him, and he can destroy my career before it gets started. He's going to get tired of it sooner or later."

"Tired of what, wielding his power over a beautiful woman? When he's through with you, he won't keep you around to talk about it; you'll be the first to go. Cut your losses, Gia."

He talked to her about the situation for over an hour, and his conclusion was always the same. The affair was going to backfire; the very thing she was using to try to save her career would damage it in some way. When and how it ended would determine the extent of the damage. The longer she allowed the affair to continue, the worse the ramifications. She didn't agree entirely.

The situation was terrible, but it would work itself out, she told herself. She'd wanted Curtis to tell her everything would be okay until then. However, Curtis wouldn't do that, and his dire warnings made her feel worse.

An hour after ending her conversation with Curtis, Chase turned up at her door without calling or even asking if she wanted his company. He strolled in casually, opened a bottle of wine, and with few pleasantries, went to her bedroom and waited.

While she stalled in the kitchen, trying to think of a way to get rid of him, she spotted an envelope addressed to her he'd dropped onto the counter. She opened it to find an invitation to a party celebrating his engagement.

"Daddy, how are you feeling today? Do you want me to go out and get you some lunch? How about some shrimp salad; you like shrimp salad, right?"

Marvin stared at Brenda with no hint of recognition, then grunted.

"It's time for me to go to church," he said. "They're waiting on me, and I can't find my car keys."

"Daddy, it's Tuesday. Nobody's waiting for you, and you haven't driven a car in a year."

"That's a lie. That's a lie. I can drive. I never had an accident or a ticket. Why are you lying like that?"

Brenda sighed. He hadn't recognized her for two weeks now. The changes in medication had helped in some areas, he hadn't been as agitated or restless, but his confusion seemed worse. They'd called his physician but received the answer they expected. He has Alzheimer's, and it is what it is. Some days would be better than others, but overall, his condition would decline.

"How is the home health aide working out?" Brenda asked her mother when she'd gotten back downstairs.

"He doesn't want to have anything to do with her. Every time she tries to give him his medication or help him get dressed, he starts fussing. I asked her to help me with the housework so I'm free to tend to him, but she got mad. 'I'm not a maid,' is what she informed me. I don't know what to do."

"Momma, if it's not working out, tell the agency. Maybe they need to send someone else who's more willing to help. Don't give up so easily. This is a trial, but if you're not giving any feedback, how are we to know what to do?"

"I don't want these strangers in my house anyway. How do I know I can trust these people? I could've sworn I had twenty dollars sitting on the table yesterday, and it disappeared."

"Ma'am, I explained to you I didn't take your money!" A heavy voice from the other room yelled.

"That's another thing. I can't have a private conversation in my own house without people listening in."

They heard fast, clambering footsteps, and the front door slammed shut.

"She's gone. Thank the Lord," Corene exhaled. "I don't know where they got her from."

Brenda's mouth twisted as she perceived where the conversation was headed.

"When did you say Sarah was leaving?"

Brenda checked her watch, "Speaking of—I've got to go pick up her prescriptions."

"Well, it's just that it seems like the two of us together could handle—"

"Momma, he needs full-time professional care, and when Sarah leaves my house, I'm no longer in that line of work. I want to enjoy being his daughter for whatever time he has left. I don't want to be his caregiver. As I told you before, I'm changing careers."

"What are you going to do?" Corene said arms folded, tapping her foot. "You've worked with the elderly all of your adult life, and now when we—I need you, you're changing careers. Make your change when I get too old to care for myself, but now is not the time. I would've thought you'd realized this since we haven't heard much from your siblings. It's just you and me."

Brenda rose to her feet, determined not to argue or comply. Ever since her father was diagnosed, her family had been telling her what her responsibility was. She refused to keep fighting, nor was she going to continue to defend herself. She'd pray about it then do as the Lord directs without seeking their approval.

"'Bout time you got here, thought I was going to sit up here and starve to death. I know you want to get rid of me, but is that your plan?"

Brenda placed the plate on Sarah's tray and slammed the utensils down beside it. She hated showing the older woman her irritation. Still, Sarah was another person trying to dictate where she was supposed to be and what she was supposed to be doing as if she were incapable of deciding for herself.

"It's like that, huh? Who ruffled your feathers?"

Brenda silently opened the bottles of medications and placed the pills beside a glass of iced tea. She then turned and left the room without making sure Sarah took them.

"And where are you runnin' off to?" is what Brenda heard before she closed the door.

"How is your sister faring in her new business venture?" Lawrence said to his son Kevin, who'd stopped by for a visit.

Kevin snorted as he took a bite of the pizza he'd brought with him. "What business? The only business Stephanie is in is finding a sugar daddy to take care of her."

"She didn't come to you and ask you to—"

Kevin shook his head. "She knows better. I don't believe a word that comes out of her mouth, and I'm surprised you do. She's not compulsive, she's a professional liar. I hear she's a thief too. You didn't give her any—"

Lawrence held up his hand," I give my daughter the benefit of the doubt, but not with my wallet," he said.

Kevin exhaled. "Good, I was scared the whole Miss Brenda thing might've clouded your senses a bit. You still seeing her?"

The doorbell rang, Lawrence grinned. "Matter of fact—"

Kevin swallowed his pizza in a loud gulp. Miss Brenda, at the door, was like hearing the cops were searching your house.

When he turned around, the woman walking towards him wasn't the church usher he remembered. This lady was smiling.

"You've grown up to be such a fine-looking young man," Brenda said, embracing then stepping back to appraise all six feet of him as he stood smiling at her. He felt like a child visiting an older relative. "When you were little, you were always trying to smuggle toys and candy into church every Sunday. Boy, you kept me busy."

Kevin chuckled; her recollection of him was accurate. He now felt awkward, like he needed to be on his best behavior. He continued standing.

Lawrence laughed. "Relax, boy. She's not the head usher tonight."

"Actually, I've given up that job," Brenda said. "It's time for me to move out of the way. You haven't visited our church lately, or you would've known that."

Kevin shrugged and sheepishly grinned as he sat down. There was an amused silence. *They're waiting for me to make up some excuse for missing church: work schedule, travel,* he thought. He'd stopped attending services, and Miss Brenda talking to him like a naughty third-grader wasn't going to change that.

"Brenda and I are going to the church Christmas play this evening. You're welcome to join us," Lawrence said.

He wanted to decline although he had nothing else to do. There was something in his father's manner, however. He groaned inwardly, then stood and pasted on a 'good son' smile, "If you don't mind my tagging along. In fact, why don't I drive?"

While at the church play, Kevin got more of a charge from watching his dad and Miss Brenda then from the production itself. He hadn't seen Lawrence enjoy anyone's company so much since his mother passed. It also amazed Kevin that she was so ordinary: a nice woman who even had a sense of humor. When Gia popped up later, as a surprise to her mother, Kevin knew he'd been rewarded for his sacrifice.

He'd had a crush on Gia from childhood, though she was a couple years older and paid no attention to him. When they greeted each other in the church foyer after the play, and she smiled at him, his insides melted.

"How have you been?" Gia said. "It's been forever."

"Yeah, I don't make it here often."

"That makes two of you," Brenda said while Gia smirked and rolled her eyes.

Someone called Brenda's name, and she moved away.

"I hear you're doing well, new house and all," Kevin said. Elated to have her full attention on him. They made small talk with their mouths, while their eyes engaged in a separate discourse. It made the noisy, crowded, church lobby fade into the distance.

"I'm holding my own," she smiled, moistened her lips, and ran her fingers through her hair. "But uh—how did those two?" She motioned her head toward their parents. "I mean, do you think it's serious?"

He stepped toward her, leaned in, and started to whisper in her ear, "Well—" he stopped as he spotted Lawrence striding toward them.

"What are you two talking about, or should I guess?"

From there, the four of them had dinner at a mall restaurant near the church.

"You know your social life is in a rut when you're going on dates with your mother," Gia said to Kevin while strolling the mall, having left their parents at the table. The older couple seemed content with each other's company anyway.

"It hasn't turned out so bad, has it?" Kevin said as she stopped to sit.

She looked up at him, crossed her legs, and smiled. He was tall with broad shoulders, and his gaze was all about her. It was like he'd dropped out of one of her dreams, Steffie's little brother, who she'd known all her life. Why hadn't she remembered how fine he was? The more they talked, the more they perceived they had in common, both ambitious professionals fighting to stay on top of their careers. When Gia's cellphone rang, she had no idea how long they'd been gone from the restaurant.

"I hate to interrupt you and Kevin while you're catching up, but Lawrence and I rode with him," Brenda said.

When they met out in the parking lot, Kevin dropped his car keys into his father's hand and hopped into the car with Gia. The young couple said their goodnights and sped off into the frigid winter night, leaving their parents looking on.

Lawrence looked at Brenda, "What happened here?"

Gia didn't believe in moving too fast into a new relationship, but to her, this didn't feel new. It felt right. They went to a small intimate nightclub, had a drink, and danced a bit. Later she took him back to his car, which was parked at Lawrence's house. After checking the street to make sure her mother's car was nowhere in sight, Gia gave him a good night kiss that lasted a half-hour. She could've kept him there all night had she wanted to, but eventually, let him go.

The moment she pulled into the garage of her townhouse, he called and was at her front door within fifteen minutes. She flung open the door, abandoning her restraint; there were no slowing things down to gain perspective. Kevin was what she needed to set things straight in her life. She closed the door behind him, fell into his arms, and, dispelling her usual caution, dived into the new relationship.

PART TWO

14

"Have you considered getting a second job, Stephanie? Until you get back on your feet. I mean, you owe everybody. You need to try living within your means for a change?"

"I don't need a lecture; I need some cash. Do you have it or not?"

"Not," Margo, Stephanie's younger sister, said, then she heard the phone beep. She wanted to throw the device across the room but remembered how much she owed on it and placed it in her pocket.

Everybody had advice, but nobody was giving her the money she was asking for. If they gave her some money, maybe she'd listen to what they had to say. What good was a bunch of words to her now?

If only I hadn't gambled away my paycheck, she thought, but there was no sense crying about that. She'd left her rent money at the riverboat casino and was now close to three months behind. Her roommate threatened to put her belongings out on the street, and she had no doubt the dingbat would have her thug boyfriend do it. *Where am I going to go?* She asked herself, then became angry when she thought of her dad, who, although he'd sold his larger house, still had more room than he needed; he wouldn't let her foot in the door. If she visited for longer than fifteen minutes, he started to panic.

Upon arriving home, the scene was worse than she'd expected. Tammy, her roommate, had carried out her threat and then some. Her belongings were dumped in the parking lot of the apartment building —after being picked through and trampled over. Her prized wardrobe was ruined, her shoes strewn everywhere. Her papers and other personal effects were in a pile.

She picked up what was left and looked around for her broken-down vehicle, which had been in the parking lot for months. She didn't see it.

"Your car was towed," Frank, the apartment maintenance man, said.

"Why?" She moaned breathlessly

"Tammy called the office and said you're not a resident here any longer. We had no choice; this parking lot is reserved."

Stephanie started putting her belongings into the borrowed vehicle she was driving, but there was no way everything would fit. Then she remembered her bedroom set and some other furniture items.

"You have nothing else up here. The Salvation Army picked up your larger items this morning Stephanie. I told you I wasn't playing with you, and you went and gambled anyway. You got nobody but yourself to blame for this!"

"You can't just give someone else's stuff away. That's theft."

"I didn't keep a thing of yours, even though you owe me two grand, I know I'll never see."

"Darn right!" Stephanie yelled as she ended the call.

"Hi baby brother, I need a place to stay for a couple of days. My new place isn't quite ready yet," Stephanie said, her voice thick with sweetness.

Kevin checked the caller ID to make sure it wasn't a wrong number. Stephanie had never been that nice to him in his life. *I hear she's borrowing money all around town. I doubt there's really a new place...I know I'm going to regret this...*

"Couple days is it, Stephanie, and whatever you use, you better replace."

She nearly swallowed the phone. Kevin had been her last resort, and she hadn't thought she stood a prayer. He never believed a word she said and was probably right not to.

He hung up the phone. Stephanie was a rattlesnake; it didn't matter how nice you were or what you did for her; she was going to bite you. She only cared about herself. The only reason he let her stay at his place was that he wasn't home much anyway. He'd been spending his time at Gia's and was so happy with life; he even had some benevolence for the lying con artist sister he despised.

He sat at the computer in his cubicle, about to make some business calls, when his cell phone rang again. He grimaced, figuring it was Stephanie asking for something else, probably money. One could never do one favor for her; her requests always multiplied—this time, however, it was Gia.

"Hey," he said, leaning back in his leather office chair. He loved hearing Gia's voice, and when she called, he found it hard to concentrate on anything but listening to her.

"You don't sound like you're working very hard," Gia said, loving the fact that Kevin was never too involved to stop and talk with her. She, on the other hand, had to ask him to stop calling so much during the workday; his feelings were hurt when she had to end the calls abruptly. "Looks like I'm going to be late tonight. Do you want me to stop off and pick up dinner?"

"You know better than that. You come home, and I'll have dinner and maybe a bubble bath waiting."

"You need to stop spoiling me," she said, giggling. Kevin's spoiling was the reason she'd let him practically move in with her in just the three months they'd been seeing each other. She loved coming home to him. His being there also kept Chase from dropping by.

It was evident from the relaxed way Gia was sitting at her desk, smiling mischievously and twirling her hair in her fingers, her phone conversation was of an intimate nature. She'd shut out the world, including Chase, who was watching her from his office.

He wanted her to see him, to know he was watching. She'd been dodging him lately, always in a hurry, embroiled in some client crisis, no time for small talk or to meet up for a drink. He'd guessed it was intentional to keep him at bay. She was seeing someone and had lost interest in their affair. She needed to make up her mind what was more important to her, this new boyfriend, or her career.

He left his office and strolled into her cubicle while she was facing the opposite wall.

"You're terrible. You need to get back to work," Gia whispered. Chase cleared his throat.

She swung her chair around, to his cold grey eyes boring into her.

"I've got to go," she said, then turned off her phone and sat up straight.

"Come into my office for a second."

She checked her watch and stood to grab her computer. "Actually, I'm on my way to—"

He stopped and turned, "my office—just for a minute."

She followed him, leaving the door open until he motioned for her to close it.

He sat down behind the desk; she stood.

"Have a seat."

She rechecked her watch.

"Funny, you didn't seem to be in such a hurry a few minutes ago while on the phone with the new boyfriend, I'm guessing?"

She folded her arms but remained standing.

"I want to see you tonight."

"I can't. I have plans."

"Break them."

"Am I being harassed? Because if I am, I think HR needs to know this."

"Who's harassing you? No one threatened you. We're both adults in a consenting relationship."

"I choose not to consent any longer."

"That wouldn't be a wise choice. You want to go far in this business, and you need me on your side."

"Sounds like a threat to me."

"You can't prove I said it, but I can document every time you've screwed up and every time you will. Try me, and you'll be out of here in thirty days."

Gia started to sweat under her arms. She needed her job. Maybe if she knew she and Kevin were going to be married, she could tell Chase to kiss off. The truth is she was unsure if she'd want Kevin around another week; with her, it was day by day.

Her job was her constant, and she couldn't allow this man to take it from her, no matter how she hated his demands. She'd play along for now but work on her exit strategy.

"Don't see one without the other these days. Should we be happy about it or concerned?" Brenda said to Lawrence.

"What difference does it make? They're grown and are going to do what they want anyway. Who knows, they may end up married."

"Gia married to a good boy? That would be nice. Kevin seems to be good for her; she's not running the streets with a bunch of married men anymore. I guess I can be thankful for that."

"Is she going to break his heart, you think? The boy is head over heels."

"I hope not. Gia gets bored easily, but it's been a few months. Gia never sees one guy that long. Either she's growing up, or your son's doing something right."

"He is my son," Lawrence said, laughing, and Brenda threw a pillow at him.

The two of them were sitting in her family room, having coffee and dessert after dinner, when the doorbell rang. Brenda answered, and it was Kevin.

"Hey, Miss Brenda."

"Are you looking for your dad? He's—"

"No, actually, I'm looking for Gia. I've been trying to get in touch with her all evening, and she's not answering her phone. I was wondering if you knew—"

"I talked with her earlier. She didn't mention anything to me about what she'd be doing this evening."

She stepped aside, expecting Kevin to come into the house. He hesitated until he saw a look cross Brenda's face; he'd better enter the house and speak to his dad, or she'd drag him in by the ear.

"Speak of the devil," Lawrence said at the sight of his son.

"You were talking about me?"

"We were discussing you and Gia," Brenda said, entering behind him. "We're surprised by your whirlwind romance."

Kevin nodded. He was surprised by it too but had no interest in sitting around with the old folks chitchatting about it. He wanted to know where Gia was. She wasn't with her mother or the girlfriend she'd claimed to be going out with that night, who he'd run into at the mall. He wanted to know who she was with.

He made it out of Miss Brenda's house an hour and two hunks of her incredible lemon coconut cake later. When he got back to Gia's place, she wasn't home but had sent him text messages still claiming to be with the friend he'd run into.

He went into the house and sat in the dark bedroom, wondering how he wound up hung up on a woman who'd turned out to be a liar. He hated liars, which is why he couldn't stand Stephanie.

After an hour in the same spot, he decided to pack up his things and go home. It'd been four happy months, but he was obviously cramping Gia's style. He wasn't going to sit around and wait for any woman, not even her.

He was half-packed when he heard her key in the lock.

"Hey, sweetie," she said, smiling and walking into the bedroom. Her smile froze when she saw his bag packed. They stood facing each other in silence. She then sat down on the bed, unsure of what to say and wondering what he'd found out.

"What?" she held up her hands.

"I'll come for the rest of my stuff later."

"What's wrong? I thought we were happy."

"It couldn't go on like this forever, Gia. You apparently need your space, or you wouldn't have been lying to me all night. I'll go home, and we'll talk in a couple days."

It didn't matter to her how he'd found out she'd lied; it devastated her that he knew. Chase had demanded they meet that evening. She couldn't tell Kevin the truth about where she was going because then she'd have to come clean about the affair.

"I'm sorry I lied. I met someone, a man, we had dinner," she blurted.

He threw his packed bag across the room. "Why didn't you trust me, Gia? I don't have any claims on you. Why did you disrespect me like that? All you had to do was tell me you needed your space."

"You know me. I want my cake. I wanted to see that guy, but I didn't want you to leave."

Kevin shook his head and sat down on the bed beside her. "You're unbelievable. Was he worth it?"

"He was a waste of time; that's why I couldn't wait to come home," she said, wrapping herself around him.

"We're going to need to talk, and soon," he said, as she buried her face in his neck. "We can't go on this way."

Commitment was never high on Gia's list; neither was seeing the same man for four months, especially if he was single. *I can't lose him,* she told herself, as she listened to the rhythm of his breathing, and felt his hand caressing her back. Being with Chase made her feel as though she'd been rolling around in mud; she needed Kevin to make her feel clean again.

"Mama, are you sure you don't need some help today. I don't mind."

"No, thank you. I know you don't like me depending on you, so I'll do the best I can."

Brenda then heard her father wailing in the background but couldn't make out what he was so upset about. "Mama?"

"He got up this morning looking for his car keys again and is convinced I'm hiding them from him. He's been throwing a tantrum all morning."

"He hasn't fought you, has he?" Brenda was shocked. She'd seen her father in a bad state, but never so out of control.

"No, he's broken some dishes is about all."

Brenda hung up the phone and quickly got dressed. "Sarah, I—"

"I know, I know, it's that crazy father of yours. You go on, I'll take care of myself even though I'm not sure what they're payin' you for."

It was best Brenda couldn't spare the time to argue with Sarah; she was ready to give her a good piece of her mind. She then remembered Keith called and said he was coming to town the following week to tour some facilities. Sarah would be gone soon anyway.

Brenda rushed out of the house and climbed into her Buick. Before backing out of the driveway, however, the front of her house and yard caught her attention. The house needed paint, the flower bed she and Lawrence had planted the year before had been abandoned, and the front lawn had brown patches. Running between her own and her mother's house was robbing her of the time to do those things she took pride in. She tried to keep her yard presentable and frowned upon her neighbors, who didn't make an effort. *Guess I better ask Lawrence to help again.* Her free time on the weekends was so limited, she struggled even to make time for him.

She smiled and shifted the car into reverse. Lawrence was always willing to help and loved when she asked him for the smallest thing.

Brenda let herself into her parents' house, and once inside noticed it was quiet—too quiet. She didn't even hear the television her mother always kept turned on. There was the smell of something burnt; in the kitchen, there was a pan with charred contents in the sink.

"Mama, where are you?"

"Brenda, is that you? Come up here. I need help!" Her mother called out from the second floor.

When she got to the top of the stairs, she saw Corene lying on the floor, her leg stretched out in front of her at an awkward angle. Her father was sitting on the bed, sobbing.

"I'm sorry. I didn't mean it," Marvin said, quietly repeating to himself.

"I had an accident and can't put any weight on my ankle. I asked your father to get the phone and call 911, but he won't stop crying."

"I didn't mean it..."

Brenda helped her mother to a chair.

"It's probably just twisted," Corene said, but Brenda knew a broken ankle when she saw one.

She called Gia, who was able to leave work to take Corene to the emergency room, while she stayed with her dad. He remained troubled and melancholy the rest of the day, but brightened up, when Corene came home, complete with an air boot and crutches.

"Where did you go?" he said to her. "I've been waiting for you to come home all day."

Gia's eyebrows raised. She hadn't spent much time around her grandfather since he'd become ill and was surprised at how he'd changed since she'd seen him last.

"Hey, grandpa," she said. Marvin blinked as if he wondered who she was talking to.

"Say hi to your granddaughter, Marvin. She's a big girl now; she took good care of me."

Marvin eyed her suspiciously as if he didn't believe she was his granddaughter.

As Brenda watched all of them, she wondered what she was going to do now. Her mother could no longer care for her father; then there was Sarah.

"Oh, Lord Sarah! I've been gone from home for hours. Gia?"

Gia sighed and looked at her watch. It was going to be a late night at work anyway, one more stop wasn't going to make a difference.

"I'll check on her, Momma, but I've got to go now."

"I'm going to have to bring Sarah over here tonight, then I'll start making phone calls tomorrow. We need to get a social worker on your case because you can't care for him anymore, Momma. I've already called my brothers and sister and told them what happened today. Maybe this will be their wake-up call, even though Darwin stopped short of accusing me of lying."

Then the telephone rang, and Brenda knew it was one of her siblings calling to check on their mother.

"Momma, I'll be in town tomorrow," Darwin said.

"There's no need for that. I'm fine."

"How can you say that when Brenda let this happen to you. If she'd been where she was supposed to be—"

"Darwin, I had an accident; that's all, and accidents happen to everybody..."

Brenda rolled her eyes, "Now he wants to show up and save the day," she said, walking Gia to the door.

"Ma, if you need me to, we'll stay at your house tonight and give you time to get organized."

"We?" Brenda said, with a slight frown, until she remembered Kevin. "Are you two still playing house? Not under my roof, no thank you."

Gia laughed and rolled her eyes to the ceiling. "He'll sleep on the couch, Ma."

"And why can't he sleep at his own house?" Brenda said with a hand on her hip.

"We like to be together."

Brenda snorted then opened the door, "Give me a break," she said, knowing she needed Gia's help. There was no way she'd get Sarah out of that house tonight without catching hell about it. She was going to have enough of a fit with a day's advance warning. "You and Kevin can stay at my house tonight, but you tell that young man he'd better behave himself or I'm going to tell his daddy. I might come and check up on you."

Gia laughed as she walked to her car. "We're not teenagers."

"You're not married either!" Brenda yelled as she drove off.

"What do you mean, she's not coming home tonight? What am I supposed to do, look after myself? I guess she forgets, she gets paid to care for me, not her crazy father. And who is that I hear. There's somebody in this house."

"That's just my man, Aunt Sarah. He rolls with me."

"Oh, does he now? And just what does that mean?"

Gia laughed. "I'm not a cook. I'll have to get you something to eat and then go back to work for a couple hours. If you need anything, Kevin will get it for you."

"You will not leave some strange man in this house. Make sure you take him with you."

Gia sighed loudly; she didn't know how her mother could stand Sarah all these years.

Rummaging through the refrigerator, they found leftovers to eat and to feed Sarah. Brenda's leftovers were better than anything she could cook or buy. Then ignoring Sarah's protest, she left Kevin in the house watching television while she went to work to tie up loose ends and prepare for a big meeting the next day.

She arrived at the office, surprised to see Chase's Lexus still in his parking space. Were it not been for the work she had to do that night, she would've turned around and left, to avoid being alone with him. When she entered the office, however, she heard him on the phone and in the middle of a nasty argument.

"You do what I tell you to do...what do you mean who do I think I am, I'm the one who will destroy you. Don't try me!"

Gia waved at him through the glass wall of his office, so he could quiet down, and she wouldn't feel as though she were eavesdropping. Still, she wondered who he was talking to.

"Yeah, so I married you, but that doesn't mean you control my life."

She nearly fell to the floor, Chase and Maria had only been married for six months. They'd had a storybook wedding, an Italian honeymoon, and rumor has it, she had plenty of money.

"You try to divorce me, and I'll take a chunk out of your hide...what I do when you're not around is none of your business. Who was I with last night? Someone a hell of a lot more interesting than you!" He ended the call then pounded on his desk, causing a paperweight to crash to the floor.

He grabbed his burgundy leather briefcase, and briskly left the office. Gia kept her eyes down, hoping he'd glide past, but his soft loafers stopped inside of her cubicle, and he plopped down into the chair she kept in the corner. She glanced over at his face, which was flushed with anger. Beyond that, no one would know he had a care in the world. He was a tall, slender man, impeccably groomed, with dark black hair combed back, every strand in complete control.

Here we go. With Kevin at her mother's house waiting for her, there was no way she was going anywhere with Chase tonight. Her stomach tightened, knowing a refusal could mean her job.

"You think you want to marry this boyfriend of yours? Take my advice, forget it," he said.

She wanted to tell him if he'd stop treating his wife and every other woman he was acquainted with, like dirt, his relationship will probably work out, but she was in no position to lecture him.

"Do you like me, Gia?"

"Sure," she murmured.

"Somehow, I seem to stop short of being a nice guy. I intend to be, but the other me takes over. She deserves better, and so do you."

"I don't deserve anything except the opportunity to be the best at my job I can be, and not have it threatened," she said. She had work to do, and he was keeping her from it.

"I shouldn't have gotten married. I should've just told you I was attracted to you."

She stared at her computer screen and waited for him to leave, having no interest in his confession or his regrets.

"See you tomorrow," he said, standing abruptly.

She mumbled a response and held her breath until she heard the elevator chime, and knew he was on his way down. Hopefully, he'd do some soul searching, and things would change, so she wouldn't have to deal with the situation anymore.

Brenda's home phone rang while Kevin was in the kitchen, scouring the fridge for more leftovers. His father's name flashed across the screen.

"Hey dad," Kevin said, picking up the phone.

"What are you doing there?"

"Gia dragged me over here; has me babysitting her aunt because she had to work late. You'll catch Miss Brenda on her cellphone. Her mother had an accident today and broke her ankle.

Lawrence's eyebrows raised as he wondered if there was anything Kevin wouldn't do if Gia asked him to. Caring for Sarah was going the extra mile.

"What's up with you two? I mean, you and Gia are inseparable these days. You're moving fast, are there any plans we should know about?"

"Well..." Kevin said the line became quiet, and Lawrence could sense his son wanted to talk. "I don't know dad, we'll see."

15

Lawrence was dozing in his recliner after a hard day at work and awakened thinking of his children. He was proud of all three, although Stephanie stretched him. But only one of the three, Margot, had a family and seemed to have her spiritual priorities straight. The other two were into their own lives, their own worlds. Kevin was building his hopes around a woman, again, and Stephanie was in another orbit entirely.

Was it me... is it my fault? He asked often, but the Lord never answered him, probably because it didn't matter. Each of us, our children included, are accountable for the lives we live. Whatever he did wrong, God will make it right, but his children must let Him do that.

Brenda...Brenda Collier...Brenda Lawrence. He was in love and when the time was right; when the Lord gave him the word, he was going to propose. When he thought about the men who'd let his precious jewel pass them by, because she was prickly around the edges, he knew God ordered everything, especially love. *He's the God of love—in fact, He is love.* Lawrence leaned back and smiled.

"Momma, we've got to tour this facility today. Please keep an open mind," Brenda said to Corene. They'd been working since her mother's accident to find a suitable accommodation for Marvin Sr. Unfortunately, as her ankle healed, the more Corene insisted she could care for her husband in their home with 'occasional' help from Brenda.

Brenda was willing to do what her mother wished but was convinced she couldn't manage her father alone, even for short periods. "You're not a young woman. Must I remind you of what happened to your ankle?"

"I told you I fell, it had nothing to do with him."

They'd had the same circular argument for months. Corene wasn't lying intentionally; she'd talked herself into believing something that wasn't true.

They toured the Isaacson Retirement Center later that day. It was the second time Brenda had visited, having done a preliminary screening to narrow down the options for her mother. She'd put this one at the top, as she was impressed with the quality of the facility, compared with others in their price range. Predictably, her mother complained about everything, but they had one spot available. If she didn't apply for it, it would be gone that same day. Corene agreed to complete the paperwork, and if all went well, Marvin would have a room within the month.

"Peace at last," Brenda said as they returned to the house. She put her purse down on the kitchen counter and started a fresh pot of coffee.

"I'll go check on your father. Who knows what that woman is doing by now, she's probably asleep," Corene said, referring to the home health aide.

Brenda watched her, now walking with a cane, climbing the stairs muttering to herself. She was eager for the day when she wouldn't have to hear her gripes about the home health care workers, although she suspected her mother would redirect her complaints toward the staff of the nursing facility.

"So, you're putting my dad away, like he's some unwanted nuisance. Shame on you, Brenda," Darwin said to her, during a family conference call, later in that week.

"He's got an illness, and momma nor I can care for him. I think we've given all of you ample time and opportunity—"

"Why are you preaching to us again," Christine, her sister said. Brenda was surprised by the hostility in her voice, as she'd been the least vocal during the entire ordeal.

"I'm sorry. I didn't mean to sound that way," she said. There was nothing left to fight about. She and her mother had decided what was best, and she was at peace. Guilty consciences at the other end of the phone line were not her concern.

Brenda's apology softened the tone of the conversation as the truth sunk in; the responsibility they'd been dodging had been shifted in another direction. She prayed that any bitterness built up over the past year would vanish so they could bond again as a family.

"I'm sorry, Brenda," Christine said. "You don't realize it, but this is hard on me. He's my dad...it's so hard." Her voice broke as they all consoled her.

Not everyone can function during a crisis, and Brenda didn't judge them for their lack of movement. She, in turn, hoped they didn't resent her for the actions she'd taken. In the end, somebody had to do something.

"Brenda, I know it's taken a long time, and you've had your own family issues to deal with, but I hope you understand. My sister and I had to take our time and make the right choice for our mother," Keith said to Brenda. He and his wife Jill were having Sunday dinner with her, Lawrence, and Sarah, who made a rare and reluctant appearance at the dinner table.

"We've made a choice. Mom, this will be your new home. The Horizon Assisted Living Facility. It has a theater, a health club, and a variety of activities."

"Who needs that?" Sarah said, throwing the brochures back at him. "I'm not going to that phony place. I told you what I want, care in my own home. More than I get here."

"We can't afford that. I've explained it to you, and even if we could, I don't think—"

"Who asked you to think? I told you—you worthless sack of dirt. I wouldn't give two quarters for you or your sister. Don't think I'm going to that place because I won't. Do you hear me?"

Brenda rose from the table. "That's enough. You do not use that kind of language."

"You can go straight to hell too! All of you," Sarah said and used her walker to pull herself into a standing position. She was unable to leave in the flourish she wanted to, however, needing Keith to assist her back to her bedroom. She cursed him every step of the way.

"She's so mean, and he tries so hard," Jill said. "When I think of the effort, he put into finding somewhere suitable, and how little she appreciates it. I can understand why Kathy doesn't bother."

Brenda nodded as she sipped her glass of iced tea. The room was awkwardly quiet until Lawrence started a conversation on a lighter topic.

Keith returned from Sarah's room looking somber, and Brenda wanted to reassure him he was doing the best he could under the circumstances. Jill squeezed his hand, however, and the look that passed between them let Brenda know his wife gave him all the encouragement he needed.

"You two have been together a long time now. How many years has it been?"

"Twenty-one," Keith said to Brenda, his eyes fixed on his wife. "She's kept me together, despite everything. That's why as rough as my mother can sometimes be, Jill keeps my head lifted."

"That's wonderful," Brenda said in awe. When she glanced at Lawrence, he was gazing at her in much the same way Keith was looking at Jill. She felt a lump form in her throat when he reached over and squeezed her shoulder.

Sarah would soon be leaving. Her father, Marvin, was in a difficult transition but was becoming acclimated to his new routine. As the clouds were lifting over her life, she saw Lawrence and wondered: could they be as happy as Keith and Jill seemed to be? Could she take that plunge again, risking everything, her whole heart?

She smiled at Lawrence and patted the hand that was on her shoulder. Yes, she believed one day she could. From what she'd observed, Lawrence Foster was a man who was worth the risk.

16

"Daddy, how are you feeling?"

"I don't have time to sit around here. I've got to get down to the church. What time is it?" He paced the floor of the small room. "These people took my keys. Do you have a car; can you give me a ride?" He stopped and turned to Brenda as he stood beside the door, waiting.

She spun away, searching for something to divert his attention. His room was comfortable enough, being it was in a hospital. He'd had a roommate initially, but that arrangement had been a disaster. Marvin was restless during the night and frequently accused the other man of taking his belongings, especially his car keys.

The new room had taupe-colored walls instead of the dull white. It was decorated with sparse accessories: a walnut-colored accent table near the window with a plastic vase holding an artificial bouquet of cattails and wildflowers. Brenda focused on the décor to avoid being distressed by her father's rambling.

"We had apple pie for lunch," he said, finally sitting down. "Corene, when am I going home? These people won't even let me go to the store. You gonna take me to the store Corene?"

She blinked. It was the first time her father had called her by her mother's name; she was undecided if that were better than him, not recognizing her at all, which had become the norm. She checked her watch.

"Daddy, I've got to go. You want me to bring you more cookies the next time?"

"Cookies...you brought me cookies? God bless you."

He'd had the same reaction an hour before when she'd given them to him.

She left him and strolled through the facility, asking herself did he really belong there. The second thoughts and feelings of guilt assaulted her each time she departed. *Maybe in his weakened condition, he shouldn't be cared for by strangers; perhaps he should be protected and sheltered from the outside world in his own home.*

Lord, why did he have to get sick? There were plenty of mean people who weren't thinking about you who could've been stricken with Alzheimer's. He was a faithful servant until he couldn't sit in church anymore. And humble. Never wanting accolades or glory just going about doing what you called him to do. What broke her heart the most was seeing how he couldn't serve God as he desired. His spirit was yearning, but he no longer possessed the faculties. Every time she visited him, he talked about getting to church.

She sat down on a bench outside watching young people, most of whom wore surgical scrubs, as they milled about the area near the Medical school. It was a warm September day, and it was time for her to go home; Sarah was due to arrive from the senior center. She hated leaving her daddy there, however. After the battles she'd fought to convince her family he should be in a facility, she had regrets.

On the other hand, her mother had adjusted to her husband's situation effortlessly. Having lived with him during the years of his decline, she now openly admitted, the facility wasn't the perfect solution, but he was better off.

Brenda's heart ached, and once again, she asked God why; she had yet to receive an answer. Maybe the Lord was telling her she should appreciate that Marvin was still alive, and she could see and talk to him whenever she wanted. However, he was no longer the father she knew but a shadow of the man he'd been. It seemed unfair for him to live out the rest of his life that way. Given the choice of an extended illness or death, he'd rather be in heaven.

It was a sobering lesson; loving God means we accept His way of doing things, whether we agree or not. We can question and even disagree but must recognize He's sovereign and knows best. *Thank you, Lord...* She stood up straight, inhaled deeply, and pulled her shoulders back. Placing one foot in front of the other, she headed toward her car in the parking lot, forcing herself to move on with the rest of her day.

Gia rolled over and checked the clock on the nightstand. It was nearly six o'clock; Kevin would soon be home waiting for her. She was in a hotel room across town with Chase, who wasn't ready for her to leave. *This has got to end,* she told herself as he slid in close, putting his arm around her waist in the large king-sized bed.

She'd stopped lying to herself months ago; that the affair was being forced upon her against her will. She was willing enough. There was something about the deed that compelled her, excited her, and kept her yielding to his demands. Kevin wouldn't understand, nor would he have any respect for her if he knew. It was the lying. He could deal with another man in her life but couldn't accept her deceit.

So, she and Chase put phony meetings on their calendars, hooked up in luxury hotels, and were usually home by dinner time. Occasionally Kevin would ask. *Why couldn't I reach you this afternoon? Why was your cell phone off...*She always had the same answer; *I was with a client.* It would seem like he'd stop asking since he routinely received the same response; unless he suspected she was lying...

Chase's wife was out of town this weekend, so he had all the time and the world. Gia, however, needed to get home.

Kevin sat at the bar near Gia's house and stared into his beer. It was Friday evening; the happy hour crowd had gone home, and the real drinkers remained. The ones who couldn't stop with the twofers and would be driven home in a rideshare sometime later that night.

The baseball game played on the screens around the bar, and a group of noisy patrons sitting behind him was cheering on the Cardinals. He barely glanced at the score. Gia had disappeared again, dropped right off the radar; he was more than suspicious of her absences.

Where the hell is she, and why is it when she says she's been with a client it sounds so...contrived? It happens suddenly. They're together all the time, go everywhere, are in constant contact, then he can't find her, can't reach her; then she reappears. Saying all the right things, with reasonable explanations, but her manner says something else. She's distant, distracted, oozing desperation at the same time. Clinging to him, *but does she really want me*—is what he asks himself. He was unsure if she loved him, although she said so occasionally when prodded. *If it's true, why can't I feel it?*

When he looked up, an attractive blond across the bar was giving him the eye. He met her gaze briefly, then returned to his beer. What if he did hook up with someone, and Gia couldn't find him for once? She'd have a fit. She occasionally accused him of other women, even though they'd made no commitment to monogamy. Still, she couldn't tolerate the thought of his having a drink or meal with a woman and often queried him about his work relationships. He thought her jealousy was cute, but what if there was more to it than that?

He placed cash on the bar then left, resuming his moping in the car. Maybe that was it, someone at work. She'd never invited him to any after-work gatherings, and Kevin had yet to meet anyone she worked with, although they'd been together for nine months.

He redialed her cellphone; this time, she picked up.

"Hey baby, I was just about to call you. I'm just leaving—"

"Another meeting with a client," he said, completing the sentence for her.

She caught the sarcasm in his tone; it wasn't the first time. "Have you had dinner—do you want me to bring you something? How about I stop off and get your favorite bottle of wine?"

"No, thanks. Look, I'm going home tonight. I've got to deal with things there," Kevin said, and it was true. His leech sister Stephanie was dismantling his house, and he needed to get her the hell out of there.

"You can do that tomorrow, Kevin. You know I don't like—"

"It's not about you tonight, Gia, okay," he said, ending the call then turning his cellphone off.

When he arrived at his house, he found it as expected. Stephanie was out for the evening, and from the front door to the basement, the place was a pigsty: dirty clothes, dishes, trash. If he were moving back in, and it appeared he would be, she would have to go. Some of the clothes strewn around still had price tags on them, which meant she'd done a lot of shopping. He hoped she'd saved moving money, though he knew his airhead sister and doubted it.

The doorbell rang. When Kevin opened it, Gia was standing there with a bag of food, which smelled like barbecue, and a bottle of wine. She was smiling, but her eyes widened as she looked behind him, catching a glimpse of the mess.

"Oh my God," she said, partially relieved, assuming Kevin's irritation was with his sister instead of her.

"What are you doing here, Gia?"

"You said you were coming home, I just kind of invited myself. Can I come in?" She said, not exactly sure she wanted to.

He turned away without responding. Gia also noticed he hadn't kissed her or appeared happy to see her.

She followed him into the living room, as he picked up trash along the way, placing it into the garbage bag he was carrying. "I missed you."

"Did you?"

"Would you like some help?" She said, clearing a spot on the cocktail table for the food and wine.

No, I want you to tell me where you've been all afternoon. I want you to tell me who the mystery 'client' is, and I want you to stop lying. Kevin thought as he grabbed a broom and swept.

She sensed she should leave. Something was bugging him, more than Stephanie trashing his place; it had to do with her. She was better off, not knowing what it was. *Don't I know anyway?* She didn't leave, however. Instead, she made him and herself a plate of the food she'd brought, sat on the couch, and, while he worked around her, she ate.

"Why don't you sit down and eat?" She said, turning on the television.

He wanted to tell her to leave but couldn't. She knew how to stroke his ego. Her willingness to sit there patiently while he ignored her was too much for him to overcome, and he couldn't stay angry. After two helpings of barbecue ribs, beans, potato salad, a slice of sweet potato pie, along with the bottle of wine, everything seemed alright again.

"Gia somethings up with you. One day you'll trust me enough to tell me what it is," he said, with a full stomach and his head cradled in her lap.

"Only thing up with me is you. That's all you need to know," she said, stroking his hair.

He knew he was being conned and was suspicious of why she felt the need. She was trying hard to divert the questions he had about her.

They fell asleep fully dressed on the living room couch and were awakened when Stephanie burst through the front door, loud, drunk, and dragging company.

She guffawed when seeing Kevin and Gia.

"What you doin' here? The lovebirds got tired of the little love nest. You didn't lose your house, did you, Gee? Hope you don't think you're going to move in here; I don't have no space for royalty." She laughed raucously at her joke, and her male companion laughed also.

"Funny Stephanie, but you won't be laughing tomorrow when you have to find another place to squat," Kevin said.

"Loosen up, boy. You don't have to be like that," Stephanie said.

"Naw man, you ain't got to—" her companion echoed.

Kevin pointed his finger, "Brother, I don't know who you are but get out of my house."

Stephanie took on the posture of someone ready to fight, but her friend lifted his hands, backed up, and headed toward the door. "Baby, it's been real," he said before the door slammed.

"You fool!" Stephanie yelled at Kevin. "He had money, maybe he could've helped make your house payment."

Kevin laughed. "That bum. What's wrong with you, are you that drunk?" He knew his sister was always looking for a free ride but had she sunk that low? He doubted if that guy had a job. If he did, it wasn't a legal one. "I don't need anybody like him paying anything for me, and you need to sober up real quick because you've got to go. We can't live under the same roof. This was just supposed to be a couple weeks, and it's been months."

"You're not even here. You live with the princess over there, or is there trouble on the love boat?"

He refused to answer; it was his house, and she wasn't his responsibility. He'd given her a break, and she'd stretched it into six months, but her luck had run out. It didn't matter if he didn't spend a night there for another six months, Stephanie had to move her bottomed out life, out of his place. She wanted to be a bum; she could go camp out on the street for all he cared. He glanced over at Gia, who was wide awake watching everything going on like it was live theater. *I got my own problems.*

The following morning, Stephanie awoke with a hangover and the reality that the previous night had been real; she'd been kicked out of what she'd come to think of as her house. Her hard-luck became even more evident because Kevin and Gia came back later that afternoon and started clearing out her belongings.

"Take your hands off my stuff! What's wrong with you?"

"Better get it moved today, or you can get it out of the dumpster tomorrow," Kevin said.

"You can't do me like this. You can't just put somebody out on the street. There are laws."

"Those laws are for people who pay rent. You don't pay a darn thing so I can do what I want."

"Okay, you want money. All you had to do was ask. I'll pay; how much do you want?"

Kevin snorted. "You don't think I'm that stupid, do you? An agreement with you is worth less than you are." He'd never see a dime; she'd simply use the time to take her money and find a new place, which she should've been doing all along.

Stephanie marched to the kitchen, picked up the phone and dialed it rapidly while her body trembled with rage. "Daddy, it's me. No, everything isn't all right. He's putting me out. Just like that, no warning. He's moving back in and wants me out. What am I supposed to do?" She then held the phone out to Kevin, who snatched it out of her hand.

Gia watched the scene in fascination. She'd never had any complaints about being an only child and resented her father for having more kids, twin boys who she had no relationship with. She didn't like to share and understood Kevin cutting Stephanie loose.

Kevin held the phone without speaking, while both Gia and Stephanie could hear Lawrence's voice on the other line.

Stephanie took the time to start planning her next move; she had no choice. The odds her father would convince Kevin to change his mind were slim; that he'd give her a place to stay himself even slimmer.

She quietly slipped out of the living room, went to the bedroom where she stored most of her belongings and started looking through phone numbers. She'd lived on the edge a long time and made a habit of collecting phone numbers of new acquaintances; people who didn't know her well enough to avoid her.

By the time Kevin had ended the phone call with their dad, she had a fish on the hook. A man she'd met a couple weeks back. He wasn't much to look at, but was single, had his own house, and seemed desperate. Just the way she liked them. She'd pack up her belongings, put everything in storage, and fall in love, all in the next twenty-four hours. Stephanie had to dig out his business card again to remember his name:

Laron 'Bookie' Hughes, Master Barber. Long as he wasn't a serial killer or devil worshiper, she'd be fine.

Lawrence finished the call with his son, ending his half-hearted lecture. Kevin knew he was going through motions, given that he wouldn't let Stephanie set foot in his house. He commended his son for allowing his sister to stay so long, although he hadn't really been trying to help her. Kevin had Gia on the brain for the better part of the year; his house had been an afterthought.

He'd almost expected Kevin and Gia to make some type of more permanent arrangement by now, but it seemed his son was moving back home to put some space between the two of them. Lawrence recalled a conversation they'd had a while back.

"I don't know how she feels about me, really. Sometimes it seems like I'm in this thing by myself, and she's just going along for the fun of it. But then she can be so sweet and behaves as if I'm the most important person in the world to her. Then I wonder if it's my own insecurity."

"Trust your instincts. If you feel she's holding back, you're probably right," Lawrence said and stopped short of preaching.

Thinking back to that conversation caused him to ask himself, why do our children, who are taught God's way, spend so much of their adult lives trying to find the loophole? You do things His way, or you ultimately fail. God won't allow anything we do to work out if He's not the center of it. It's the kind of tough love we can expect from a caring father. It's the way he tried to love his own wayward daughter Stephanie.

He started to call her back, to make sure she had a plan for her next move, but changed his mind, making himself breakfast instead. Stephanie's hysterics were too much to face on an empty stomach.

"She doesn't talk to me much about her male friends or relationships, but seems to be crazy about Kevin," Brenda said to Lawrence while they were having dinner at a restaurant later in the week.

If she'd been talking with anyone but Lawrence, she would have dropped the subject, reluctant to reveal how little she knew about her daughter's personal life. Instead, she asked, "they're doing okay...aren't they?" What she wanted to know: was Gia treating him right, was she trying to make him happy, or was she breaking Kevin's heart.

Lawrence looked back at her then down at his hands, clasped on the table in front of him. "You know your child, and I know mine. What do you think?" He saw the shadow of sadness and concern settle over Brenda. "Smile, sweetheart. They're adults and must go through life. We were their age once, took our lumps, and survived."

She nodded, feeling her shoulders droop. What good was it for her to have learned a thing or two about life, if not to share her wisdom with the one, she believed needed it the most. She wanted Gia to be happy, but Lawrence was right, her daughter's happiness was up to her. *We make choices in life; happiness isn't an accident we stumble upon; it's a choice God gives us.* Her pastor often said.

"I almost forgot," she said, shaking off her sad thoughts. "I picked this up for you today." She reached into her purse, pulled out a small jewelry box, and handed it to him smiling.

He opened it to find a gold tie pin, engraved with his initials. "You didn't think I was going to forget your birthday, did you?"

Lawrence smiled so hard, Brenda thought he'd bust, and it pleased her to bring joy into his life. Suddenly she hoped to have the opportunity to make him happy for a long time. Watching him fuss over the pain caused her to smile.

"What's so funny?" He said, seeing her smirk after he'd attached the tie pin.

"Saw a vision of you and me; two old folks standing atop a wedding cake. Isn't that funny?"

His eyebrows raised, "Yeah? Keep looking, Miss Brenda, and tell me what else you see."

Sarah swung her legs over the side of the bed and reached for her walker. She needed to use the bathroom and hated approaching the tedious undertaking by herself. Nobody was in the house, however, but that little girl and her boyfriend. That was like having nobody at all. The mother, as has been her habit on weekends, was out and about with her man friend. The one she thinks was going to marry her.

"You alright, Aunt Sarah?" Gia called on the intercom.

"If I wasn't, what good could you do me?" Sarah muttered but didn't attempt to speak into the machine. "She can bring herself in here and check to see if I'm okay?" By the time Gia made it to her door, Sarah was exiting the bathroom, headed back to her bed.

"Aunt Sarah, I told you to call my cell phone or use the intercom when you need me. I even programmed it into your phone for you to press 3. Gia said, then demonstrated again that the number 3 on the phone keypad caused her cellphone to ring.

"I forgot; you can't expect me to remember everything," Sarah said, having no intention of calling Gia on the telephone while they were in the same house—pure foolishness. If she had to do that, the girl might as well go home and take that useless boy with her.

Gia looked at her watch; she was ready to leave sour old Sarah but promised her mother she'd wait until she returned home. She didn't have time to spar with her tonight, however. Kevin was hinting about leaving without making any mention of her coming with him. She'd been stalling him, so she'd be ready to leave when he did, but Brenda was taking too long.

When she returned to the family room, Kevin was waiting with his coat on, planning to tell her goodnight.

"Goodnight, where are you going? It's early."

"I told you an hour ago; I'm going home, Gia." He draped an arm around her shoulders and kissed her, but as she reached for him, he pulled away.

"When my mother gets back, I'll come over."

Kevin closed his eyes and let his head drop; he'd been telling Gia for two hours he was going home alone. *Why hadn't she listened?*

"—or not..." Gia said, stepping away from him, her lip quivering as she folded her arms. "I don't understand. What did I do to make you treat me this way?"

They'd had the same conversation for months now, and he couldn't go around in circles with her another time. He'd asked Gia a hundred times in a hundred ways to tell him about her other life, but she denied it existed. Denied flat out with no explanations for her secrecy, her mysterious disappearances, or the fact that she didn't want him to meet her coworkers. She expected him to ignore all of that and pretend he didn't have a problem with it. He hated the way she dismissed it, each time he brought it up. He pulled open the front door and, as he turned to leave, nearly collided with Brenda, who neither of them heard drive up.

"Oh!" Brenda said

"Sorry, Miss Brenda. Hey dad," Kevin said to Lawrence, who was following a few steps behind.

Before either of them could make small talk, Kevin darted around them and headed to his car, leaving Gia standing at the door, biting her lower lip.

Seeing the hurt in Gia's face, Brenda wanted to ask her about it but knew any question coming from her wouldn't be welcomed.

Behind her, Brenda heard Lawrence say, "Come on and smile, girl. He'll come around."

"I don't know what I did," Gia said, her voice shaking.

Brenda awkwardly hung up her coat in the closet. When she turned to take Lawrence's, she noticed Gia standing at the door, as if she had nowhere else to go.

"You want me to make you some hot cocoa the way you like it with whipped cream and chocolate syrup on top?" Brenda said. It was the best she could do, and Gia seemed to like her attempt at consolation; it brought a sheepish smile to her face.

"There's that smile," Lawrence said. "Girl, don't ever let anyone take your smile away. People laugh at me, but I can keep smiling through the worst of anything."

The three of them had cocoa and sat at the dining room table. Gia wanted to talk with Lawrence but didn't want her mother to be a part of the conversation. Lawrence, however, had no desire to be her confidant.

The dissatisfied daughter left Brenda's house after an hour of trying to pump Lawrence for information. He suspected, however, she might turn up on his doorstep sometime in the next few days.

What's next...What do I do, how do I fix it. I need him...he can't know. I can't tell him, can I—should I. What do I do? Gia was pacing around her house from one room to the other. Open bottle of wine on the counter, the half-full glass on the coffee table, and she was wearing out the carpet as her mother would say. She made herself sit on her leather sofa, it felt cold and stiff because Kevin wasn't sitting on it with her. He made everything in her life warm and comfortable, welcoming. But now he was cold and distant and blamed her, but she was never that way towards him. She held herself and stroked her arms to calm the shivering. When he moved back to his house, she followed him there and he'd let her stay. Until he couldn't reach her for two days.

She'd gone on a business trip with Chase, at least that's what Chase had told his wife, to Miami—The Four Seasons. Gia couldn't call Kevin because he would've tried to keep her on the phone, wanting details of where she was staying and what she was doing. Instead of lying, she turned her phone off.

When she returned to town, Kevin's locks were changed. He claimed he did it to keep Stephanie out, but then never gave Gia a key, and still hadn't. It was a violation of the unspoken arrangement she believed existed between them—*he's supposed to be with me*, but he's choosing to be by himself. He claimed he felt like he was alone most of the time in their relationship, anyway, said she was too distant. *I can't lose him, but I'm in too deep on both sides.* No matter how she looked at her alternatives, she was a loser. She'd lose a lover a career or both; there had to be a way to salvage something.

She picked up the phone, "What are you doing?" She said when Kevin answered. She then heard a woman's laughter in the background. "Who the hell is that?"

"Don't question me, Gia, unless you're ready to answer some of my questions."

She gripped the phone and paced faster. *He's entertaining a woman!*

"Gia, I've got to go."

"Wait, am I invited to your little party, or is it private?"

"Good night Gia," Kevin said and ended the call. He'd been playing hard to get for months now and was getting under her skin. It was going to take more than her petty jealousy to bring them back to where she wanted; it was going to take honesty and full-time participation. He doubted she could do it. She was accustomed to playing games from all angles.

As for his guest that evening, her name was Kim, and she wasn't the vivacious beauty Gia was. Her face was pretty, her figure plump, but she was fun to be with. They'd been friends for some time, and though she'd let him know she was interested in him, he never followed up on it until now. She called him, they met for a drink and now here they were.

She was down to earth, which is what he needed, and she was good for his ego, flattered by his attention, captivated by his charm and gen-uine. *Bet a brother doesn't have to worry about where she is on a Friday afternoon.* He asked himself just how far he wanted the evening with Kim to go. It would serve Gia right if the woman spent the night, and she was giving off those signals. Would he then have another problem on his hands, like getting rid of her?

It wouldn't be fair to use her, as revenge against Gia, who he felt was stringing him along. Gia wanted him on a leash, like a pet, while she was noncommittal and shady.

While his next move was going through his mind, the evening was progressing along on its own. One kiss and he found Kim on his lap, trying to remove his tonsils with her tongue.

"Kevin," she hissed. "It's been a long time...I don't want you to think—"

"Think what?" Kevin said, all the while Kim was hastily unbuttoning his shirt.

"You look good to me, and sometimes I just have to go with the flow—you know what I'm saying, right?"

"Long as you respect me when it's over," Kevin said as they both laughed and rolled off the couch onto the living room carpet.

Kim made Kevin a full course breakfast the next morning and asked if it will be okay if she called him every now and then; she was into having fun, not relationships. "You strike me as a man who's discriminating. My guess is that you're just out of a relationship?" Kim said, taking a bite of buttered toast. "I can't stand men who sleep with everything. You and me, we could have some fun, no strings attached." Then the doorbell rang.

Kim could see by the way Kevin winced; he knew who it was.

"Maybe I'm wrong; maybe you're still in a relationship. Maybe that's her now. I'll be in the other room getting dressed," Kim said, as Kevin went to the door.

When he opened it, he found Gia standing outside fuming. "Whose car is that?" She said, and before Kevin could answer, pushed her way into the house. "You have company?"

"Yes. What are you trying to prove?"

"I just want to see her, that's all. Is that why you moved out of my place and locked me out of yours, because of her. Why didn't you just come out and say so."

"Look who's talking."

They stood in the doorway, glaring at each other silently as if in the boxing ring, waiting for the opening bell, and the first punch. The only sound in the house came from Kim moving around in the bedroom.

She emerged moments later, fully dressed. "Good morning," she sang, smiling and gliding between them as she headed to the door, ignoring the daggers Gia was glaring at her with. She blew a quick kiss to Kevin behind Gia's back and climbed into her car.

"That's what you prefer over me, Miss Piggy? Oh, my God! She never saw pork chop she could pass up!" Gia squealed, then put two fingers to her nose, simulating a snout and made snorting noises.

Instead of responding, Kevin folded his arms and studied her; her mood instantly shifted from mirth to anguish. She trailed him into the living room, then plopped down heavily onto the sofa and stared down at the floor.

He ignored her and busied himself with the breakfast dishes, wishing she'd leave. He felt sorry for her; sorry he'd hurt her. She wanted things her way, and he now realized, she didn't handle it well when they weren't. After about ten minutes, he threw down the cup he was about to load into the dishwasher and returned to the living room. She was in the same spot, avoiding his eyes.

"I didn't try to hurt you. I'm sorry."

Gia was still trying to process in her mind what had happened. *He knew I was aware he had a woman here and slept with her anyway. As if wanting to prove to me—what. That he's single. That I'm not the only game in town? What?*

She looked up at him, her head tilted back chin jutting forward. "No need to apologize, after all, you're right. We don't have any strings on each other. And you've been right about something else. I do have another man I didn't tell you about. My boss, as a matter of fact; he's rich, and he's white. I didn't know if you'd have a problem with that, so I didn't tell you. There—the secret is out."

Kevin nodded slowly. "I hope he makes you happy, Gia."

She glared at him and stood, her mouth twisted as she spoke, "He needs to make his wife happy. He doesn't have to do anything for me, and you know what," she gritted her teeth, "neither do you." She walked out of the house, slamming the door behind her. Kevin watched from his living room window as she revved up the engine of her sports car and sped down the street.

He wondered how something as simple as love could go so wrong. She was all he wanted; to love her, marry her, and live his life with her. Why were they moving away from each other? Why had she been running from him all along?

17

"We need a new approach to our mission, a new plan of attack. The current way is too difficult, rigid, and isn't producing. We're fighting ourselves. Let's think, analyze our steps, and do things differently. We need to open things up, the old way isn't working. It's too forced, and although we've had some successes in the short run, it can't be sustained. People—where do we go from here? The answer is in front of all of us, and we know what it is; we need to bring it out. Gia, do you have any ideas?" Chase paused from pacing the conference room during their Tuesday morning staff meeting. The twelve team members seated around the table were desperate to escape. While the sound of a phone ringing on the other side of the office resonated, Chase tapped his foot and waited.

Oh God, Gia groaned inwardly. She had neither the patience nor energy for a corporate pep rally. She plastered on a smile, however, and out came the stock answer. "We could all start by making calls to our client contacts, especially one's we've had issues with during this past year and get a sense of where we're missing the mark."

Everyone around the table was relieved they weren't called upon, and happy she'd come up with something that sounded reasonable. They chimed in enthusiastically, but Chase stood up straight and folded his arms.

"Come on, you can do better than that. How many customer care calls do we need to make this year that go nowhere? I want all of you to go back to your desks and find your open issues list from the past six months and give Gia statuses. We'll start building from there."

The room was silent again as they gathered their coffee mugs, laptops, and notepads and filed out. Issues they'd hoped had vanished from the radar months ago, would now be resurrected and piled on to everything else they were expected to do, thanks to the boss man's repudiation of Gia's suggestion.

She was unaffected by the vibe radiating from them, however; Kevin hadn't called; it had been a week. He hadn't even dialed her number; if just to hang up, she checked her call log religiously. What was she supposed to do now after everything they'd said to each other? There was no casual way to call and try to crawl back into what they'd had; how could she pretend the episode with *that woman* had never transpired?

Isn't he concerned about me...is he wondering how I'm doing? Doesn't he miss me? Engrossed in her thoughts, she lingered at the conference table well after the meeting had ended.

"Gia, is there something on your mind?" She blinked, looked around, and saw that she and Chase were alone.

"Oh...Sorry, I was thinking about how I'm going to tackle this project," she said, standing and gathering her files.

He walked to the open door, made a quick check of the corridor, then closed it. "I know we haven't seen each other for a while; I haven't been able to getaway. I'm attending a conference in New Orleans next week. Why don't I buy you a plane ticket so you can join me for the weekend?"

She wanted to gag. Kevin wasn't calling; Chase was the last person she wanted to be with.

"Um, I don't think so. Maybe you should invite your wife instead," she said, the words rolling off her tongue felt sweet and long overdue. She had two choices: apologize quickly or allow her words to stand as stated and let him deal with it. Choosing the latter, she stood facing him squarely, wondering what he'd do next. The skin under his shirt collar turning crimson was the only indication of his discomfort.

His gaze back at her was steady, his tone even. "That wasn't necessary, Gia. A simple no would have sufficed."

She pursed her lips and held his gaze; she'd challenged him and couldn't back down. He was going to either leave her alone or find a reason to fire her. At that moment, she didn't care.

He sat down in the black leather chair at the head of the table, without taking his eyes off her. "Have a seat," he said, nodding to a chair next to him.

"No, thank you." She folded her arms and, while shifting from one foot to the next, looked up at the ceiling.

"I'm sorry. Am I keeping you?" She remained silent. He then cleared his throat. "We're going to forget about this conversation. Apparently, you have other things on your mind."

"Is there anything else?" She scowled and looked at her watch.

Blood rushed to his face; Gia turned and moved to the door. Once in the hallway, she peeked at him through the side window. He sat frozen, staring down at his notebook. She was in for it. It would take him a couple days to regroup, then she'd catch pure hell. Grinning, she skipped back to her desk, wondering would the consequences be worth it.

I wonder where she is right now. What she's doing. Has she been with him...has she been thinking about me? If I call her at work, will she lie to me and claim she's busy working. I've heard that one before. She's sleeping with her boss. Man! Kevin was in his cubicle, trying to focus on his job and get his mind off Gia. She was the woman of his dreams and had been his for a moment; he'd been happy, so he thought. It was a lie, however. She couldn't have loved him, or she would've been straight with him. All he asked for was honesty, not perfection; she'd pretended to be perfect, and they'd lived a lie. *I just want to hear her voice.*

She'd be his again whenever he chose to make a move and go backward. The part of her she'd given him before, he'd have back, but she'd keep the rest to herself. She'd keep her secrets, and tell him what he wanted to hear, and act the way he wanted her to. *That isn't good enough.* He picked up his cell phone and fumbled with the buttons. *Or is it?*

He leaned back in his chair, stared at the dull grey walls of the cubicle, and thought about the color she'd given his life. He decided to call her, then his desk phone rang, coming from conference room one; he was late for a meeting. He grabbed his notebook and hurried down the hall, grateful he'd been diverted in his moment of weakness.

"I had some money in my pants pocket, and now it's gone. Know anything about that, Stephanie?"

Shaking her head and shrugging, Stephanie continued to file her nails while lounging on the king-sized bed in the expansive bedroom. Focusing on her nails prevented her from having to look at Laron, her current lover/meal ticket. He was overweight, bald, in need of a dentist, but was serving his purpose. Tonight, however, he was in her way. Glancing up at the clock, she filed even faster while concealing her irritation. She needed to get ready for her date, but baldy was still hanging around the house, bugging her.

"You're a liar. I saw you through the crack in the door going through my pockets. Give me my money now, or you're going to need the paramedics to come and put your thieving butt back together again!"

Stephanie rolled her eyes and exhaled as she pulled the roll of bills from her bra and threw it at him. "What's your problem? Not like it's a million dollars. If you would've given me some money when I asked—"

Laron stood in the middle of the room so angry his nostrils flared, and fists were clenched. As young and pretty as Stephanie was, he couldn't trust her for a minute. He wanted to beat the crap out of her just so she'd get the message he wasn't to be played with. That wasn't how he was raised, however; even a no-good woman like her was still a woman, and a real man keeps his hands to himself. Besides, she wasn't worth even a night in jail.

"It's time for you to leave before I do something I'll regret. This isn't working out."

"What do you mean? It's time for me to leave. You can't dismiss me like that," Stephanie said, throwing the nail file across the room. They had the same conversation once a week, and each time she managed to talk herself into more time. She was working on a new landing spot but needed a couple more weeks. "I'm your woman, and I live here. What kind of relationship is this when a man puts his woman out on the street over a couple dollars?"

"I don't know what kind of relationship this is. I ask myself that every day. Do you always steal from your men; is that what you call a relationship?"

"I didn't steal anything from you. I asked you for some money. If I asked, it's not stealing."

Laron stared at her, blankly with his mouth open. She could twist things around so fast; he was often left speechless.

"I needed the money to buy some food. There's nothing to eat in this house. What do you expect me to do, go to the supermarket with your maxed-out credit cards?"

He continued to stare at her. She hadn't set foot into the supermarket since she'd moved in, insisting they eat carry out all the time. Pointing out that fact was useless, however, Stephanie always had an answer.

He then sat down in the chair and watched her get showered, dressed, and made up; to go to the supermarket. When she was done, the black and gold V-neck micro-mini dress hugged her curves, and the black suede high boots showed off a hint of her toned thighs. She stood in front of him, allowing her perfume to cloud his senses, then held out her hand. He gave her the same roll of bills she'd thrown at him.

"Hurry back...from the store." He said while watching her shapely behind bounce out of the room and out of the house.

As Stephanie drove down the street in Laron's car, she felt a twinge of guilt; it surprised her. He was a lonely man chasing after a woman twenty years his junior. He saw through her lies and deceit but was no match for her; she talked circles around him then did what she wanted. *That's not how you treat people...you know better.*

`

"Hey baby," Ian said, whispering in Stephanie's ear, while she was busy losing Laron's money at the black-jack table. She cut him a look before going back to her hand; he was over an hour late but showed up at a good time; Laron's cash was drying up.

"Do you have some chips for me?" He said, and she scowled at him again. It was the second week in a row she'd given him money. *Why is it, the ones you want are always broke?*

She dug in her purse and took out some of her own money, proceeds from the paycheck she'd cashed that day. *Before we get together, we're going to have to iron out this money situation,* she thought. Stephanie didn't want to take care of herself, much less him.

"Thank you, baby," Ian said and squeezed her thigh. They gambled a while longer before going to the buffet for dinner then checking into a cheap motel for a few hours. Laron threw a fit if she wasn't home before daybreak.

"Ian, I can't wait until we can go home together," Stephanie said. He smiled and nodded as they dressed to leave the motel. She got high just looking at his curly, shiny, black hair, smooth brown skin, and the whitest teeth she'd ever seen. The real attraction, however, was his silky, slick manner; it reminded her of herself. He thought he was hustling her, but Stephanie knew she was going to hook him. "You can't play a player, baby. I know all the tricks. I invented a few of them," she'd tell him, and his response would always be a flash of that smile.

She was going to tame him, and knew they'd be perfect together; they understood each other. When she told him this, he'd nod in agreement, smile, then they'd make love. Later before parting, she'd press him again, and he'd claim to want what she wanted. Then the next week, they'd hook up and repeat the sequence all over again.

Stephanie, tired of using men to get by, and tired of Laron, wanted more. She longed to be with a man she wanted, and that was Ian. He claimed to be unmarried, employed, and heterosexual but was vague about his current living arrangements. She suspected, like her situation, a woman was paying the rent, but still saw a future where the two of them made their own way. Time was running out, as Laron was growing weary of her antics.

"You've been great, Brenda. Thanks again for your patience and all you've done. I know we've taken a long time to make a decision, but we wanted to do it right," Keith said. "My mother is such a difficult person and isn't satisfied with anything we do; I need to know inside myself, I'm making the right choice." He sat back on the couch in the family room and took the steaming cup of coffee from the tray Brenda held out to him.

She took a seat opposite him and began stirring cream and sugar into her own cup. *It's really happening...* She'd been anticipating hearing those words for four years now, and the day had finally come; Sarah would be leaving within the month. She'd be the sole occupant of her home for the first time ever, getting the chance to start her life over again.

"I'll be darned if I'm goin anywhere. They ain't locking me away in that place like some convict. I got rights, and I still got my right mind. It'll be a cold day in hell before I let them stick me in that place. Those people with their phony smiles; bet they beat the mess out of those poor old stiffs soon as the family leaves. I see through em—all of em. Figures he'd fall for it, worthless, that's what he is. No, thank you. I'll stay right here. You ain't much, but you ain't killed me yet."

Brenda stood with her arms folded, listening. *Not going to miss this ...* "Did you stop to think that staying here isn't an option? Maybe I can't do this anymore. I have rights also."

"You wouldn't dare put me out," Sarah said, pointing, her hand shaking vigorously. "Your God will judge you if you do that to me.

You'll pay. And tell you another thing, I'll die before I go to that place. You tell em! My death'll be on their heads, yours too. I'm too old for this. I'm not gonna take it. You tell em!"

Brenda sighed and went into Sarah's bathroom to get the bottle of tranquilizers her doctor had prescribed. The old woman had been so agitated when told she'd be moving, Brenda feared she'd give herself a stroke. Sarah was terrified at the prospect of a new environment. Keith reassured Brenda, however, that the new facility had an excellent medical staff equipped to address her health concerns.

Sarah's fear hit a soft spot inside her, however, and for the first time, Brenda asked herself if she should put a halt to it. It was out of her hands, however. The papers had been signed, and everything was all arranged. Sarah was moving whether she had a change of heart or not.

18

"I've been increasingly disappointed with your job performance during the last few months."

"Really?" Gia sneered at Chase. "Just what performance are you referring to, during work hours," she leaned across the table toward him, pursed her lips, and cocked an eyebrow, "or after?"

Chase, his wide eyes darting at the overhead camera in the conference room, wondered if they were turned on and who might be watching.

"I don't know what you mean by that, Gia, but—"

"Oh, don't you? Should I remind you of the places and dates?"

"That has nothing to do with anything."

"Sure it doesn't," she said, rolling her eyes, unsure where her bravado was coming from; her worst nightmare was being realized. She'd stopped accepting his 'meeting requests,' and now he was going to fire her; she was perplexed as to her next move.

He presented her with a document labeled 'Written Warning' and watched her fume as she scanned it. He'd been through the process enough times until it had become a routine. When one of his subordinate romances went sour, he'd initiate the paperwork for termination; mostly show. He'd never had to go beyond this first step.

After a one or two weeks cooling down period, he'd offer the woman a deal, an excellent reference if she'd disappear. For Gia, he even had leads on some open positions he'd be willing to help her land, but she needed to play along. Her insolence, however, indicated she was ready to fight. He'd give it a couple weeks and hope by their next talk, she'd be reasonable, or he'd have a big problem on his hands.

Gia went back to her desk and grabbed her purse while ignoring the blinking message light on her phone and the string of unanswered e-mails that had greeted her that morning. She needed air, or she'd march back into Chase's office; he'd need an ambulance after she was done. *If I'm going to get fired, it might be worth it to go out leaving my mark,* she thought while flying down the five flights of stairs. She kicked open the door on the ground floor and stood outside, facing the parking lot. It was a chilly, early morning in late autumn, cold enough for snow, but she was boiling.

The momentary image of violence made her smirk as she headed for her car. It was tempting but not smart; she needed to be smart. Her life felt like it was crumbling despite her striving to master her own reality. The men in the production that was her life had all gone off-script. Kevin had walked away, and as good as she was at her job, Chase was going to fire her.

She'd willingly walked into the career trap, thinking it would be easier, a shortcut to the top. The trade-off, however, was her brains, and hard work was secondary to her willingness to continue to play along.

She drove around the area of mostly high-rise office buildings, wanting, of all things, to run to her mommy. Brenda feared no one and would know how to put this situation in the right perspective. The idea of showing up at Brenda's house and telling her, 'I've stopped sleeping with my boss, and now he wants to fire me,' was unimaginable, however. Before the sound advice, she'd be bombarded with an earful of reproach. *But I deserve it...*

Instead, she went back to the office and buried herself in work until late that evening, then went home and worried herself into a state of anxious insomnia. At two a.m., she broke down and called Kevin, who came right over as if he'd been expecting her call.

"You have rights, Gia. I mean, the guy just promoted you, what a year ago? Now he's going to fire you. Tell your HR department your side of things and the real reason your job is being jeopardized," Kevin said the next morning while they were having breakfast.

"It's not that easy. It's his word against mine, and I'm sure he's covered his tracks."

"Come on, Gia. You give him too much credit. How much covering can the guy do? It doesn't matter anyway. Resign and marry me. I'll take care of things until you find something else."

Gia, who'd been chewing on a piece of toast, almost bit her finger. Kevin coughed, choking on what had come out of his mouth.

Idiot—you... can't even trust her, much less marry her, he thought as they finished breakfast in silence, neither acknowledging his gaffe. On his drive to work, he wondered what possessed him to say such a thing to Gia that morning. He was doubtful he wanted her as a lover, much less a wife. He resented her dishonesty; felt she'd treated him like a brainless fool. He loved her. However, no amount of hurt or anger could change that.

"Ian, where are you? Call me as soon as you get this message. It's important." Stephanie said, ending the call. She then gnawed on a manicured fingernail and paced the bedroom. *Where is he!* She lightly kicked Laron's dog, sending him scampering out of the room. She hated dogs, especially that dog; Laron treated it better than he treated her. She was sick of them both. It was time for her to disappear anyway, and her escape plan was nearly complete, but she needed to hear from Ian.

She'd found an apartment for the two of them, but because of her credit history, the landlord required a chunk of cash upfront, plus she'd need a co-renter. Ian had assured her he was in, but she needed him to stop talking and show up with the cash. He'd had three weeks; if they didn't sign the papers by Monday, the place would be gone, and she'd have to start all over again. It wasn't easy finding a landlord willing to rent to her with her long trail of unpaid debts. *What is up with him?* She asked herself. Ian sported a great wardrobe and was always meticulous in his grooming, from haircut to nails. He looked like money, but Stephanie noticed he rarely had any.

She'd yet to see him drive a car he owned; his wheels were always borrowed, much like her own. He'd claimed to be free, single, and employed, or at least he'd never said he wasn't when she asked. *I did ask— didn't I?* They'd had no contact for two weeks, and her calls, to the one phone number he'd given her, all went to voicemail; she had no address. She couldn't even remember if he'd told her the part of town he lived in or where he worked.

"Stephanie, what did you do to my car?" Laron yelled as he slammed the front door.

She cursed under her breath, then checked her hair and make-up in the mirror. "What did you say, baby?"

Lawrence had thought about it, prayed about it, thought about it more, then waited to hear from God, and although the lightning bolt never hit his living room and no voice thundered like many waters, he was sure; Brenda was the one. God had had plenty of time to tell him if she wasn't. Not only was she the one, but now was the time for him to make his move, and for them to start making plans.

She'd changed in the most beautiful ways; change Lawrence knew only God could've brought about. Brenda Collier loved him and wasn't afraid to show it. He was a blessed man.

Finding two good and Godly women to share his life with was more than he deserved. He'd assumed when God took Yvonne, he'd spend the rest of his life content with memories while making the best of being a widower. Yvonne had been the best wife in the world, but he'd been lacking as a husband. He'd failed to see her and treat her like the queen she was.

She'd raised their three children almost single-handed while he focused on his career; the more she did, the more he came to expect. She worked a part-time job, threw herself into work for their church, and did other volunteer functions without ever complaining. Lawrence was oblivious as she'd pushed herself too hard, putting her own health last until it was too late. He would always regret not caring for his late wife the way he should have. God was giving him another chance.

He leafed through the resort brochures he'd present to Brenda after Christmas when he'd ask for her hand in marriage. He wanted to take care of Brenda; he wanted them to take care of each other. His only question was, would the strong-willed Brenda Collier allow him to do that?

Chase waited for three weeks for Gia to approach him in desperation, to appeal to him, to beg him to salvage her career. She didn't. In fact, she behaved as though nothing had happened, as if he'd never given her a written warning like she wasn't afraid of him. Now he didn't know what to do. He could back down and do nothing; their situation would end in a stalemate. He would have to accept that she'd won.

Her triumph would be a private one, but he was willing to bet, she'd find subtle ways to remind him. He'd already detected bold defiance in her demeanor in the way she looked at him. He sensed a sneer, a smirk when she talked to him. Seemed at times like she was looking down on him, challenging even provoking him. She said all the right things, and her words respected his authority, but her eyes defied it. Because of this, he was going to have to make another strategic move against her. He couldn't have an employee mocking him to his face, even if he'd brought it on himself.

Gia was surprised things had been so calm at work since Chase had shoved that stupid paper in her face. Since that day, she'd come to work with the attitude—*Do what you gotta do-put up or shut up.* She wasn't going down by herself. Kevin had been right; Chase had as much to lose as she did, if not more. He had no desire for rumors of their affair to surface, even if it turned out to be her word against his. Then she *stumbled* on his paper trail.

After doing some after-hours snooping in accounting one evening, she'd found records and receipts that coincided with assignations at various hotels and restaurants in and out of town. She discovered Chase had other companions; he'd been busy. She was prepared to present her ammunition to HR when the time came and waited patiently for his next move.

A month went by, however, nothing happened, and she relaxed. She doubted Chase would let it go but wondered what he was doing. Was he collecting data to build a case against her? The thought came to her to go to HR first, but she was reluctant; why get them both fired for no reason. She decided to intensify her job search, call up colleagues, put out feelers, write her next chapter before Chase did that for her.

"Daddy, pray for Aunt Sarah, she moves to her new home to-morrow," Brenda said, sitting across from her father in the dining room of the nursing facility.

Marvin nodded his head while looking around the room with agitation. Brenda could tell, he wasn't sure where he was at that moment and was irritated because of it.

"Corene, did you bring me candy and some soda pop?"

"I'll bring it next time," Brenda said. It was pointless telling Marvin his doctors had restricted his sugar intake due to diabetes; it would upset him more.

"Can we go now? I'm ready to go home and take my nap. What's Gigi doin'? You bring her to come and see me. Corene and I will watch her for you."

Brenda smiled and stood. "Okay, daddy. I'll do just that. I've got to go and finish getting Sarah ready to go. She's giving us a real fit about this move."

"Don't blame her. Who wants to leave their home? You don't want to die in a place like this. You want to be in your own home."

Brenda was stunned and sat back down in her seat. His moments of clarity of thought and speech were so brief and unexpected that when they occurred, she tried to hold onto them as long as she could; to have her father back if only for a moment.

"I'm sorry you feel that way, daddy. It's just that—"

Marvin lifted his hand to let her know he understood. They both stood, and he reached for Brenda's hand and held it tight as they walked back to his room. She helped him get comfortable in bed for his afternoon nap, then kissed his forehead and left.

"I've tol' you, I ain't goin to that place. I'll die first. Do you hear me?" Sarah yelled. Most of her belongings were packed in boxes along the perimeter of the bedroom. Looking at them seemed to make her even more furious, but it was too late for Brenda to do anything about that. The following day she'd be moving.

Sarah had worked herself into a dreadful state. Her blood pressure was up, and she was flying into waves of anxiety and rage, breaking and throwing whatever she could get her hands on. The only thing that calmed her was the strong tranquilizers, but she'd taken her prescribed dose, and the next one wasn't due for some hours.

"You're going to have to calm down. You're a grown woman, and sometimes grown folks have to do what they have to do."

"Get away from me! You wait till you get my age. I hope they do the same thing to you you're doing to me and what you did to your father. You're going to get what you deserve. My only regret is I won't be alive to see it."

Brenda moved a chair from the wall to Sarah's bedside and sat down to face her. "Sarah, we've been together for a long time. While it's true, we've never grown to like each other. You know I did the best I could for you. I've cared for you, and I've prayed for you, and I only want the best for you. I think I cared more for you than you cared for yourself, but I can't do it anymore."

"You won't; there's a difference. There ain't nothin' wrong with you. You're gettin rid of me. It ain't right! I'm too old for this, and you know it. You know I don't wanna be around a bunch of old people. You coulda told them to do what I wanted. They listen to you."

Brenda shook her head. After the years of Sarah's complaining and accusing her of poisoning, she was now indicting her for abandonment. Her children were placing Sarah in a facility with a monthly rate equal to some people's mortgage payment, and still, she was angrier than ever. No one could win with Sarah.

Later, after giving Sarah her sedative so she'd rest, Brenda prayed for her. She asked Sarah to join her, but she'd spit at her instead, something she'd never done in all their years together. It hurt her deeply; the old woman was leaving as mean or meaner then when she'd arrived.

The next morning, Brenda made sure to arise early, as Sarah's transport to the new facility was due at her house at 8 am.

As soon as she entered the room, she detected it, felt it, sensed it, the stillness. It had happened enough times when she'd worked in the nursing home. She ambled reluctantly to the bed and peered down. Sarah's eyes were open, her mouth was open, her fists were clenched. She was dead.

19

Several family members turned up for the funeral of Sarah Jean Faulkner, more than had visited during the later years of her life, Brenda noted: probably more Sarah's doing than theirs. She did her best to carry out Sarah's last wishes—no church funeral, one song, a closed casket. Some of them were too ridiculous and spiteful, such as listing her late son Russell in the obituary as her only child.

Her son Keith appeared sorrowful, Kathy, his sister, relieved.

The entire event was the saddest Brenda had ever been a part of, not due to any sentiment she'd held for the old woman, although she missed her, meanness, and all. The proceeding, however, lacked any hint of emotion or love, and no one pretended. They understood Sarah wasn't for it. She was buried next to her son Russell Jr., who was next to his father. Then it was done.

Kathy and Keith thanked Brenda and showed their appreciation with a generous and unexpected monetary gift, equal to nearly a year's salary, in a card that read, 'You've earned this. Enjoy the next stage of your life'.

Indeed, she would. The first person she called when she'd found Sarah, had been beside her whenever she needed him, and was with her now, Lawrence. He'd taken the day off work to pay his respects and had been a comforting companion, helping her bear the burden of the loss of Sarah's life and her own conflicting emotions.

When she walked around her house knowing she didn't have to attend to Sarah or listen to her caustic remarks, a feeling of freedom descended upon her. When it hit her that the old woman's death had liberated her, she felt guilty though she knew she had no reason to. *It'll sort itself out in time,* Lawrence told her, and she believed it. She'd been a blessing Sarah never appreciated. God knows he gave her the grace to put up with the old woman's abusive language and provocation day after day. She'd treated Sarah right like she loved her, and in a way, she did. She'd loved Sarah because God loved her and mourned her for that same reason.

"Momma, she could be a mean old lady, but I'm going to miss her. Maybe because I was one of the only people she was ever nice to," Gia, who'd also taken the day off of work, said as they sat in the family room of Brenda's house after the rest of the mourners had left.

Brenda laughed. They could never figure out why Sarah had taken a liking to Gia, but she was the only person the old woman didn't talk badly about.

Gia smiled at her mother and watched her, wondering when she'd started being happy. The Brenda who'd raised her didn't laugh easily and barely smiled. Where did this pretty, free woman come from, who sat with her feet resting on the coffee table as she threw her head back and ran her fingers through her hair? She wasn't frowning about the short length of Gia's skirt; in fact, she wasn't frowning about anything. Everything seemed fine in Brenda's life, even though it all wasn't how she wanted. When had Brenda Collier stopped trying to force her will upon the world?

"Why are you looking at me like that girl? Do I look funny; is there something hanging out of my nose?" Brenda said.

"She's admiring your beauty, and so am I," Lawrence said, walking into the room with three servings of lemon pound cake.

"That's so sweet," Gia smiled and meant it, even though watching them caused her heart to hurt. While she was happy for her mother, she was sad for herself and Kevin, who was keeping her at arm's length.

"Am I getting a new step-daddy soon?"

Her mother rolled her eyes but then leaned over whispered her response. "Mind your own business, but if it happens, you'll be the first to know," she winked.

Gia stayed with her mother a while longer until she caught the vibes that the couple wanted to be alone. While in her car, she thought about Kevin and called him. He didn't answer, which was probably intentional. In the past, it would've propelled her to show up unannounced at his door, but she wasn't in the mood to get her feelings hurt that night. Unlike most men she dated, Kevin could resist her and had been getting plenty of practice lately.

"Where will we live, my house or yours?" Brenda said, playing along with Lawrence's conversation, the mock wedding plans, again. They played this game often lately: talking around the what's, where's, what if's, and what wills.

"My house is a rental, yours is paid off, but if you'd like, you can sell this one, and I'll buy you a new house."

Brenda put a hand to her chest and pretended to swoon. "Oh my."

"—and a new car, some new clothes, and new jewelry. In fact, to show you I'm a man of my word, I'll start right now." Lawrence pulled a burgundy velvet ring box from his pocket. Everyone in town knew the store that color box came from. Brenda's blood rushed to her ears as she stared at it.

He held it out patiently; you didn't rush Brenda Collier. He allowed her a look at the box to gain an understanding of where the conversation was going. A smile appeared at the corners of her lips, and he knew he had the green light. When he opened the box, her smile widened, and both hands covered her face. He removed the ring and held out his hand. Without a word, she gave him her left hand, and he slid the ring, the fit a bit loose, onto her finger.

"My Lord," she said, gazing at the four karats. She'd seen bigger diamonds but had never owned one even close.

"Do you like it? You know I'm not a cheap man. You want a bigger rock; we can do that. I picked out what I like."

Brenda waved her hand, "It's perfect. Just like you."

"Guess that means you'll marry me, or do I need to get down on these bad knees of mine."

"Stay off the floor, Lawrence Foster. Yes, I'll marry you."

He laughed loud and booming, and Brenda was sure the neighbors could probably hear it. She decided if she could make a man laugh like that, her neighbors could complain all they want.

"Ian, what happened to you? I've been trying to reach you for weeks. I lost a place because of you," Stephanie said, walking fast behind him while he looked around, trying to evade her. They were in their usual casino meeting place, but he acted as if she was a stranger.

"Uh, sorry, baby," he said, mumbling and looking over her shoulder as if she wasn't there. "Some things came up. You know how it goes."

"What?" She said, then stood directly in front of him, forcing him to look at her.

"Look. I was trying to tell you I had some things going on, but you weren't hearing me. Sorry, it didn't work out, but that's life." He walked around her, and when Stephanie turned to follow, a woman was waiting; she was older and expensively dressed. Her lips were tight, and her eyes darted between Stephanie and Ian. Once he joined her, Stephanie didn't need to read lips to know what the woman was saying.

"Hope she beats him up for me," Stephanie mumbled under her breath, then grabbed a drink and went back to the blackjack table to take her mind off her problems, which were more significant than Ian.

She was in trouble. Big trouble this time. Laron had discovered some stuff missing, cash, jewelry, checks, and knew she was the culprit. He was threatening to turn her in to the cops, which she thought ridiculous. How could she get arrested for taking things from her own home? She lived there and had found some stuff he didn't use; it took long enough for him to find them missing. She needed cash, however, to go around and buy back some of the stuff she'd pawned, hoping to shut him up about the bad checks she'd written. Figuring if she could win something that night, she wouldn't have to use her own money, but she was down big-time. If her luck didn't make a turnaround soon, she'd be going back home without a dime, then what would keep her out of jail?

"Hi Gia," Stephanie said, standing at the door of her townhouse.

Gia was stunned and speechless, wondering how Stephanie knew where she lived and what the heck she wanted.

"Don't you act like I'm a stranger. You and I have known each other most of our lives—we go waaay back."

It was true; having been raised in the same church, they'd known each other for a long time. She and Stephanie were the same age but had never been friends. More importantly, she'd had a glimpse of how Stephanie lived her life these days; her reputation as a user was all over town. People like her always looked for old friends. Gia should've expected this visit at one time or another. Now how was she going to get rid of her?

"Well, can I have a tour of your place?"

"Stephanie, I'm on my way—"

"You don't look like you're going anywhere." Stephanie looked down at Gia's sweatpants and the slippers on her feet.

"Okay, I'll be real with you, Stephanie. I wasn't expecting any visitors, and I'm not in the mood for any. Call me some time," Gia said, stepping back and closing the door.

"Gia, please. I've got some problems. I just need to talk. I know we haven't been close in the past, but none of my so-called friends want to be bothered with me. Can you make some time for me just for family sake? Rumor has it we're going to be sisters soon."

Gia sighed. "Rumor has it..." she said as she opened her door and let Stephanie in. Brenda and Lawrence had invited both families together for a special dinner the following weekend, where a surprise announcement would be made. They could've simply called it an engagement party because the forthcoming announcement was clear to everyone.

Gia was ecstatic for her mother, who, in her opinion, had sacrificed her own happiness for years. But thinking of her sometime lover, Kevin as her stepbrother felt weird. She'd always hated the idea of siblings and certainly didn't need a parasite like Stephanie calling her sister.

"Hey, this is nice. Nice and classy, just like you," Stephanie said. "You know I've always looked up to you. You're a girl who knows how to get what she wants, and you're not waiting around for some man to give it to you. I want to be more like that. I want to be independent and have my own like you. But no one has been willing to help me out. It's like the people in my life want me to stay down," Stephanie said, sitting on a high-backed stool at the dining room counter.

"I don't believe that, Stephanie. I know your dad will do anything for you," Gia said, placing a glass of wine and a bowl of chips in front of her.

"Don't let that smile of his fool you. He won't even let me stay with him for a while so I can get myself together."

Gia thought back to the way Stephanie had wrecked Kevin's place and how he was forced to evict her. *Can't blame her dad for that.* Recalling that the young woman showed up at her door claiming to want help, she decided to fulfill that request. Nothing helped more than the truth.

"Maybe that's your fault, Stephanie," Gia said. "Maybe you haven't shown you can be trusted. If you want people to help you, you need to start building some bridges."

She sounds like my self- righteous, holier than thou brother... Stephanie thought, taking a long gulp of wine to prevent herself from lashing out. Her nose had been in the air from the moment she'd answered the door, and Stephanie wanted to fix it for her, but needed pity from someone she hadn't burned already. Gia was a long shot, but Stephanie was desperate.

"What's happening between you and my brother? Seems like there might be some trust issues in your life also. I thought you two would be in a double wedding with the old folks."

Gia, who was standing in the kitchen, stiffened. "Things happen," she said, avoiding Stephanie's eyes. "We're working on it."

"Yeah, that's what I'm saying. Things happen. Life doesn't always go the way we expect, and next thing you know, you're in trouble and don't know how you got there."

"Don't know how you got there?" Gia said, her eyes wide. "I have my share of problems, but I also know how I got there, and most of the time, it was me; nobody else."

"I'm not perfect, either. At least you have your mother. My mother's gone to heaven. I sure miss her," Stephanie said, letting her eyes water a bit for effect. Gia wasn't close enough to their family to know she and her mother never got along. Her words were sincere though, it's ironic how she'd give anything to have her mother fussing at her again.

"People can be there, but that doesn't mean they're there for us. In my life, I haven't always felt free to be open with my mother as I've wanted to be. Maybe in your case, if people didn't feel like you're trying to rip them off, they'd be more willing to help."

"Oh, is that what you think I'm here for?" Stephanie said, cocking her head to the side.

Gia placed a hand on her hip. "You and I haven't ever been friends, and you show up here out of the blue, talking 'bout we're almost sisters. Yeah, that's what I think."

Stephanie grinned, then held out her wine glass for a re-fill. "Girl, I like you. You tell it like it is."

"What do you want, Stephanie?" Gia said, pouring the wine.

"I need some money, a loan.

"I don't loan money. How much do you need?"

Stephanie gave her a figure; Gia sent a Cash App payment to her phone, right then and there. She wanted to kick herself for not asking for more but hadn't expected anything.

"There you go, you got what you came for. My only condition is you don't come back. This will not be a repeat. I don't care what you do with the money, but if you get in another bind, don't come over here sister dear. I'm not doing this because I feel sorry for you. I'm doing it because I can, and if it helps great. If you crack it up, drink it up, gamble it up, or whatever, enjoy the ride baby, cause it's the only one you'll take on me."

Stephanie went to hug Gia, but she stepped back.

"Our business is done; we don't have to be friends," Gia said.

Stephanie smiled at her while fishing for her keys. She'd gained respect for Gia, who'd seen through and cut through her bull but helped her anyway. Skipping out of Gia's door, she vowed to repay her. Probably not with money, but in some other way. Maybe help her and Kevin get it together...

"Thank you, family and friends, for joining us, but we're a bit disappointed," Lawrence said, to the group of about thirty assembled guests, "you've ruined our surprise." Everyone laughed because there was a table in the corner of the room heaped high with engagement gifts when the engagement hadn't been announced.

"I told him to forget the surprise," Brenda said.

The party was held in a nearby restaurant banquet room, but Brenda had done the bulk of the cooking.

"I'd like to make a toast," Gia said. "Momma, I love you, and I love Mr. Lawrence. You two are going to be incredibly happy. Can I come along on the honeymoon cruise? Promise I won't get in the way."

"Love you too, but no. We'll see you when we get back," Lawrence said to a room full of cheers and laughter.

"Y'all got the honeymoon all planned, when is the wedding date?" Brenda's mother said, which generated more laughter.

"I wanted us to be related, but this wasn't what I had in mind," Kevin said when he'd found Gia alone in the lobby of the restaurant.

She knew he'd be there watching her the entire evening while he hadn't called her at all that week.

"Let's take a trip," she said.

"You mean to go on the cruise with them?" He laughed.

"No, I mean us. We've never gone away together."

"That's because you were too busy going away with other people."

"Why are you throwing that up in my face again? When are we going to move beyond that? It happened, but it's over. You haven't exactly been a monk. Who was that girl I saw you with two weeks ago?"

"She wasn't my boss," he sneered, then strode back to the party room. Once there, he wondered why he'd been so cruel.

20

"I thought this might interest you," Chase said to Gia, sliding a piece of paper across his desk. He'd summoned her to an impromptu meeting that Tuesday morning to present her with a document describing a job opening at another brokerage firm. She scanned the details but saw nothing in the position that interested her; it wasn't a promotion, and that firm had a reputation for being cheap with salaries.

"I can talk to some people, and the job would be yours."

"No, thank you," she said, sliding the paperback across the desk. "What is it you wanted to discuss?"

"You really should reconsider," he said then slid the paper toward her again. "It would be a great opportunity for you to start afresh."

This time she only glanced at the paper. "I don't want a fresh start. My track record and my career have been built here. I'm not walking away." Times were tough in the securities industry: firms were closing, and brokers were losing their jobs left and right. Their firm was one of the few who'd seen the storm coming and had prepared for it. It didn't matter what she and Chase had been through, she refused to walk out on her career because he wanted her to. She'd leave for the right position. If he thought he could force her out before then, he would have to try harder.

"Don't push me, Gia. I'm trying to be fair and give you the chance to leave on your terms."

"Thank you, but I choose to stay on my terms," she scowled while crossing her legs and leaning back.

"Are you prepared for the consequences?"

"Certainly, but not without a fight. Are you?"

His mouth twitched as they stared each other down; she seemed to be getting larger by the minute, towering over him. "You're forcing my hand Gia. You've had a great career here, but it's time for you to move on. In fact, your numbers are down."

"So are yours, so are everyones. Have you seen the stock market lately?"

He ignored her, "It's obvious you're unhappy here, as evidenced by your work. I'm trying to help you."

"That's very kind of you," she pursed her lips.

"You need to take this seriously. My next step is HR."

"Then stop stalling and do it, Chase. I'm ready to take my chances with anything you throw at me, armed with my legal counsel. If you're ready to rumble, so am I."

His face turned bright red, and he nervously tugged at his tie. He couldn't afford a scandal or lawsuit, and surprisingly, given his poor judgment with female subordinates, this was the first time he'd been threatened with one. He'd been careless, leaving it accessible for any two-bit lawyer to put the pieces together. Gia was smart and resourceful; if she said she had a case against him, it meant she'd done her homework. Bluffing wasn't her style.

He cleared his throat, then leaned back in his chair and took a deep breath. His office phone was ringing, but he ignored it. "I'm sorry, Gia. I've underestimated you. I'm going to take a step back."

Gia, arms folded, sat silently, staring at the wall behind him.

"I... don't know how we got here. I guess I let pride get the best of me. Maybe I'm angry about the way things...happened. You had every right to move on, but I didn't like it." She bit her lip but said nothing.

"I'd like to start over if we can. Try to rebuild the working relationship we lost. We were a formidable team before all the personal stuff got in the way." He then stood and offered her his hand. "I'm willing to try if you are."

She stood and shook his hand firmly. Leaving the office, she felt like a heavyweight boxer who'd scored a knockout punch; she restrained a laugh until she was back at her desk. Once in her cubicle, however, she couldn't sit; her heart was racing. Grabbing her purse, she pranced across the street for coffee so she could calm down. All she could think of was how God had pulled her out of another of her messes.

Once seated in the coffee shop, however, the mirth evaporated. This was no victory; Gia had been using sex to try to get ahead on the job and deserved everything that was coming to her. She promised God and herself better decisions going forward.

"Hi Daddy...Um...can you come down to the jail and get me. I need to be bailed out; there's been uh...a little misunderstanding."

Lawrence posted Stephanie's $2000 bond; the charge was forgery and writing bad checks. When they brought her to the waiting room, he simply shook his head. She wouldn't meet his gaze, instead kept her eyes down on the floor, like a five-year-old who knew they were getting the belt as soon as they got home.

"What's this all about, Stephanie?" Lawrence said once they were in the car. "And don't give me any of your stories; I want it straight. Whose name did you forge on those checks, and how much did you steal?"

"I didn't steal anything. The checks belonged to my boyfriend; he's mad because I broke up with him, so he called the cops."

"You didn't forge his name?"

"I signed his name, but...he knew about it."

"Then, he told you to do it."

"No, I'm telling you he knew I did it. I told him afterward, and he was always cool about it until now."

Lawrence exhaled loudly while sitting at the stoplight. As usual, Stephanie's story didn't add up, but it was easy enough to piece together. She was using some man again and helping herself to his bank account. He let her slide for a while, but even the idiots Stephanie hooked up with, got tired of being played.

"How much?"

"I don't know."

"You have some idea. Hundreds, thousands..."

"Five grand, I guess. Laron closed the account without telling me. See, I'm telling you he set me up."

"No, I see you set yourself up. If the guy isn't writing the checks himself, that probably means you weren't welcome to his money."

"He was supposed to be my man."

"Oh really," Lawrence smirked then pulled into an IHOP parking lot. This is going to keep them laughing at work for a while. "I want something to eat, are you hungry?"

"While they were eating, Stephanie unloaded her whole sob story of the day. She had a new place, which is what she'd used Gia's money for, but no food, furniture, or reliable transportation. Her clothes were still at the boyfriend's house, and he'd given her a week to retrieve them. Then there were her legal fees, and she needed a way to get to the job that she now needed as bad as ever.

The most essential thing Lawrence heard was she had a place. At least she wouldn't be trying to make him feel guilty about that. Lawrence would have directed her to the nearest shelter. At some point, she needs to learn there are no free rides. As for transportation to the job, that's what public transport was for.

"Daddy, you can't be serious. I only get on a bus if I'm desperate."

"Sounds like you don't have much choice. I'd call that desperate."

"But can't you—"

Lawrence looked up; the forkful of pancake that was headed to his mouth had stopped in mid-air.

"Sorry, I just thought..." she said, shrinking under his stare. Lawrence had another vehicle he'd let her use from time to time, but then there had been that incident...

"That's great. I'm happy for you, Gia, but watch your back. Don't think it's over," Kevin said, sitting on his couch, holding the phone with one hand, flipping television channels with the other.

"Let me buy you dinner. I owe you that much," Gia said.

"Some other time, maybe. I'm—"

"I know you're busy." He was always busy when she wanted to see him. "We can go right now for a quick bite; I'm sure that won't interfere with your busy schedule." When they'd lived together, Kevin had plenty of free time for her, too much, really. His current unavailability was all about her past affair with Chase. He didn't respond to her counteroffer, and there was a tense silence on the line.

"Have it your way," she said, ending the call. She'd begged, pleaded, bought, and even tried to sleep (when he'd let her) her way back into Kevin's life, and all she'd received was rejection. She'd told herself she'd wait for him no matter how long it took, but now she was making a fool of herself. He had no respect for her; she'd fallen head-first off, the pedestal he'd placed her on. He was a good man and had loved her more than anyone in her past, but she'd messed up—time to accept it and move on. But go where?

She scrolled through her contact list, and every name in it bored her. She'd left her past social life behind, and there were no new numbers. The thought of calling one of the old girlfriends to run the streets with was even less appealing. Getting dressed and going out was more work than it was fun once she got there. That lifestyle had been more habit than enjoyment, and she was reluctant to start it up again. She picked up the phone and called her mother.

"Hi, what's wrong?" Brenda said. Gia rarely called; when she wanted to see her, she put her key in the door, like she still lived there.

"Nothing. I just thought it was time we start working on your wedding."

That same night after getting off the phone with Gia, Brenda received another out-of-the-ordinary phone call. A man's familiar baritone. "Hi there, stranger. I hear congratulations are in order. Are you busy?"

21

Raymond Collier, Brenda's newly divorced ex-husband, called to congratulate her on her engagement. He also wanted to get together.

"I haven't a clue why he wants to see me," she said to Lawrence. She didn't mention the years she'd dreamed of receiving that phone call and had never gotten it. In the past, when Ray rang her up, it was for advice about Gia; he'd once even asked her for relationship help. To Brenda, he viewed her as super-human; he used to call her the rock that couldn't be shaken, failing to consider, as steady as she was, she had feelings. When he'd left her for a younger woman, he alleged it was because Cookie, his new wife, made him feel needed, while Brenda, who handled everything, rendered him unnecessary.

"I guess you'll find out, won't you?" Lawrence said as he spooned generous helpings of the dinner Brenda had prepared: fried chicken, macaroni and cheese, and collard greens, onto his plate. He had no trepidation about Ray Collier; the man was a fool to leave a woman who cooked like her.

"Don't you want to be there?"

He shrugged, "I'll be there if you want."

She smiled, knowing Lawrence's presence would prevent her ex from going into his sob story, then the walk down memory lane. Over the years, while never trying to reconcile, Ray had tested the waters a few times, to see if he could get her sympathetic ear. Brenda shut that down quickly, knowing he only missed the part of her that had made his life easy.

"Momma. This is the dress you're going to wear. Trust me," Gia said.

Brenda shook her head. "I'm not spending that kind of money for one day."

"I told you I'm paying."

"And I told you, I'm not letting you spend that kind of money." Before Brenda finished the sentence, Gia gave the bridal store clerk her credit card and the dress. A cream, floor-length gown which was form-fitted with a beaded design across the waist. The hem flared out into a modest train; the top was sleeveless, and the same beaded pattern from the front formed a sheer back panel. Gia thought the classic gown possessed the right amount of understated pizzazz for her mother's coming out party.

"They'll call you for your fittings." She raised a hand to silence her mother.

Brenda smirked at the gesture, reminiscent of herself. "Okay, bossy, Miss Brenda," she said, and Gia smiled.

"We've got an hour to shop for your shoes before we meet with the caterer. If you don't behave, I'll do this thing without you."

The humor left her face. Gia had taken over the wedding plans and was turning it into something outside of her comfort zone. She'd anticipated a private ceremony, then a simple gathering, maybe at her house. Gia was purchasing designer gowns, for the two of them, had reserved a luxurious facility and was now hiring a caterer. She'd failed to consult Brenda about anything, insisting on giving her the wedding she wanted her to have. She liked it but wondered where the money was coming from. Her daughter made a good salary for a single girl, but looking at the four-figure price tag for her gown alone, made her question if it was that good. She also speculated how involved Gia would be with her wedding, had Kevin been more involved with her.

"You should be taking this more seriously, Miss Foster. You've written numerous checks on Mr. Hughes' bank account, and he's made a statement he'd never authorized any of them. He'd even closed the account. In this state, that's called grand larceny, and it's a felony. You may escape jail time, but it's going to be difficult to keep the conviction off your record. I'd advise you to change your attitude," Daryl Jackson, her court-appointed lawyer, said.

Stephanie let out a loud breath, looked up at the ceiling, and sank down in her chair; the whole situation was unbelievable. *Why is the entire world against me, and why are they taking Laron's word as gospel and ignoring mine?* They were meeting in his downtown office, during her lunch break; she needed to get to work but also needed to avoid going to prison. She had a looming court date, but due to the backlog of cases, the prosecutor's office was amenable to making a deal. Laron would need to agree, however.

Daryl watched her as he sat on the side of his desk. He knew he had to keep things professional, but Stephanie Foster had a shapely pair of legs and a figure to go with them. If he could keep her out of jail, he wouldn't mind taking her out.

When she sat up, she followed his eyes.

"Alright, Mr. Jackson."

"Daryl, please."

"Daryl, I'm at your mercy. Please, I don't have anyone else to help me. Tell me what I should do."

He advised her, off the record, to mend bridges with Laron Hughes.

"He feels like you've used him in the past. He's all done with that. Be his friend, do some things, like paying him back some of what you owe, to show him you want his friendship..."

Three weeks later, the lawyer's counsel had worked. Stephanie had taken Laron to dinner a few times, and humbly apologized for her behavior. She told him how she'd changed but didn't throw herself at him, doing her best to demonstrate she was rebuilding her life. She also claimed to be in therapy for her gambling problem.

She was in therapy, alright, it was called survival, and it was cold turkey. The longing for the casino still haunted her, but she had other problems, like a roof over her head. Everyone she knew had heard about her arrest, and doors were slammed in her face. Old acquaintances went in the opposite direction when seeing her on the street. Her family was also less than enthusiastic to hear from her.

Laron came through and told the prosecutor's office that she'd made full restitution, even though she hadn't. They agreed to reduce the charges to a misdemeanor. She received probation and a fine with community service.

Once she completed her plea, her lawyer Daryl, treated her to dinner, and they spent the night in a downtown hotel. She blissfully thought she'd met the right kind of man, but after that, he refused her calls. She was no longer his client.

At work the following week, she struggled to hold back tears. She was broke, having spent her last few paychecks to stay out of jail. There was no money left to secure an apartment.

She'd bounced from house to house, but the few friends she had left were tired of her. For the past month, she'd alternated sleeping in her car, and a homeless shelter when she could get a bed. She'd hoped things would click with Daryl.

And people have the nerve to judge me, she thought, when considering all the users and pretenders in the world. She and Daryl, she and Ian, she and all the others, users, out to get what they could from whoever was dumb enough to give it up. She wanted out of that category forever, finding it difficult to remember when she'd started down that road, stopped trusting herself, and started using others. She narrowed it down to her sophomore year of college when she'd ditched academia for a married professor. He swore to her he was leaving his wife, then dumped her. She keyed his car, squealed to his wife, and the rest is history.

"Congratulations, Sarah's dead, and you've shut daddy away. Now you can get married and live happily ever after. Proud of yourself?" Darwin, Brenda's younger brother, said, during a family dinner at their mother's house.

"God bless you too."

Darwin glared at Brenda as Lawrence stepped between them. "Nice to meet you, I'm Lawrence Foster, and it looks like we'll be family."

Darwin sniffed and walked away from the two of them.

"Bet you haven't been to visit Daddy since you've been in town," Brenda said to Darwin's back as he exited the living room.

"I wish you two wouldn't," Corene said.

"Talk to your son, Momma. He started in on me." Brenda, incensed by her brother, forgot about the house full of guests who were quietly watching her.

"On behalf of Brenda and I," Lawrence said, addressing the room. "We're delighted to see you this evening to celebrate this great occasion, and I hope we'll also see you at our upcoming wedding."

The room was comprised of assorted relatives, mostly from Brenda's mother's side, celebrating Corene's 75th birthday. Darwin had come to town as a surprise, but Brenda wished he'd stayed where he was.

Gia made a late entrance, and Brenda could tell, she considered the crowd old and boring. She wouldn't be sticking around unless Kevin turned up.

Banners, streamers, and balloons decorated the dining room. The table was stocked with fried chicken, ham, roast turkey, and the usual side dishes all prepared by Brenda the night before. Her cuisine was a guarantee the party would be a success. People would show up to eat even if they didn't know what was being celebrated.

Brenda beamed at the plates piled high with food, but her expression suddenly clouded as Ray Collier, her ex-husband, strolled into the room. He hadn't been to Corene's house in years; he'd rarely visited when they were married unless coerced.

"Happy Birthday Corene," he said, handing his former mother-in-law a large silver and black decorated box.

Brenda watched stunned. He'd never given her mother a gift before.

He scanned the room, smiling when he spotted Brenda and crossed the room toward her. She stood, placed her hand on Lawrence's shoulder, and made a quick introduction. Ray nodded politely at Lawrence, then turned his gaze to her.

"It's been a long time," he said. "You've changed. I like it."

Her brow creased as she started to inform him how little she cared about what he liked. Lawrence grabbed her hand and gently squeezed it.

"It's great to meet you, sir. Your daughter Gia is such a treasure, I'm sure you're immensely proud."

Brenda sucked her teeth and walked away as Gia slid up next to her. "What's he doing here?" She said out of the side of her mouth.

"Don't know. Go ask him, then take him with you," Brenda snapped as she carried an empty food tray into the kitchen.

Gia laughed before turning, then cooing loudly for the crowd and her father's benefit, "Hey Daddy!"

"You invited him where?" Brenda said to Lawrence, later that evening as they were cleaning up from the party.

Corene was upstairs resting from the excitement and was probably asleep for the night. Darwin, who'd said he'd take care of the cleanup, was missing. He was also MIA on the money he'd promised to contribute, for the party and their father's expenses.

"I think it's best if we sit down with Ray and bring things out in the open, before the wedding."

"Why? I don't owe him anything. He hasn't given me the time of day in over ten years and now?"

"That's another thing. It's time to put the past behind us. I don't want you to still be mad with Ray once we're married."

Brenda put down the plate she was washing and turned to him, folding her arms.

He held up his hands, "I didn't say I won't marry you. I'm saying it's not the best way to begin our life. If we've got the chance to clear this stuff out of the way, we should try."

"And just what do you think this will accomplish?"

"I don't know," he said, grabbing the stack of clean plates and placing them into the cabinet. "Let the Lord take care of all that."

Brenda turned back to the sink full of dishes. Lawrence was right, but she was doubtful of her ability to release the pain of her past with Ray. She'd love for that weight to disappear from her life, however, having discerned how much of it she was still carrying.

"I'm happy for you two. Really, I am," Ray Collier said, sitting at the dining room table of Brenda's house the following week. "If you're who Brenda wants, then I can accept that."

Brenda, who'd prepared a savory meal of grilled, blackened catfish, dirty rice, green beans with ham hocks, and homemade biscuits, silently concentrated on her plate. She figured, filling her mouth with food was the best way to refrain from saying some of what she was thinking.

As she listened to the two men conversing throughout dinner, she was convinced Lawrence Foster could have a conversation with a corpse if he wanted to. She suspected Ray didn't want to like him, but after five minutes in the man's company, one couldn't help it.

"That's a good start, my friend. Now say what you mean," Lawrence said, pushing back what was left of the apple pie a la mode Brenda had served for dessert.

Ray's eyes widened as he placed a coffee cup to his lips.

"Come on, we're all grown here. You didn't show up out of the blue because you're happy for us." Lawrence grinned at the other man as they faced each other across the table.

The shift in conversation captivated Brenda, who'd grown weary of Lawrence's Mr. Nice guy act. She was seated at the head of the table, sipping coffee watching them.

A half-smile appeared on Ray's lips as he shot a side glance at Brenda. She felt his eyes but chose not to meet them. "Like I said. I want what Brenda wants. Just maybe she might realize she doesn't want you as much as she thinks. We were married for fifteen years, and I've known her for nearly all my life. Frankly, I think I know her better than you do. We've both been through a lot and learned a lot during our years apart. I want her to know marrying you may not be her only option if she doesn't want it to be."

Lawrence nodded, smiling. "Now we've gotten to the point. I understand what this is about."

"I'm not sure you do," Ray said, placing the coffee cup on the saucer, hard, causing a loud clinking sound. "Until you showed up, Brenda was still in love with me, and of course I was in love with her," he coughed slightly "I'd gotten entangled in another situation; didn't know what I'd thrown away until it was way too late."

"HAH!" Brenda exclaimed, shaking her head at the ceiling.

Ray's expression darkened. "I'm not perfect. I made mistakes and didn't treat you all that well, even before I left you. But Mr. Lawrence here isn't perfect either, I don't care what you think. There are no perfect people, but you and I have a history together, and you were willing to live with my imperfections back then. I think you should consider giving me another chance. That's what I came to say. Mr. Lawrence, I don't mean any disrespect."

Lawrence shook his head and lifted his hands.

"But for Brenda and me. I think we can—I can make things right again. I can't let you marry this man before I let you know how I feel. Do with it what you will."

Lord, how many years did I dream of hearing those words? Is it another man that caused him to come back, is that what would have done it? No... It's because SHE dumped him, that's the only reason he's here.

Brenda was tempted to call him out, but sat stoically, her heart filled with laughter. She saw the picture clearly, and this time it was okay. It was okay that Ray wasn't really interested in her; Lawrence was. She was free of the weight of having been rejected by him, released from being a casualty of his war with himself. He'd eventually find another woman to take care of him. Thank the Lord, it wouldn't be her.

Ray tried a few more times to appeal to their history together in his effort to sway her, to no avail, as Lawrence looked on amused. Finally, she'd had enough.

"You know what Ray," she said, cutting him off in mid-sentence. "I pray for you and hope you find what you want out of life. Mr. Lawrence here," Brenda said, walking around the table and placing her hand on his shoulder. "He's the man God sent me, and I'm not going to return the gift."

"I see. I bet this is about that rock he's placed on your finger," Ray said, his head motioning toward the hand on Lawrence's shoulder. "You know I can't compete with that. You disappoint me, Brenda. I thought it would take more than money and jewels to win your heart; guess I was wrong." He then stood and retrieved his coat and hat.

Brenda wanted to laugh but restrained herself. Ray wasn't trying to win her heart; he was shopping for a home.

"I guess I'll say goodnight," he said then moved toward the door, as Lawrence stood and followed him.

"Congratulations again," Ray said, with a lump in his throat, avoiding eye contact with the other man. He then turned toward the street, and Lawrence watched him walk, not to a parked car, but toward the bus stop.

"You know I worry about you. Why haven't you called?" Lawrence said to Stephanie. He hadn't heard from her since she'd informed him, she'd dodged the legal jam she was in. He'd done plenty of praying on her behalf and was relieved she'd only been convicted of a misdemeanor. She hadn't given him her new address, however, and never answered her cellphone. He'd finally tracked her down at work, glad she'd held on to her job. He simply showed up at the front desk, asking for her.

"I know Daddy. It's just that I've been doing a lot of thinking since— you know. I don't like myself much right now. I understand why everybody else runs the other way when they see me coming. Even you do, sometimes," she said. The two of them were seated alone in the staff breakroom.

Lawrence leaned back and rubbed his chin.

"I'm trying to rebuild my life and my reputation. I know it's been a while, but I was determined the next time you heard from me, it would be a joy, and you wouldn't worry about keeping tabs on your wallet," she then stood. "I've got to get back to work. I'll call you. I promise," she said, walking away.

"Come on, don't leave so soon. I want to talk to you."

Biting her lower lip, she hesitated. She worked at a call center, as a debt collector of all things, and was good at it, but that day she was behind on her numbers. She also wasn't in the mood for one of Lawrence's lecture/sermons; she sat back down anyway.

"You don't have to drop out of sight waiting until you think you're perfect. If that's the case, we may never see you again. The fact that you're trying is good enough."

She smiled and nodded. "Okay, daddy. I hear you."

"You will be at my wedding, won't you? We wanted to send you an invitation, but nobody knows where you live."

She assured him she wouldn't miss it, while at the same time dreading it. She'd be face to face with Gia and Kevin and was embarrassed about the person she was when she saw them last.

Her brother had practically given her his house, and she'd treated it like it was nothing, then when she'd gotten into another jam, she went to Gia of all people, and hit her up for money. In some ways, she wished she still didn't care. The old Stephanie didn't give a darn and never looked back. It was hard trying to change when her past kept showing her reruns.

"It's good to see you, sweetheart. I've missed you." When Lawrence said he missed his daughter, he meant his little girl and the woman he always knew she could become. The girl standing before him reminded him of his Stephanie, and it was nice seeing her back again.

Stephanie looked at her dad with surprise; she was the last person anyone wanted to see coming. "I've got to go," she said, standing and kissing Lawrence's forehead. "Love you, Daddy."

Lawrence fished in his pocket for his wallet, but she was gone before he could offer her any money. She still hadn't told him where she lived.

Brenda had been going along for the ride. In the beginning, she'd been foolish enough to think it was her wedding, but now well into the preparations, she knew the truth. She was a prop, as significant as the plastic bride on top of the cake.

Momma, you are going to go here... go there...wear this...wear that. Stop complaining Momma, just do it. Be happy, Momma I'm doing this for you. Don't worry about how much it costs—you're not paying for it. Do something different for a change, Momma. I don't care if you don't like it—I'm paying for it. Leave it to me—you'll see. This is going to be a small, simple affair, but it's also going to be classy and elegant like you. Trust me, I know what I'm doing...

Gia had transformed Brenda's vision of her wedding into something she didn't recognize, having approached every detail as if it was a major corporate undertaking. *Lord, I just want to get married. It doesn't take all of this to say, 'I do.'* 'Momma, this is not going to be some night in Whoville. I'm planning a sophisticated event.'

Brenda wondered what her daughter was trying to prove. Especially once she saw the final guest list.

"I gave you a list of fifty names. There are over 100 people here, some of them I don't know." She said to her daughter over the phone, having called her at work. She'd stumbled upon the guest list by accident, along with receipts showing what Gia was paying for everything.

"Look, Momma," Gia said, lowering her voice in her cubicle. "I'm taking this opportunity to do a little business networking, which is why everything has to be perfect."

"Networking?" Brenda repeated then comprehended; Gia was using her wedding to impress colleagues and clients while spending loads of cash to do so.

Later that evening, when Gia stopped over after work, her mother gave her an earful. She sat in the den and listened quietly, then gave her mother a partial explanation of the extravagance by confiding vague details of her job struggles. She was using the opportunity as a kind of real-life resume.

"A stylish affair with excellent food and wine will leave a favorable impression with my business associates. I know it's not your style, Momma; it's a little over the top, but go with it, please. Relax and have fun, I promise you and Mr. Lawrence will enjoy it."

"Fine, Gia," Brenda said, sighing and shaking her head. "I wish you would've told me this upfront." The wedding plans, while overdone, were alright now that she understood the real purpose. Neither she nor Lawrence had much interest in wedding arrangements and were pleased to have someone, free of charge, take care of them. If the lavish show would help Gia's career, she was happy to oblige.

During the weeks leading up to the ceremony, Brenda sat by while Gia combed over every item. The color schemes for the décor of the ballroom, the menu, the wine selection. The only thing Brenda insisted upon was that they exchange vows at her church, standing before her pastor. Gia tried talking her into moving the ceremony to the hotel so the guests wouldn't need to move locations, but she stood firm.

"My first wedding was at the courthouse. This one is going to be in my church, in the sight of God and everybody else." It was non-negotiable.

She had also attempted to put her mother on a crash diet and exercise routine so her dress would fit better. Brenda ignored her. "For as much money as you're paying these people for that gown, they'd better make it fit even if they have to let out a seam or two on the day of…"

"That sounds excellent. No, I haven't received all the responses back for the dinner, but since we're such a small wedding party, I'm going to reserve for all of us. If there's a change, I'll let you know…" Gia ended the call with the manager of the venue hosting the wedding rehearsal dinner. With a stroke of her finger, she checked the item off her list.

Overall, she was pleased with her attention to detail and was looking forward to seeing her efforts rewarded. Her mother was going to have a luxurious wedding reception, and Gia was thrilled to do it for her. The story she'd told her about impressing the clients was just to end her complaining; she was doing it for Brenda. It was her time to be unselfish and Brenda's time to be spoiled; she wasn't going to allow her mother to ruin it for either of them.

She had, however, taken the opportunity to purchase a maid of honor gown for herself that was a stunner. For the person whose attention she hoped to corral, the groom's best man, Kevin.

"I'm hurt. I didn't get my invite to the big party," Chase said, taking a seat in the chair beside her desk. "Since you're spending so much of my time planning this."

"That's a bit of an exaggeration, isn't it?" Gia said, smiling sweetly. "I'm sorry, and I'll try to be more mindful of the time I'm spending. By the way, have you seen my numbers for this quarter?"

"No, I haven't," he coughed as he stood and turned toward his office.

Liar. He knew everyone's numbers before they did. "They're better than ever," she said to his back.

"Humph" was his response.

It had been a while since she'd been forced to put him in his place. Since then, things had been tense, even borderline hostile, but she could handle it. Wisely, she'd been putting out feelers and had some strong prospects. She just needed to hold still a little while longer.

She'd kept things on a professional level, and neither her staff, peers, nor clients suspected she and Chase were engaged in a silent war. It would harm her professional reputation if that type of information got out, and in her business, how you carried yourself mattered. An inter-office affair here and there was no big deal, it's how one behaved *after the love was gone,* that was important.

Thank you, Lord, again. Some days it was what got her through, a simple prayer. She realized how vulnerable she was and how much of her life was beyond her control. Yes, she was young, cute, and smart, but there were plenty like her getting kicked out the door of some corporation every day, and unlike her, they'd played it straight. They hadn't been fooling around with the boss.

"No, Gia, I haven't gone to the formal wear shop yet. We've got time. A few weeks, isn't it? I didn't think I was expected to be fitted for my tuxedo so soon," Kevin said. His dad had told him how viral Gia had gone with the wedding plans, and now he was experiencing it, being she was calling him at work. *How long does it take for a tux to be ready—a week?*

"I know it's early, but it would be nice to have it done, and out of the way, so I don't have to worry. I'll make a deal with you. Meet me there after work, and I'll buy you dinner afterward."

"I didn't know you were so into weddings. The way I hear it, you have this one planned down to the color of the toothpicks in the meatballs," Kevin said to Gia over dinner. They'd walked from the formal wear store to a small bistro in the area. It was noisy and crowded, but he liked the distraction; it kept a distance between them.

"Very funny," she said, flicking water at him from her glass. "She's the only mother I have, and it's her first real wedding. I want it to be right. She'd do the same for me. If—"

He became engrossed in something playing on the television screen over her shoulder, and she got the message. She, in turn, looked around the crowded restaurant, observing other diners, families, and some couples. An interesting gentleman seated at the bar came into her view. His well-tailored suit said he was a professional, and she imagined the newspaper opened on the bar in front of him to be the Wall Street Journal. He seemed comfortable and unfazed amid the noisy crowd.

"Don't mind me," Kevin said, wide eyes staring at her, "If you'd like to go over and make his acquaintance."

"Thank you, but that's okay," she stole another quick glance before returning to her drink. "If I wanted to talk to him, I wouldn't ask for permission.

Why am I jealous? He asked himself, looking down at the table. It was why he stayed away from her, determined to avoid being caught in her games. They'd been together for a mere hour, and she was already looking around the restaurant at other men.

Abruptly, she stood, pulled out her wallet, and placed some cash on the table to cover the bill. "It was great seeing you again," she said, pulling her car keys from her purse.

"Same here." He slid the bills back toward her.

"My treat, remember?"

"That's okay. I don't need anything from you." He threw his own wad of cash on the table, and made a hasty exit through the side door, leaving her standing there.

"Ladies and Gentlemen, may I present to you, Mr. and Mrs. Lawrence Foster," the pastor announced to the congregation. Lawrence drew Brenda to him and planted a fiery kiss on her lips that elicited a loud reaction. Even the pastor was amused.

"Let's get this reception over with, I think Deacon Lawrence has other plans."

Brenda shot the pastor a look, then elbowed Lawrence before they walked down the aisle, the small wedding party trailing. Brenda was breathtaking in the ivory, satin, gown, with matching long gloves. An elaborate pinned up hairdo, a beaded headpiece, and a short veil completed the visage.

Gia served as the maid of honor, and the style of her tea-length mauve dress was like her mothers, also with a matching headpiece. She strolled down the aisle, arm in arm, with Kevin, the best man. He donned a black tuxedo with bow tie and cumberbund, the color matching her dress. The wedding party was complete with Lawrence's daughter Margo as the bridesmaid, her husband Neal, a groomsman, and their two children were the flower girl and ring bearer. Lawrence had wanted Stephanie included, but they could never work things out with her schedule.

Kevin and Gia were all smiles, neither speaking nor looking at each other, but she knew they were eye candy. After all, she'd arranged it that way. During the planning, she'd been optimistic about a reconciliation, but their blowout a few weeks back had squashed any hopes of that happening. Hanging on his arm felt great, however, so she pretended he was still her man, held on a little tighter, and smiled. It was a wedding after all; dreams were what weddings were all about. She would live her dream that day because she had footed the bills to make the fairytale happen, for her mother anyway. Kevin would play along; it was his dad's wedding, and he could return to hating her tomorrow. As they stood in the reception line, she spotted a photographer's camera and nudged him. His smile broadened right on cue.

Kevin felt like a prop in a Hollywood production. Gia was beautiful, close, but impersonal. He loved being close to her, hated the show, but it *was* an excuse. He took in her perfume, as she was on his arm, for the benefit of the cameras. When they weren't being photographed, he noticed, she still held onto him. He liked it but wondered if he was simply a part of her outfit that evening.

During the reception, as they moved from table to table, greeting guests, Stephanie called them out. "I thought you two broke up. You look like you just got hitched, did I miss something; was it a double wedding?"

"Shut up. What are you babbling about?" Kevin said through clenched teeth, while Gia smiled.

"Um-hmm," Stephanie smirked. "There's something up with you two, and it has nothing to do with the old folk's wedding," she said as they moved away.

For the first time that day, they shyly turned and faced each other, taking in the moment. Neither spoke until Gia saw Brenda signaling to her from across the room.

"I, uh, I've got to go," she said quietly.

"I think you'd better," he said, brushing her hand and looking after her as she walked away. Stephanie sidled up to him, and he gritted his teeth. "Why do you always have to open that big mouth of yours?"

"I was just trying to figure out what was what. Seems like you have some figuring to do yourself."

Kevin and Gia caught up with each other a half-hour later, while Lawrence and Brenda were on the dance floor.

"You really look beautiful," he said.

"So do you." She brushed lint off his collar.

"I'm sorry about—a few weeks ago."

In the dimly lit ballroom, she wrapped her arms around his neck, rested her head on his shoulder, and whispered, "I'm sorry about... so many things."

The beauty and elegance of the day overwhelmed Brenda, and Lawrence reveled in her happiness. After the throwing of the bouquet, cutting the cake, and more pictures, the newlyweds departed on route to their Hawaiian honeymoon.

As the guests trickled out, Kevin stayed behind and waited for Gia.

When she finished her business with the hotel banquet manager and found Kevin waiting, she ran and threw her arms around him, looking into his face.

"I knew you still loved me."

"Never said I didn't."

"What's next?" She said as they held hands and strolled toward the hotel lobby.

He shrugged. "You want to stay here tonight?"

She stopped. "I'm not talking about tonight. I'm talking about us— after tonight."

He released her hand and looked down at the floor. "I can't answer that. All I know is what I want tonight."

She folded her arms, "*That's* not good enough."

He stepped forward and kissed her forehead, then shoved his hands into his pockets and shrugged. "I'm sorry." He looked into her eyes, and seeing she was close to tears, knew he had to retreat to keep from saying what she wanted to hear, things he'd regret the next day. He backed away, turned, and exited the hotel.

This is so hard, Stephanie thought, pacing around her room, walking by the toilet on one side and hotplate on the other. Someone with a sense of humor labeled it a studio apartment. *Living right is boring.* The dingy walls, dirty windows, and musty smell of the place were getting to her, but staying in, meant she wasn't spending any money, and she had none to waste. That had never stopped her before. Just then, her cell phone rang. She checked the number, and it was her dad.

"Congratulations, newlywed," she said.

"Why did you leave so early? We wanted you in some of the pictures."

"I didn't feel right. You guys looked so great, and I felt out of place in what I was wearing."

"Nobody cared about that Stephanie, but if that's the case, why didn't you let me buy you the dress I offered?"

She was quiet on the other end.

"I'm sorry, Baby. I just called to say I was happy to see you, and that we're on our way to the airport."

"You guys have a great time. Tell Miss Bren—um, what do I call her now?"

Lawrence laughed and asked his bride. "She said, Brenda, is just fine."

"That's a beautiful dress, Gia. How many hours ago did the wedding take place? You are still a vision of perfection."

Gia smiled at the lie and took another gulp of her drink. Having never left the hotel, she was on her way to intoxication. After Kevin walked out on her, she'd hit the hotel bar, meeting up with James, the catering manager. He'd been throwing hints for weeks, and the look in his eye said he sensed an opportunity; she wasn't that drunk yet.

"It was all so perfect," she said, lifting her glass of wine.

"Yes, it was," he said, watching her like a cat waiting for the right time to pounce.

He was good looking, professional, and much too agreeable. Personally, Gia wouldn't trust him with her pet goldfish, but he knew his job;

the reception had been exceptional. He was also nice to have around when a girl needed an ego boost.

"Are you married?" Gia said, leaning over the table so she could look directly into his eyes while he answered.

"Separated," he said, the word getting caught in his throat.

Liar.

There was a time when she preferred married men. Now she didn't know what she preferred, so she studied him.

Seeing she was not the easy target he expected, his eyes shifted to his watch.

"Am I keeping you? Maybe you need to get home to the little woman?"

"Hmm—no I told you—"

"Yeah, right," she lifted her glass to toast him, and he chuckled. This time his laugh was genuine.

"How did you know?"

"I have wife radar."

"Does it matter?"

"To her, maybe, not to me."

"You're something else," he said, sipping from his glass of scotch.

"So, they tell me."

Just then, the jazz band started to play, and Gia getting lost in the music, started dancing, and stopped drinking. Full of confidence and wine, she danced alone at first but had no problem attracting partners. She lost track of James along the way but appreciated that he'd taken care of her bar tab before he left.

She'd acquired a good number of drunk admirers and was forced to slip out of the hotel before the lights were turned up, announcing the closing time. She arrived home before three in the morning and found Kevin asleep on her sofa.

'You idiot,' she murmured, watching him. Instead of waking him up, however, she went to her bedroom and locked the door. She awoke to the rattle of the doorknob around daybreak, and when she didn't get up, heard her front door close.

"Well, well, the last time I saw you, you were knocked out on my sofa," Gia said to Kevin as he stood at her door several days later. She'd expected him to call to explain what he was doing there that night, but she'd heard nothing.

"Yeah, I've been meaning to talk to you about that. Can I come in?"

She stepped aside and closed the door behind him.

He stood rubbing his neck as he spoke. "I'd started to feel bad about what I'd said to you. Started having second thoughts, the way I always do when it comes to you. I guess it was best you weren't here. Where were you anyway?'

"The hotel bar, getting my groove on," she said.

Kevin nodded, "I see. Guess I was wasting my time feeling bad. You switched gears and moved on to something or someone else. Who was it that beady-eyed manager? I don't know why I fall for your act every time, because that's all it is with you."

"If you're done, give me my key," Gia said. It was the equivalent of surrender. While he had a key, it was a guarantee he'd show up sometime.

"I left it at home," he said. "Humor me, am I right, was it him?"

"Was it him what, Kevin?" She said, folding her arms. "We had a drink, and he skedaddled home to his wife."

"Married, just your type, right?" He caught her hand as she tried to strike him.

"Get out! I hate you."

He pulled her to him and kissed her, causing the intensity of the moment to dissipate.

"The more I say I'm going to leave you alone, the more irresistible you become," he said, encircling her.

"You have plenty of resistance when it comes to more than one night at a time. This is going to stop. I mean it. It ends here and now," she pushed him away and held out her hand.

He fished in his pocket for her house key, dropped it into her palm, then rocked back on his heels. "This is what you want?"

She kept her head down, staring at the key, unable to trust herself to answer him, and remained that way, until she heard the front door close.

The grass in front of the apartment house was green with brown patches, and the wrought iron gate surrounding the property was rusted and needed paint. A warped plank of plywood in the center of the yard had become home to various birds and insects. Everything was damp and moist, the midwestern air heavy and thick. The space depressed, Stephanie. *They could at least pick up that piece of wood,* she sighed. Sitting on a wooden bench plopped awkwardly in front of the house was preferable to going inside and staring at the four dingy walls of her rented room. She chose to take in the not so fresh air.

They did keep the lawn trimmed and the leaves raked. She guessed the next time the handyman, the landlord's cousin, came around, he'd move that plywood. *Where did it come from?* She glanced across the street at a house with all but one window boarded up. *Crackheads will make a home anywhere.*

"What's wrong with you, girl? Why you have that look on your face like something stinks up your nose?" One of her neighbors, Mattie—Hattie, she forgot which, was watching her. They were always watching her, the bunch of losers. She wished they'd mind their own business.

"I smelled something. Should have known you were nearby," Stephanie said, without turning.

"You sure have a smart mouth. If you're so much, why are you here? Cause you're broke, that's why. Those looks of yours don't pay the rent, do they?"

"Did for a while, and it was fun while it lasted," she said, then stood and turned toward the older, heavyset woman. "Bet you can't say that."

The woman reared her head back and laughed. She was still laughing as Stephanie watched her waddle down the porch steps to the sidewalk, on her way to the bus stop.

"Glad I made your day," she called out.

Just then, a car crept slowly down the street, an older Cadillac Stephanie had noticed before. The driver was a senior man based on the style of hat he wore. She guessed he was waiting for encouragement from her as it had been happening for about two weeks. When she saw the car approaching, she usually kept her head down in a book or walked into the house, amused. *What does this old man want? He should know—Stephanie will take his money and turn him out of his own home. He'd better take the hint.*

She was bored, however, and hadn't been on a date in forever. There'd been offers, but she was tired of the mechanics of the chase. *What's in this for me, what do I give up to get what I want?* Like, love, relationship, those words were foreign to her. But here was this old man driving five miles an hour down her street trying to get her attention. She thought for a second, then stood, ran her hands down her hips, and sashayed toward the car. *Harmless fun, I'm not going to hurt this old dude. I just need a good laugh.*

"Hello, beautiful," he said, stopping the car and grinning at her. He wore a straw hat, sunglasses, and a gold tooth sparkled from his smile.

Older than I thought. I'm not this desperate. Stephanie waved and starting to walk down the sidewalk away from the car.

"Wait a minute, girl," the man said. "I don't mean no harm. I know I'm old, but you can spare me a minute, can't ya?" He called after her. She stopped and turned.

"I've been seeing you sitting in that same spot every day. Looks like you need a friend."

"A friend?" Stephanie laughed, edging closer to the passenger side window.

"That's right, a friend. Everybody can use one. Not much fun living life all alone; I don't know you, but you seem kinda lonely to me. Pretty girl like you, I'm sure you have plenty of joy to give."

"Uh-huh," she said, nodding slowly and folding her arms.

"That ain't no pick-up line, girl. Old as I am, I got no business trying to pick up nothing as young as you. I'm not a fool, plus my wife would kick my old ass." She doubled over in laughter.

The man smiled as he watched her. "That's right. You need to do more of that. That's what God wants. That's what he's been telling me to tell you. Tell her she needs to laugh. Tell her she needs my joy so she can bring it to the world."

She stopped laughing. "Who are you? Some preacher or something. Jehovah's witness? You trying to get me to go to some church?"

"Girl, I'm a messenger with a message, special delivery from God to you. He loves you that much. Mr. Tim is my name. When you thank God for the message, say a little prayer for me too. Be seeing you beautiful," the man said, tipped his hat, then moved on down the street, still driving five miles an hour.

She stood frozen watching as the car made a right turn at the corner then disappeared. She hadn't heard the voice of God often in her life but knew when he talked to her. "Wow," she said out loud.

When she turned to walk back to the apartment house, she found a couple of her housemates watching her. Brick, a young guy, just released from a half-way house, who'd been trying to hit on her for weeks, was speaking to Otis, the owner.

"Hey Otis, look who's got themselves a new boyfriend. She likes caddies," Brick said. "You shoulda told me that, Baby, I would've borrowed one from my cousin. Then me and you can take a ride."

Otis looked at Stephanie, chuckled, and then went back to reading his newspaper. She stepped past the two men and went to her apartment. *Maybe I spend too much time moping around this place like a loser.* Thoughts of a second job or enrolling in school had been rolling around in her head for some time, and she'd swatted them away. They interfered with the pool of self-pity she was swimming in. The old man in the caddie, and his message, might have been the jolt she needed to lift herself out.

"You've been sleeping with my husband. I know it, and unless you stop it, I'm going to your superiors."

Gia held the phone; her hand was shaking, and she felt herself sweating. Her affair with Chase had been over for months.

"I don't know where this is coming from."

"Like hell, you don't. You're Gia Collier right. I got the info from someone in your office, so don't tell me you don't know what I'm talking about."

"Maria, I don't know who this person is, but I'm telling you office gossip is not reliable. If Chase is having a relationship with someone in this office, it isn't me."

"You weren't in Palm Springs last weekend?"

Gia exhaled. "No, and if I need to prove my whereabouts, I can."

There was a long pause on the line.

"I guess you're not the one."

"No, I'm not."

"I'd advise you not to discuss this conversation with my husband. You may not be seeing him now, but I know he's been with you. I followed him to your place one night some months ago."

"That was—"

"Not business, not that time of night." The line went dead.

Gia stared at the receiver until the off the hook signal reminded her to hang up. *She's dangerous, but can she hurt me? How long has she been following him and building her case—they've only been married about a year, and he and I haven't seen each other in what—six, seven months. Nothing more deadly than a chick that's pissed off at her man, and he's started up another affair. Chase has no clue what is coming his way, but I do. His ship is going down. Time for me to bail...*

PART THREE

24

Gia spent the rest of the morning combing through her contact list and making calls. She knew the right questions to obtain job leads without letting on she was looking.

"Hey Holly, how have you been? How did things go with the Croft account? Yeah, wow sounds like a nightmare, who was the project manager—Jeff, what's his last name? Oh yeah, I know him, I met him last Christmas at the project launch session. Yeah, he's trying to leave—thinks he may have an offer. Good for him. I might just give him a ring and congratulate him. Not yet—huh—everything's still under wraps. Okay, I hear you. Well, I just called to see if you need anything; we have to look out for each other. Yes, I do have news on that, as a matter of fact..."

She hung up and quickly dialed another number. "George, hello, this is Gia Collier with Titan Brokerage. I hear your firm is bidding for the Nelson Electronics Pension account. I may have some research available that would help you with your bid. I can give your project Manager Jeff Richard's a ring, if you'd prefer, I thought it best to bring it to you first. Hit me up if you're interested, my number is..."

She made five more similar calls that morning. Then satisfied she'd sowed enough seed, congratulated herself with an expensive lunch. Seated alone at the Chef Antini Bistro, she lifted her soda glass and toasted Mrs. Chase Weller, thanking her for the heads up. Even if Gia's name happened to come up in a scandal, months from now, she'd be long gone; her exit negotiated on her own terms.

"I want to be happy. I want to be with the woman I love. I want to be able to trust her and know she belongs to me."

"Man, you sound like a soap opera. There's money to be made and women to be had, and all you do is drag yourself around here day after day and whine about the one who doesn't act right. There's more to life than one woman. If you don't get it together, you won't have a job either," Gerald, Kevin's co-worker said.

"I do my job," Kevin said, staring at the walls of his cubicle.

"No, you show up to work on time every day. When you come in, you might as well be absent. I'll be honest, I'm not the only person to notice. Your lack of presence has been noted in some meetings and has been brought to Zach's attention."

Kevin sucked his teeth. "Whatever, man. I do what I need to do."

"Barely, and as a friend, I'm telling you, you need to show some interest in being here. There are smarter, more experienced guys ready to take your place, for less money. It's a tough world out there, better wake up, son." Gerald then picked up his computer and briefcase. "Off to meet with clients for the rest of the afternoon. You'd better get some meetings on your calendar."

Kevin watched him go and knew he was right. He'd been telling himself the same thing for months but hadn't the energy or interest to push himself in the direction he needed to go. He was good enough at doing his job, but in the technology sector, just doing your job didn't cut it. You had to prove your value in clients and dollars. Burying himself in e-mails, databases, and correspondence just to get through each day, while everyone around him was hustling would get him nowhere.

Later that same day, while staring at his computer screen, he was jolted by Zach, his manager, standing in his cubicle.

"Kevin, do you have a minute?"

Recognizing the tone, he stood and sighed. *Maybe this is the wakeup call I need to get my butt moving again.* He plodded into Zach's office and shut the door.

"I got a talking to at work today. Seems my boss doesn't feel I've been pulling my weight."

"Is he right?" Lawrence said. "You do seem out of sorts."

Kevin held up his hand, "I know. I don't know why I can't move on. She's just a girlfriend. I've broken up with girlfriends before. Maybe it's the way, or the reason, or that she is or was desperate to get back together. Part of me wants to run back so bad, but I know she's not committed to anybody but herself. Maybe that's what's killing me on the inside. I want to give all of myself, and I know I won't get that back from her."

"Eat up, Brenda won't be happy if you don't clean your plate."

Kevin smiled. "I see why you married her. Does she cook like this every night?" He attacked the plate of smothered chicken, wild rice, and fried cabbage. "You'd better slow down, pop, you've put on a few pounds already. How long have you been married, three months?"

Lawrence laughed, "Can't help it, but we joined a gym last week. I pledged I wouldn't deprive her of the joy of cooking, but we'll have to work these calories off one way" he cocked an eyebrow "—or the other. She dragged me to the gym the next day."

Kevin stopped eating and watched his dad. "You're happy, huh?"

He nodded, then pushed back from the table. "My wife made a peach cobbler for dessert."

After preparing servings for them both, Lawrence handed a bowl to Kevin then sat back down.

"Now, let's talk about what will get you out of this funk. I don't care how much you think you love her or how much you think she's wronged you. Gia is not the problem. It's you."

"Yes, Marvin, everything is going well. Your father is in good hands. Brenda and Lawrence take good care of me. In fact, I'm thinking about putting this house on the market. They've told me they'll have plenty of room in their new house, and the proceeds from this can help towards paying for your father's care. Yes, I'm sure... no, you don't have to worry but come visit sometime. Your father's not getting any better; each day he's still with us is precious. Okay, love you too."

Corene put the phone down and sighed as she scanned the house where she'd spent nearly fifty years of her life. Selling it made sense and was the right thing to do. It was too big for her, and she hated living alone. She would've moved into Brenda's current house had there been a room on the ground floor, besides the one Sarah died in.

Brenda and Lawrence even offered to take Gia's old room upstairs and let her have the one on the first floor, but she declined. The closing on their new house was now only a month away.

It was time to pack, to throw away, and walk away from memories that were gone forever. *Who can remember fifty years?* When you're surrounded by it, you don't have to. Now she was leaving; trying to cling to that past was crushing. None of it, her husband included, could ever come back again.

It was sad in a way, no one comprehended. They all produced quick, anecdotal responses. 'At least you have your health, your children, your house...' What about the years, what about the husband who barely recognized her, what about her life?

Whenever these dark thoughts took her over, or when it was time to start packing, she hid. Went to the den that had become her bedroom since Marvin left and went to bed. She'd stay there the rest of the afternoon, possibly until the next day, unless Brenda called.

That was where she was headed when the doorbell rang. She looked out of the side window to see Gia, at the door.

"Gigi, what a surprise. What are you doing here?"

"In the neighborhood, thought I'd check on you," she said, stepping into the house. "Momma wants to know if you've started packing, and I see you haven't." Gia scanned the room; everything seemed unmoved since the last time she'd visited. "Grandma, you know what you need to do. When do you want to get started? You name the day, and I'll be here."

"I don't need any help, young lady. This is my mess, and I'll take care of it, but if you want to come and see me, say early Saturday morning, and wear some work clothes. Bring that little boyfriend of yours too."

She was about to tell her grandmother that Kevin, who she was referring to, wasn't her boyfriend, but then remembered they were all family now. He wouldn't hesitate to come over and help Corene on Saturday. To Gia, it was an excuse to be near him. They hadn't seen each other in months. "That's a good idea, grandma. Kevin is your step-grandson now."

Corene chuckled and folded her arms. "I don't think he'd be coming over here for me, but girl, however you get it done, is fine."

"Hi Daddy," Brenda said to her father, who was looking at her in agitation.

"Where's Corene? She said she was going to bring me some fried catfish. I've been waiting all day."

They were sitting in the resident lounge of the nursing home, which was nearly empty that late autumn day. Most of the other residents were milling around outside on the patio.

"I don't think she's bringing it, daddy. You remember the doctor said it's not good for you."

Marvin shook his head. "It's not good for me," he then quickly shifted the conversation to a range of topics: the nurses, the food, the other residents, who he liked and who he didn't, often alternating between present and the past. One minute he'd be talking about his daily life, the next he'd relay an incident that occurred twenty years prior.

Brenda had taken up crochet again, just for those visits, allowing her fingers to work, while she chimed in when needed into his discourse. Having something to work on, gave her the patience to spend hours with him, more than the rest of her family, including her mother. Given the debilitating nature of his illness, she deemed it essential to spend as much time with him as possible.

"Corene's moving out of the house and going to live with Brenda," Marvin said. "Gigi got married, you know, Corene's going to live with her and her husband."

"Daddy, Gia didn't get married. I did. I'm Brenda," she said, laying the half-finished scarf in her lap.

"You're Brenda?" he repeated. "Gigi's my favorite granddaughter; don't tell the rest of them. Tell her to come and see me..."

Brenda sighed and reached for the Styrofoam cup of apple juice that was sitting on the bureau. He sipped from the straw while she held it, then went back to talking.

At least he's talking today, she thought, as she returned the cup. Some days when she came, he'd lay around and sulk silently. His bad moods could be triggered by anything; if he didn't like what they'd served for breakfast, or if one of the residents or staff talked to him in a way he didn't like, it would spoil his whole day. *Maybe I should speak to the doctors about his moodiness.* It was pointless; they'd offer to adjust his medications to appease her, but then remind her his mood swings were a symptom of his disease. She found it infuriating how they all did nothing, including herself. Keep him comfortable, quiet, and happy as possible, then watch and wait for him to be cured miraculously or die. Those were the options.

Lord, I know you're able. I believe you can do anything. Can you please do something? Believing God knew what was best in every situation, caused her now to be perplexed, watching her father's decline from day to day. How could this be for the best?

"NO! NO-OH-OH!" she heard a woman's screams from somewhere down the hall. It was a common occurrence in the retirement home, but it shook her out of her thoughts and into reality. Her father took no notice.

This isn't just me, my life, and my family. The whole world is suffering, suffering is a part of this life. How can I sit here questioning God about my situation, when death and disease come to everyone's house?

Tears formed in her eyes as she packed away her crochet. "I have a treat for you, daddy. Here." She held out a candy bar, a Butterfinger. His favorite for as long as she could remember. "You've got to give me a kiss first," she said, pulling it away, imitating the way he played with her when she was a child. He smiled with delight and gave her a kiss, like the child she had been.

"Okay, Grandma, where do you want me to start?" Gia said as the doorbell rang.

"I don't know," the older woman snapped, as she went to the front door. "That's what you're here for." When she opened the door, Kevin and another man were standing there in jeans and work gloves.

"It's for you," Corene laughed, speaking over her shoulder. "Did you young men come to take us girls out on a date?"

"Wherever you'd like to go, Miss Corene," Kevin said, grinning, then introducing his friend Mike.

"Thanks for coming over. Gia is the boss of this project." She took a seat nearby to supervise in case Gia tried to throw away something she wanted.

They started with the garage, and after four hours of work, Gia knew they'd need to rent a dumpster.

"Grandma, have you thrown anything away in the last forty years?" Gia said, standing amidst the piles of trash, they'd run out of containers to dispose of.

"Why? Once my kids moved out, I had so much space, didn't need to."

Gia grumbled, "My mom would have a fit."

"That's why she's not invited. She would've taken care of this, but I don't want to endure the fussing that goes along with her help."

After another couple of hours of work, Kevin caught Mike watching Gia and launched a picture frame at his head.

"Fool, are you crazy? I'm going to file charges."

"Get your mind on work. I'm not paying you to stare at her."

"You're not paying me at all," Mike, the taller of the two men, said as he walked up to Kevin and pushed him in the chest. In seconds, the two were in a wrestling match on the garage floor yelling and laughing as the debris they'd spent hours sorting into piles was being knocked all over the place.

Gia and Corene stood in the doorway, watching.

"Whose idea was it to invite Kevin?" Gia said to her grandmother.

"I thought the boy had more sense than this," Corene said. They turned from the scene, shaking their heads.

25

"That's a good question; what do I want to be?" Stephanie said out loud to herself while sitting at a computer in the public library, researching colleges. The people seated around her on other computers paid no attention. "What do I like to do besides spend money and look cute?"

"I know that's right." a woman sitting a few feet away from her said. "That's the kind of job I want. Forget cleaning up after folks."

"Is that what you're doing, looking for a job?" Stephanie said to the older and shabbily dressed woman.

"Yes, I been laid off for ten months now. I've picked up a little work here and there, but it's tough out here."

She needs some help. She looks tired.

"I've got an interview later on today for housekeeping at a hotel."

"Good luck," Stephanie said, eying the bird's nest of hair she had tucked under a wool cap. The woman needed an emergency miracle makeover; there was no way anyone would hire her the way she looked.

"Are you going home to get ready?"

"Girl, this is as close as I got to a home. I lost my place months ago. I get a bed in the shelter at night, then I come here."

"Those clothes you have on?"

"This is the best I have."

Stephanie jumped up. "What size do you wear?"

The woman frowned but told her. "Are you alright, Miss?" she said, remembering Stephanie had been talking to herself a few minutes before.

"How long are you going to be here?"

"Until it's time for me to leave," the woman said.

"I'll be back. Look for me in about an hour." Stephanie hurried out of the library, with plans forming in her head. She knew the woman probably thought her strange; maybe she was, but couldn't in all conscience let that woman go to a job interview looking the way she did, when so little time, effort and cost, could make a huge difference.

It took Stephanie ten minutes and five dollars to find the woman a suitable skirt and blouse from the Goodwill across the street from the library. She then went to a drugstore and purchased some inexpensive cosmetics and hair accessories, then stopped by her apartment for hair products. When she returned to the library, the woman was waiting for her; probably having nowhere else to go.

"My name is Norma, by the way," she said, standing and smiling as she observed the bags Stephanie was carrying.

"I'm Ste—"

"No. I'm going to name you Angel because God sent you my way."

"Whatever, you say, Miss Norma," Stephanie said, rolling her eyes and shaking her head. "We've got to get to the restroom to work on that hair. How much time do we have?"

After a quick shampoo in the library sink, it took an hour of water, hair grease, gel, and furious brushing for Stephanie to tame Norma's hair into a conservative bun.

"How did you do this? These clothes fit perfectly, and you saw me all of five minutes. Girl, you are gifted. How much do I owe you?"

"Chick—if I thought you had any money, I wouldn't have bothered," Stephanie said, packing away the hair products. "You have forty-five minutes, and I've got to get to work myself. How 'bout I drop you on the way, so you'll be nice and early; make a good impression."

"You think of everything," Norma said, and Stephanie's heart stuck in her throat at the sincere admiration in the woman's voice.

I've done nothing worth all of that; nothing she couldn't have done for herself.

"When you've been down as long as I have," Norma said, admiring her profile in the bathroom mirror. "You forget, you can do things differently; that you don't have to look bad, just because you feel bad. I know you didn't spend much money, but that's not the point. You took the time, and you cared."

Stephanie, who'd been rummaging in her purse for her car keys, paused. "I couldn't let you go to an interview for a job you obviously need badly, without helping out in some way. It's not a big deal. Don't get the wrong idea. Trust me. I'm *not* a good person."

"Yes, you are. Stop thinking like that," Norma said, as they left the restroom.

The security guard at the front door looked at them as they passed. "What happened to Norma? She went in there, and *you* came out?" He said grinning.

Norma laughed. "Go on, Fred. Thanks to my angel here, you may never see old Norma again."

"I'm worried about Stephanie. Have you heard from her?" Lawrence said to his daughter Margo.

"Daddy, you know she and I don't talk. I have no time for her, and no money to give her."

"What's wrong with you and Kevin? She's your sister and a human being. I know she's got some rough ways, but the two of you don't seem to care whether she's breathing or not. Isn't her welfare more important than your agitation? If she asks for money, just say no, at least you'll know she's safe."

Margo sighed, "You don't need to worry about her, she'll take care of herself. I pray for her, but that's all I can do."

"I think you're wrong. The last time I saw her, she declined the money I offered. She hasn't called and asked for a thing since."

"Which probably means she's found somebody else to pay the freight. Stop worrying, daddy; she's a hustler. She'll turn up when she needs something."

Lawrence's hand tightened around the phone as he bit his lip. He wanted to tell his daughter about her self-righteous attitude; wished to point out a few things about her life she needed to work on. Her shortcomings, however, were not the point of the conversation, neither was Stephanie's.

"I'm going to end this conversation by asking you to check on your sister. I'm concerned she isn't feeling welcomed, and I don't care what she's done in the past. We're still a family. Can you do that for me?"

Margot sucked her teeth. "Do you have her *current* phone number?"

"Lawrence, what are we going to do with all of our old furniture? We're buying items for the new house, and we've got your furniture in storage, this furniture, plus my mother's."

"Did you check with any of the kids to see if they want any?"

"Kevin has made his claims. Margo and Gia both say the items aren't their taste, and we haven't heard back from Stephanie."

"She left me a message," Lawrence said, "—said her place is too small for furniture. I'm trying to get her over here to pick what she wants, so I can place it in storage for her, but so far, I haven't been able to reach her."

"Then choose for her: a living room, bedroom, and dining room. Lord knows we have it all. She might not need it now, but it'll come in handy later."

Lawrence, who was sitting on the sofa, patted her behind as she walked by him, carrying a tray of coffee and dessert.

"Lawrence!"

He laughed, "That's what I've always admired about you. You're determined to help people, even when they don't particularly want help."

"I've gotten better."

"It's not a criticism. I appreciate your thinking about my—"

"Our," Brenda said to him while sitting on the couch. "We're one family, and I don't think of Stephanie as any less my daughter than Gia is; I'm praying that one day she and I will have a relationship. Contrary to the way people talk about her, I don't believe she's a bad girl. Lord knows Gia's not perfect, and Margo and I are having our struggles seeing eye to eye. By the way, did I tell you we're babysitting for her and her husband this weekend?"

Lawrence dropped his newspaper in his lap, "We?"

"Yes, grandpa, we."

"Look, baby, I know you're trying to make a good impression and bring us all closer, but don't get too carried away. I don't want Margot, thinking she's going to be dropping her brood off every weekend. Naomi allowed her to do enough of that."

"Lawrence, when have you ever known me to let anyone take advantage of me? When and if the time comes, I know how to speak up for myself."

He picked up his paper and laughed. "Sorry, for a minute, I forgot who I was talking to."

"It's time we spend more time with our grandchildren."

Lawrence groaned. "I've never been good with kids, even my own. I admit, my wife did the child-rearing. I went to work and worked as many hours as I could. Even in the prison, it was safer than at home."

"I would say you need to grow in that area. What do you want your grandchildren to think about you? He's that nice old man that didn't spend much time with us."

He went back to his paper, but this time he was agitated. He hated when his wife was right about things he'd never thought about; she was always finding something.

"Yeah, girl, it's been a while. Ever since I got hung up on Kevin, I've taken myself out of circulation. I'm not anxious to go back out there again." Gia was sitting in the Blaze Nightclub, talking with her old friend Monique.

"You still have your contact list, right?" Monique said. "You can dial up a number whenever you want, and it's on."

"You know how life is in the fast lane. Out of sight, out of mind." Gia pulled out her phone and pulled up her contacts. "Most of these clowns have forgotten who I am, and I can't remember half of them."

"Sounds like it's time to dump the old and start afresh."

Gia sighed. "Yeah, I can't stay a nun forever. It was okay until I told Kevin to stop dropping by. That made him disappear altogether."

"You haven't seen him at all?"

"When I asked him to come over my Grandma's to help her start packing, he showed up with one of his friends. They spent the day joking around and roughhousing with each other. He paid no attention to me."

"Sounds like he brought his friend to keep some distance between you."

"I wish I hadn't taken my key and put my foot down. Even un-committed, he was better than these clowns," Gia said, grimacing at a guy walking by, eyeing her over a pair of sunglasses sitting at the bridge of his nose.

"Does he know it's midnight? He looks stupid. Who told him that was sexy?"

"You're too picky. Okay, the sunglasses are a bit corny, but look at that suit. I wish he was looking at me. I think he's fly."

"Help yourself. I'm sure he won't mind." Gia said, picking up her drink and looking away.

"I think I will; be back," Monique said as she freshened her lipstick, checked her hair, and went off to find the man with the sunglasses.

Gia seeing her glass was empty, was tempted to order another choco-late martini, then remembered she was driving and had no intention of hanging around that spot much longer.

"Can I buy you another," a male voice said; it came from the stairway overlooking her table.

"No, thank you," she said, and when she looked up, saw an attractive, mature man smiling at her. *Now he's handsome,* she thought, noticing his well-tailored clothes and laid-back manner. "But I would like to dance."

"My pleasure," he held out a hand and led her to the dance floor.

She ended up staying at the club much longer than planned. Reginald, her new dancing partner, was the type of man who made her comfortable. He was accommodating, without being pushy, but confined all his attention to her.

"I haven't been doing the club thing for a while, but you've made my night very enjoyable," she said to him.

"I'm glad to hear it. Can we go someplace quieter and talk?"

"How quiet?" She'd heard all the lines. When a man suggested going someplace quiet, that could mean anywhere from a sleazy corner of the bar, to a luxurious hotel.

"Not trying to violate any boundaries," he said. "There's a spot I like about a mile from here, Nottingham's?"

"I know it. How about I meet you there in about an hour. After I check on my girlfriend."

Monique had moved on from Mr. Sunglasses but had found another playmate.

"Time to go, boo. Tell your new acquaintance good night," Gia said, to her tipsy friend.

"Girl, I'm staying with my new man Jason."

"My name is Justin," the man said, who was practically holding her up. "Yeah, she's going with me."

"No, she's not," Gia said, then turned to Monique and grabbed her purse. "I brought you, I'm taking you home. Exchange numbers, addresses, and whatever you need to do, but I'm going to drop you at your door. What you do from there is your business."

"Wow, baby, you don't have to be so mean. You can come too; the more, the merrier."

Gia rolled her eyes then clenched her teeth at Monique. "I got a date, so let's go."

Monique sighed, "Sorry, Chris. My girl looks out for me. We have an agreement; we don't leave each other, especially when one of us has had too much to drink. I think that one of us is me," she said, then burst into laughter, nearly tripping in her high heels.

Gia got her to the car, while Monique was cussing her the entire way. "You messed me up. I really liked him. He was gonna take me out."

"I know where he was going to take you. Believe me, you should be thanking me for this. You did not want to wake up tomorrow morning next to that—trust me."

"I trust you," Monique said, once seated in the car. "You're my girl forever, through thick and thin, Gee." She was snoring quietly minutes later.

"Hi, I was afraid you weren't coming," Reginald said as he stood to greet her at Nottingham's Grill.

"Sorry, I'm a little late. My girlfriend had a bit too much to drink, and I had to make sure she got home safe."

"You're a good friend."

"No, there are too many crazies out here, and I couldn't live with myself if something happened to her. I try to get her to take it easy on the alcohol, but that doesn't always work when someone else is buying the drinks."

"They continued their conversation well after the bar closed. The restaurant was open twenty-four hours, so they ordered breakfast.

"You have a hearty appetite. Not obsessed with your weight like so many other women. That's refreshing," Reginald said.

"My mom is a great cook. We don't talk about calories in her house. I have to hit the gym hard, but it's worth it."

Gia discovered through conversation that he was a lawyer, recently divorced, and had three children.

"Recently divorced, that explains why you're so—"

Reginald raised his eyebrows.

"Different, calm, relaxed. Not like most men that hang out in clubs."

"I guess that's because I don't hang out in clubs. I sometimes go when I get bored. My kids are with their mom's this weekend, and I'm not seeing anyone right now; I was restless. They say the worst place to meet someone is in a nightclub.

"They're right," Gia said, spooning a forkful of eggs and hash browns into her mouth.

"I don't know; you seem awfully nice. Grounded, real, as well as beautiful."

Gia laughed, "You're absolutely right, but you see, *I'm* the exception."

"And confident.

Gia then looked out the window and saw the signs of sunrise. "It's been a long time since I've been out all night. Thank you for being great company," she said, taking her wallet from her purse.

He held up his hand. "We've had a lovely time. Please don't insult me."

My kind of man, "I was simply trying to show my appreciation."

"Then, that means we can see each other again?"

"That means it's possible. Yes," Gia said, standing and extending her hand.

Reginald stood also, shook her hand, then placed a hand on his chest and made a slight bow as she walked past him and out of the restaurant.

By the time she was in her car, leaving the parking lot, she wondered if anything would happen between them. He seemed to be a true gentleman. The Gia she used to be wouldn't have given him a second thought.

"I got the job, thanks to you."

Stephanie, who was seated at a library computer, a week after meeting Norma, turned toward her and smiled, pleased because she was maintaining her grooming. Her clothes were worn but neat; she'd done her hair and had applied some modest makeup.

"Good for you, but don't credit me. You got the job, I just tried to help."

"Never underestimate the value of a little help. Girl, you made all the difference. I walked in there with a totally different attitude. Once the interview was over, and the manager reviewed my qualifications, he decided I'd be a waste in housekeeping and hired me for the front desk."

Stephanie laughed and gave Norma a high five.

"I've got a little money can you walk over to the thrift store with me and do what you did last week. I need some clothes for my new job, and I don't have the eye like you do."

Stephanie, who'd been trying to do some research on applying for college, hesitated.

"That's okay, you've done enough already," Norma said, starting to walk away.

"No, wait. It's just that I don't get the chance to get here very often, and I'm trying to move my life in another direction. Every time I get to this point, I end up staring at this computer screen. Last week, I stopped completely to help you. If you can give me some time—"

"Maybe I can help," Norma said.

Stephanie looked at her watch and realized she only had another ten minutes of her allotted computer time left anyway. She shrugged and grabbed her belongings.

They went into the coffee shop, and Norma told Stephanie some of her story.

"I've worked in human resources before. You can't tell by looking at me, but I've managed a staff of over a hundred people in my career. The company I worked for downsized, and my job was eliminated. After that, I just couldn't pick myself back up."

Stephanie looked at her. "And you were willing to clean hotel rooms?"

"After falling on my face and losing everything, I had no choice. I have hope now which I didn't have until I met you last week. I didn't expect to actually get a job, I was just going through the motions to keep my food stamps coming in."

You never know who you're helping.

"So, let's talk about you," Norma said. "I already know three things about you, you like to spend money, look cute, and you have a passion for helping people."

"No, helping people is not me," Stephanie said, "You happened to catch me at a rare moment. If I told you my story—"

Norma held up her hand. "Not interested. This is where we will start. Helping others is in you. I'm living proof of it."

"Well, I do like the fact that you've had a good result, and I helped you achieve it. It's a feeling I think I'd like to build on."

"Then I'm going to give you a homework assignment," Norma said. "To be completed the next time we meet. I'm not sure what my work schedule is going to be. I want you to think about what you want to do, not how much money you want to make, or where you want to work. What do you want to spend your time doing that will make you happy and feel your time is being well spent? You tell me that, and I can point you in the right direction. That was my specialty when I worked in HR. Many people go to school then take jobs looking for what they'll get. To be happy in a career, you need to feel you're making a contribution also."

"Norma, you've just said what I've been feeling. I want to do better, but I need to love what I do. When I'm reading these descriptions of jobs and even some college course descriptions, I'm not seeing—"

"Love? It won't be on that screen. A job will pay you. A college will take your money and give you a piece of paper if you finish. None of them will give you what you love. That's up to you."

Stephanie stared at the homeless woman who she guessed was nearly fifty, and marveled at her wisdom. To think, she was walking the streets without a place to live, having become too depressed to try. She wondered how many other Norma's were out there in this tight job market, displaced because they'd given up.

Maybe I need to talk to somebody: a professional.

"I'm trying to work with you, Kevin, really. You've been here for a long time, and you've been a good employee. I don't know what's up with you, but I'm willing to try to help or connect you with people who can help. The bottom line is I can't keep watching everyone else in this office moving around you. We're all moving at normal speed, and you're in slow motion. We can't have it. If this isn't the place for you, I'll do what I can to help you find something else, but you've got to ask for that help now while it's being offered."

"I appreciate that Zach and I know I haven't been myself."

"That's an understatement. You haven't finished one project I've given you in months.

Kevin nodded and rubbed his face with his hands. "I know. I know. No, I don't want to go anywhere else. I love what I do."

Zach then stood up. "You're going to have to get it together and prove to my boss and me that you want this job, or you won't have it."

Kevin stood and nodded. "I understand. Thanks for being fair."

"I like your attitude. I always have Kevin. I know you're going to meet this challenge. I have no doubt," Zach said, walking him to the office door.

Back at his desk, he checked his watch. It was lunchtime. He'd been in the habit of taking long, meandering breaks, roaming through a mall, sometimes going home, and watching television. Today he called in his lunch order to a local delicatessen and pulled out his client list, which had collected dust. He made up his mind to work through lunch and spend the rest of the day, reviewing his accounts.

God, help me get it together, he whispered earnestly, embarrassed at what God thought of him, losing focus the way he had. But he knew he couldn't conquer the gloom he'd fallen into by himself.

The house was quiet, the hour early, and Lawrence knelt in the dark, his bible opened in front of him. Sometimes Brenda would join him at that hour, but most of the time, it was his time alone with God. His prayers were mostly about the children.

He continued reading and praying until he had no more to say, then decided to take a walk. When he returned after an hour, he found Brenda still asleep, so he made her breakfast.

"Thank you, honey. How nice," his wife said, coming into the kitchen in her bathrobe, her smiling face without makeup. She went to the counter and removed two coffee mugs from the cupboard.

"What do you have planned for your day off?" she said, handing him his coffee.

"I'm going to meet with the realtor to go over the inspection report on the new house. Then I'm going to try to have lunch with Kevin. Would you like to come?"

"No, I've got enough on my plate for today. I'm having lunch with my mother, and I'm going to check on her progress with getting her belongings organized. I'm not even pushing for her to get packed. She's a long way from there."

"Kevin told me he helped her one weekend a while back."

"The way Gia tells it, he and his friend stopped by, but the two of them weren't much help."

Lawrence laughed. "Are you excited about the new house? You sure it's what you want? It's not too late to back out. We'd lose money, but I'd prefer you to be happy."

"I love the new house, Lawrence Foster. How many times do I have to tell you that?" Brenda said, nudging him to the side with her elbow so she could spoon eggs, bacon, and grits onto their plates.

As they sat down at the kitchen table, the telephone rang. It was Brenda's sister Christine calling to tell her that her husband's company had been awarded a multi-million-dollar contract.

"That's impressive," Lawrence said, once Brenda was finished with the call. "I don't recall her ever calling before, and we've been married—what three months?"

"My sister only ever calls to brag, bless her heart. I think she believes I'm jealous, but I've always been happy for her. I only wish her husband's business success would translate into some financial help for daddy. She calls to brag, but when I ask for help, she's always broke. I guess having two kids in high profile colleges is expensive."

Lawrence stood and walked his plate to the sink. "I'd better get moving."

"Don't forget, we have the kids tonight. I'm thinking we'll take them out to eat and maybe to the movies; if you feel like it."

A sick feeling came over Lawrence, and it showed on his face.

"You've got some work to do, grandpa. We have three other kids, and we'll probably have more grandkids. You'd better get with it," Brenda said, sipping her coffee and laughing at him.

"I'll be free in about an hour, where do you want to meet?" Lawrence said to Kevin over the phone while sitting in the realtor's office.

"Was that today? Sorry, dad, I should've called you. I have to cancel."

"Work picking up?"

Kevin coughed slightly. "Work never slowed down; I did. They've placed some heat under my seat; either I get moving or get out."

"Sorry to hear that, son, but I'm sure you know what you need to do."

"I do, just don't know how things got this way."

"It happens easily enough. Life is full of snares and distractions—"

Kevin tapped his pen on his desk *don't have time for a sermon today.* "You're right, dad, look gotta go. I may be working this weekend. I need to catch up on my numbers. But I'll try to come by on Saturday." He then disconnected.

Since he now had the lunch hour free, Lawrence decided to call Stephanie who he'd been in regular contact with, since his marriage, but she kept their conversations quick and vague. Refusing to divulge where she lived, saying she was embarrassed about it. She also didn't like him popping up at her job.

"Sure, daddy, I can meet you," she said, answering her phone for once. He suspected his daughter avoided his calls, then returned them when she felt like it.

She's smiling, he thought as Stephanie came through the door of the restaurant.

When she got to the table, she gave him a big, hearty embrace that nearly brought him to tears.

"My word," he said, stepping back. "All that love, are you *my* daughter?"

"Missed you, daddy. How long's it been?" She said, sliding into the booth.

"Months and you have no excuse. You *know* where I live."

"I know, and I'm sorry. I've been—"

Lawrence held up his hand, "Going through some things. You're not the only person to ever go through things. Why is it you have to cut yourself off from everybody."

"Daddy, you know what I've been like. People don't want to hear from me or see me coming. Even you at times. That's just how it is."

Lawrence looked down, then picked up the menu.

"You look like a much happier person than the last time I saw you," he said after they'd ordered lunch. "How are you?"

"You know what daddy," she said, taking a deep breath, "I've been blessed—really blessed. I don't know how else to say it."

Lawrence raised his eyebrows. "Has something happened? You win the lotto, or meet some wealthy man, or—"

Stephanie smiled and shook her head. "You're talking in the language of the person I used to be. That's not my definition of being blessed anymore. I'm about to move out of the rooming house I live in, and I've gotten a promotion on my job."

"Great,"

"One day, this old man stopped me on the street in front of my building and told me God said I need to smile more and spread His joy to the world. Part of me said the old man was crazy, but a part of me knew he wasn't. Do you know I've been joyful ever since then, about everything; the way I see my life and myself. Do you understand that?"

Lawrence smiled and nodded.

"Then, I started to think that I can do better for myself. Why was I spending my life waiting for somebody to come along and do for me? I started looking into going back to school, then I met Norma at the library."

"And Norma is?"

As Stephanie described how she met Norma, Lawrence watched her one-woman stage production, having never seen her so animated talking about someone besides herself.

"Come to find out, Norma had been a Human Resources professional before getting knocked down so hard, she couldn't get herself back up." She was gobbling fries in between sentences.

"Now, she's been coaching me, helping me find what my resources are. I think she's way off, but she's such a smart woman, I enjoy talking to her. It's like she's feeding into my life. She keeps trying to tell me my strength and passion is helping people. I keep telling her Stephanie's passion is helping herself."

Lawrence laughed.

"She won't listen to me and won't let me tell her about my past. She says it doesn't matter. She's encouraged me to do some volunteer work in the shelter where she was staying and know what? I love it. People keep saying I have a gift. Can you believe that? They say being around me makes them feel good about themselves. Then I go to work, and they say they like the positive energy I've been bringing into the office, and they asked me to be a training coach for new employees. The increase in my salary was huge. I still have a lot of debts to pay off, but I can afford a better place now. Isn't God good?"

Lawrence started laughing, and soon they both were.

"Daddy, I don't know why He loves me or puts up with me, but I'm glad He does."

Lawrence smiled as he ordered two giant brownie and hot fudge Sundaes.

When the waitress brought the desserts with mounds of whipped cream and set them in from of them, Lawrence raised his spoon. "We're going to enjoy this now. Brenda and I have a date at the gym this afternoon."

"Yes, Marvin. I know you want to come home, but look at the home-made lunch I brought for you. Don't you like it?"

Marvin looked at the plate of baked chicken, steamed broccoli, and brown rice and screwed up his face.

"Where's the mashed potatoes, with homemade gravy, and collard greens with the fatback?"

"Doctor says you can't have all that. This food is better for you."

"This ain't good for nobody," he said, pushing it aside.

Corene put a finger to her lips. "If you don't tell the doctor, look what else I brought you." She pulled out a box of jellybeans.

"I won't tell," he said, excitedly then took the box from her and grabbed a handful before hiding the rest in his nightstand. He contentedly focused on the candy during the remainder of her visit.

"Have any of the ministers from the church been in to see you?"

Marvin shook his head, and Corene sucked her teeth. She didn't want him to hear her complaining because, like a child, Marvin sometimes repeated what he heard. Still, she was frustrated by the lack of support he was receiving from their church.

Marvin had been active in everything at Grace Tabernacle Church; many of the programs sponsored by the church wouldn't have happened if he hadn't taken a leadership role. When she thought of all the long days and nights he'd spent, especially after his retirement, working for the church, it amazed her how quickly he'd been forgotten.

When he first became ill, there was someone around all the time, pledging support, but now it had been three years. Marvin was a part of their past.

I'll call the church and ask one of the leaders to visit Marvin every week, she thought. *If they hear from me often enough, they'll get the message. Not that Marvin notices, but I do!*

"Reggie, I'd love to see you tonight, but I have to work late. You'll wait, wonderful I'll call you back when I can give you a time." Gia smiled as she placed her cell phone on her desk.

"Reggie, again. This one sounds serious," Diane, an administrative assistant who happened to be standing near her desk, said. "He took you to lunch just two days ago and wants to see you again already. You must be doing something right."

"Must be. I'm not sure what, but I'll try to keep on doing it."

Reggie was a dream or seemed to be. He had all the externals: nice clothes, house, car, looks, and while she tried to avoid being impressed by the superficial, it was nice dating someone who could afford the places and things she liked.

He also wasn't pushy. They'd been to each other's homes, but there'd been no sleepovers. This was stoking Gia's interest. She loved a man who took his time.

Just as she was about to go out to lunch, her phone rang, a call she'd been expecting. "Hey, Holly, what's up?"

"Just wanted you to know, Jeff, our Major markets project Manager, is about to submit his resignation. The boss knows about it, and your name has come up. Get on it, girl."

"Gotcha, thanks babe," Gia said, then hung up the phone smiling. She sat down at her desk, car keys still in hand, planning the phone call she'd make to Jeff's boss after lunch. *Should I risk calling here, or should I go down the hall, where ears won't be listening?*

Nobody knew she was looking for a job, and if the information leaked prematurely, it could give Chase, or one of the other bigwigs, the chance to sabotage her. Even though Chase would probably pay out of his own pocket to get rid of her, one can never trust an ex-lover turned enemy.

She decided to use caution and watch herself every step of the way. Turn on the charm for Steve, The President of Titan, her current firm, so she could get a good recommendation when the time came. *Steve, I swear, this opportunity just dropped in my lap. What do you think; should I pursue it?...*

It was early yet, but she knew now was the time to make her move. Her goal was to secure the job; be everything they want and more, so they wouldn't bother recruiting, thereby eliminating all competition. She was optimistic, but still had some leads working in other firms. It paid to have a backup plan.

"George, hello this is Gia Collier, I'm not sure you remem—you do? You did? Well, thank you, that's very flattering. I just wanted to pass along a tip I received about Bedford Industries. Yes, it seems their looking for bids for their employee stock fund. It's not the kind of thing we handle, so I thought I'd pass the lead on to you. Can I give them contact information for someone in your office? Great." Gia smiled but glanced at her watch as George decided to prolong their conversation with talk about things going on internally in his organization, not the typical subject matter for someone from the outside. He was trying to reel her in, and she was letting him.

"Would I be available for lunch next week, with you and Constance?" Her smile widened; Constance Henry was the firm's CEO. "That would be a pleasure. Is there anything, in particular, you want to meet about...a job opening? Yes, I'd be interested. How's Tuesday look for you? You'll get back to me? Fantastic."

Gia nearly skipped back to her cubicle but sobered quickly; Chase was sitting in the chair beside her desk.

"Having a good day?" he said, staring at her as if he were trying to look through her eyes to see her thoughts.

"Is there something I can do for you?" She stood over him, arms folded.

"Not anymore," he sighed. "Those days are over."

"You can say that again," she said, taking her seat.

"Did my wife call you?"

"Not that I recall."

"Cut the bull, either she did, or she didn't."

"Then, no."

He leaned over, and with his mouth near her ear, whispered, "You're lying."

"Prove it," Gia said with a shrug, then turned to her computer monitor.

He stood and ran a hand through his hair. "Somebody has told her something, and I say it's you," he whispered. "When I find out for sure, you're going to wish you'd kept that pretty mouth of yours closed."

"Why does it have to be me?" she hissed. "From what I hear, you have a new little traveling companion in this office. If I came by that information, I'm sure someone else could; if they happen to be looking."

"You scheming little liar. You've been checking up on me," he said through clenched teeth, his face becoming flushed. "Accounting told me some 'unidentified' user had been in my expense records. It was you."

She stood and blocked the door of her cubicle from curious eyes. "Don't blame me if you were careless about covering your tracks. If I looked in your expense reports, it was because they involved me. After the thrill is gone, a girl has to look out for herself."

He took a step toward her, "That's wise. But if you're the one trying to sabotage me, watching your back won't help you." He pushed past her and was gone.

He's trying to blame me for the dirt he brought on himself. Like I made him cheat on his wife, using his corporate expense account. She gritted her teeth, snapping in two the pencil she'd been holding. *Glad I saw this coming.* Trouble was swirling; she could sense it and planned to be long gone before being sucked in.

"Make the most of what you've got, girl. You're not a size six, but you've got beautiful eyes and a flawless complexion. Accentuate them. Stop wearing clothes that bring attention to your flaws. Tight clothes are not attractive on all body types. When you walk into that potential employer's office, you don't want them focusing on those leopard skin, candy apple red leggings you've shoved your size twenty hips into. I don't care if Rihanna wore a pair in her last video. They ain't for you."

"You ain't got to say it like that. I ain't no size twenty," LaResha a young girl, who'd just completed her GED said, rolling her eyes at Stephanie, "My boyfriend said—"

"Your boyfriend isn't giving you a job, is he?"

"I don't like you," the girl said, turning away, but Stephanie noticed, she wasn't leaving.

"What are we gonna do, Re-Re? I've got other clients, some your age. And by the way—my track record is rather good. Everybody I've helped, if they wanted to find a job, got one. I may not know what's hot, but I know what looks presentable to an employer."

"Yeah-yeah. You keep sayin'."

Stephanie looked at her watch. "My time is almost up. There are some clothing donations—"

"I ain't wearing those hand me down clothes. I've got money."

"Then come back tomorrow with a pair of black *pants, n*ot jeans, or leggings, size—"

"I don't need you to tell me my size."

Stephanie walked around the chair the girl sat in and stopped behind her. "Eighteen, no smaller. I would suggest a nice full skirt. The blouse can have some color, but don't blind me. Your interview is when?"

"Wednesday," she snapped as she stood to leave.

"You'll thank me when you get hired. Bring some makeup, I'll show you how to work those eyes of yours.

LaResha walked out of the small classroom without speaking, and Stephanie doubted she'd be back. Some girls, especially the young ones, don't like to be told they needed to change something about themselves to secure a job. They refused to understand we are all judged by our appearance, regardless of our abilities.

Stephanie loved her volunteer job as a Dress for Success career counselor; she only wished she could spend more time doing it. There were so many who could benefit from her help; she was receiving calls and requests from other shelters, charities, even churches. In the tough employment market, applicants were looking for an edge, and free advice was highly sought after.

"I'm no expert," she's had to explain repeatedly, "I like to help people use their appearance to their best advantage. Most of the time, I'm winging it. I know what I like to see, and everyone has strengths that can be brought out in one way or the other."

The requests for her time were overwhelming, and she had to turn down more than she could honor.

While she packed up her color and fabric samples, along with the pamphlets she'd created, Victoria, the shelter director, entered the classroom.

"You certainly pissed her off."

Stephanie shrugged, and Victoria did the same.

"It's a tough world. These girls need to be told the hard truth, in a soft way. I think you're great at that."

Stephanie smirked, "Everybody keeps telling me I'm great at *that*. What? I like people, I like to talk, and I like what looks right. What is that?"

"Accept that you have a special gift, even if you don't know what to name it. All I know is I've been getting calls about you since Norma dragged you through that door. There's something about you people relate to."

"I don't know who people think I am-but—"

"I did your background check. I've seen it all," Victoria said. "You've had a colorful life; some petty thefts, domestic incidences, and other misdemeanors."

"You thought that was good, check out my credit report. That would make you really laugh. I haven't met a bill I didn't skip out on. My wages have been garnished so many times, it's a wonder I get a check at all."

"You need to stop," Victoria said, covering her mouth to hold in her laughter.

Stephanie laughed along with her but was unsure as to what the woman found so funny. Everything she'd said was straight-up truth.

"You're hilarious; a pretty woman like you who can laugh at herself, and still put her heart into helping people. I almost forgot," she said, handing Stephanie some paperwork. "The state is looking to award a contract to someone doing what you do. They call it an Employment Image Consultant. Why not investigate it? If you're going to do this, you might as well receive some compensation. It's not much, but it will help."

"Well, I'll be," Stephanie mumbled, looking over the paperwork. "An Employment Image Consultant. I like the sound of that."

"You should. There's a market for that type of work. You wouldn't believe the kind of money those who cater to high-end corporate clients charge for what you could easily do."

"Yeah?"

"Do your homework, Stephanie. Get one of those coach certifications. Your volunteer hours counts as work experience. As you're helping others, you can help yourself also. Build your dossier, and then you can start marketing to paying clients. I'm sure Norma can hook you up with some good contacts. Just because a person makes a six-figure salary doesn't mean they know how to dress or present themselves. The opportunity is out there."

"I've been looking for some direction. That's how I ended up here in the first place," Stephanie said, almost to herself. Victoria was still talking, but she was half-listening and half-dreaming.

"What does that verse in the bible say—your gifts will make room for you? I'd say the room is yours; you need to step into it."

26

"Lawrence, don't forget the grandchildren are coming over tonight," Brenda said as he was leaving for work.

"I won't forget, Grandma," Lawrence said, grabbing the lunch she'd packed for him. He was becoming accustomed to the twice a month grandkid visits, though he complained at first; he'd been wrong. Brenda had one child and wasn't close to her siblings; family was important to her, and he appreciated that. She was filling the role vacated by his late wife, and his kids, at least Kevin and Margo, needed Brenda, and she needed them.

"Also Lawrence, I want to have a family dinner; the last one in this house before we move, but I want all the kids here, including Kevin and Stephanie. Do you think you can make that happen?"

"Stephanie, maybe, but Kevin avoids being around Gia as much as possible."

"Then tell him he needs to get over it. Life doesn't stop because things didn't work out between them."

"I know, but he's still in love with her. A man has his pride."

"Yeah, yeah. I forget," Brenda shook her head and could hear him laughing as he walked out the door.

A few hours passed, and while Brenda was sorting items for their move, which was still two-weeks away, the doorbell rang. She opened it to a smiling Stephanie.

"Our prodigal girl has come home," Brenda said, smothering her with a hug while pulling her inside the door.

Stephanie enjoyed the reception and marveled that the woman so full of love, was the same usher who'd patrolled the church sanctuary like a hawk when she was growing up.

"Come in here, girl," Brenda said, leading her by the hand into the kitchen. "I'm going to fix your lunch, and then you can tell me why you won't visit us. Be honest. Is it because of me?"

"No, Mi—Brenda. Honest, it's not you," Stephanie said, sitting down. "I'm sure my dad has told you some stuff about me. I needed time to myself."

"Forget about all that. What do you have a taste for? I'll make whatever you like, people tell me I'm a decent cook."

"Are you kidding me? Your cakes are legendary, but don't put yourself out," Stephanie said, checking her watch. "I'm actually on my way to an appointment. I stopped by because my dad made me promise to pop in. He also said you have some furniture you need to unload."

"I'll show you the furniture, but you'll have to indulge me and let me make you something. I never get to see you, and Lawrence has told me good things are happening for you."

"Okay," she smiled. "Maybe a sandwich or something."

"You're a fascinating woman. Confident, ambitious, and down to earth, but I still don't feel like I'm getting to know the real you. We seem to talk around things, without ever getting to specifics. You're good at that."

Gia blinked, then looked down at her plate and began moving the food around with her fork. She and Reginald were having dinner at the Park City Bistro, after seeing a movie. The atmosphere was quiet with dim lights and low sultry piano playing in the background, ideal for intimate conversation and not her preference. "Reggie, at this stage of our friendship, I'd prefer you to see the good side. If we continue to see each other, there will be plenty of time for that other stuff."

"Other stuff?" He said, sipping his drink.

"The baggage left behind by childhood experiences, bad choices, and bad relationships; that stuff."

He nodded. "You're right about that, but isn't dating supposed to be when we lay that stuff on the table, so we can decide if we want to continue seeing each other."

"That's what's wrong with dating these days. People move too fast, in a hurry to go nowhere. My skeletons are in my closet, minding their business. You want to see them, then keep seeing me, and you'll be acquainted. If we never get beyond the friendly dating stage, then you'll never know what you've missed."

"That's an interesting way to look at things. You present it as a way of keeping control of who you allow into your real life." She looked up thoughtfully, nodded then sipped her wine.

"I see it as a way of evading commitment," he said.

"You see through me pretty well. I'm the worst when it comes to commitment. I don't remember the last time I was really committed in a relationship. Maybe never."

"Fear of commitment," he said, sitting back, crossing his arms.

"Who said I was scared? It's simply something I choose not to do."

He smiled slightly and watched her.

She laid down her fork when the waiter came to the table. As he took her plate, she retrieved her compact from her purse and freshened her lipstick.

"Have you come to any conclusions?" She closed the compact.

"No, just more questions. What are you so scared of?"

Her eyes narrowed. "I'm not afraid of anything or anyone. Everyone who knows me would agree."

He smirked. "That's what you want people to believe, but you're more transparent than you realize. I don't believe your declaration for a minute. Miss-Got-It-All-Together is a mask. I'm determined to get behind it."

She felt her armpits twitching, though she smiled back at him coolly. Having no quick or witty response, she focused her energy on appearing as though he wasn't getting to her. She pulled out her cellphone and casually started typing a text.

He signaled the waiter for the check.

Why didn't I do that?

He laid cash on the table carelessly. "Are you ready?"

She nodded and waited for him to pull her chair from the table, another of those gestures he'd requested she allow him to do.

She had thought it was cute until tonight. Now she felt Reginald using all her symbols of strength against her.

"You seem tense. I hope I haven't ruined the rest of our evening," he said, while they waited in the lobby for the valet to bring the car. "I have a bottle of wine waiting at my place. I was hoping—"

"Another night maybe," she said, looking out the window instead of at him. "You've given me some things to think about. When we get together, I want to make sure all I'm thinking about is you. I hope you're not disappointed."

He nodded and shrugged. They had sparse conversation on the drive to her house, and when he walked her to her door, she didn't invite him in.

"I'm sorry. I came on too strong," he said, as Gia stepped into the doorway of her townhouse."

"You have nothing to be sorry about. You've challenged me, and I need to know I'm woman enough to handle it. If I'm not, then we're wasting each other's time."

"What is it you want, Gia? I'll never be a man who marches to the beat of your little drum. That's not who I am."

"Good to know," she said, meeting his stare, waiting for him to speak so she could counter and have the last word. "Good night," she said finally, to his silence.

He gave her a nod and moved away from the door, then waved as he got into his car.

Wonder if I'll see him again? God, he makes me feel like a coward.

She thought about Kevin and wondered what he was doing at that moment. Without taking time to think, she dialed his number.

"Hi Gia," he said drowsily.

"How are you?"

"Alright. Work has been kicking my butt, but other than that, okay." It had been months since he and Gia had seen each other. Now, on a Saturday night, she's calling him, All he'd been hearing about for weeks was this new guy in her life. *Same old Gia.*

The phone went silent as she paced her living room, trying to figure out why she'd called him in the first place.

"Can I come over?" she finally asked.

"I wouldn't be good company, I'm beat," he said, then heard a hasty 'okay bye' and click. He thought about calling back; he missed Gia terribly. *It's just one night, I'll keep it that way; not going to get caught up in her games. She's his problem, not mine.* In the end, he knew if he did call, she'd repay him for rebuffing her. He rolled over and went back to sleep.

What the hell happened? Gia asked herself as she watched Reginald dozing beside her. He'd come over to break things off, and she was cool with that. But they wound up in bed. Somewhere between the phrases—I don't think,' and 'we should see each other again,' things heated up, and she'd seduced him. Knowing all the while, she'd made a few midnight trips to Kevin's place since she and Reginald had last seen each other. Now she felt in control.

She hoped he'd wake up soon as she was ready for him to leave. It had been fun, but Reginald, like Kevin, didn't want fun. They wanted someone they could hold onto and claim ownership. She was tired of being alone and wanted companionship but seemed unable to hold up her end of the deal.

"I've got to go," he whispered to Gia at five a.m. "I have an early meeting to prepare for. I hadn't planned on this."

"The best things in life happen unplanned," she said, stroking his chest. "You'd better go before I have other ideas."

He laughed and scratched his head as he rolled out of bed and into the shower. She had coffee and breakfast ready when he came out.

"Will I see you again?" He said, sliding onto a stool at the counter.

She shrugged, and he nodded. "I'm in your world now. No promises, plans, or pretenses. Go with the flow, huh?"

"Eat your eggs. It's getting late," Gia said, sipping coffee from a mug.

"How many other fish do you have caught up in your net?"

"Are you caught?"

"Feels like I'm being lured in."

She shook her head, "You're too serious for me."

"It's only the serious guys who get caught. Players move on," he said.

"I guess you're right."

"Answer my question. How many others?"

"You have me all wrong. I've slowed down a lot. If I were still the girl I used to be, I'd have nothing to do with you. You were trouble from day one. Nice guys always are."

He stood. "Since, as usual, I'm not going to get a straight answer. I'd better go." She followed him to the door. He stopped and turned. "What are you doing this weekend?"

"I'll be here and there. My mom and step-dad are having a big family dinner on Sunday."

"Can I come? I'd like to meet your family."

"I'll think about it."

"Is that a no?"

"You came over to break up with me last night, didn't you? You wound up spending the night, and now you want to meet my family?"

He opened the door and laughed heartily. "I admit you have me confused."

"Stay that way. I'll call you," she closed the door behind him.

"Kevin?" he turned to see Zach and a woman standing at the door of his cubicle. "This is Michaela. She's starting today and will be relieving you of all those new accounts you had to take on. You, however, have the privilege of training her."

Kevin and Michaela shook hands. *Things are looking up,* he thought as Michaela, blotted thoughts of Gia out of his mind. She was a gorgeous brunette, and their eyes met on the same frequency. He would have complained about having to train a new person, but most of them didn't look like her.

Zach saw the smile on Kevin's face and smirked, "Michaela, good luck. I'm leaving you in capable hands."

She took the chair next to Kevin's desk and crossed her long legs. Zach slipped out of Kevin's cubicle unnoticed.

"Upper management is impressed with your performance the last six months Stephanie," Maxine, the site manager told her, at their monthly meeting. "They see great potential for you at the corporate level. They've asked me to see if you'd be interested in traveling to the corporate headquarters to attend training. They're trying to recruit candidates to be a part of the national training team."

"Really. I've been here for five years and never heard of such a thing," Stephanie said.

"It's something new they're developing, trying to standardize the training curriculum at all of our sites nationwide. If you're selected, there'd be some travel involved occasionally to different sites as we take on new clients. Being that we're in the debt collection business, training our agents is of the utmost importance. Corporate sees this as a way of minimizing lawsuits and bad publicity. We all have numbers to reach, but there are certain unacceptable practices our agents use that get us into trouble."

"Is there more—"

"Money, yes, and the good part for you is, it would be negotiable. Name your price, and you'll either get a yes, or a counter. You have nothing to lose."

"Hmmm. Let's see. I'm single. Haven't sniffed a date in months. I have no kids—thank God. I'm broke. Just moved into a new place, filled with my parents' second-hand furniture, and my car runs on prayer. I have time to travel, though it might put a dent into some of my volunteer work, I'll work around that. I would have to say, yes, I'm interested."

"Thought you would be," Maxine said. "You've always been a smart girl, but lately, you've been making the right moves, and it's been noticed. Keep it up."

"I'm serving turkey, ham, roast beef, and fried chicken. Those are the main dishes, plus I've included the usual sides. I've been cooking for three days, and Stephanie, if you don't show up, I'll put out an APB for you. Don't disappoint me," Brenda said, talking on the phone.

"Sunday is my day off. I was planning on seeing you guys at church. After service, I'll come over and help you get everything together."

"That will be a treat, but I won't put you to work. Just come and keep me company until everyone else arrives."

"Can I ask you something, Brenda—why is it you seem to like me?"

"Why shouldn't I child? You're a bright and beautiful girl. I'm only sorry I never got to know you before now."

"You haven't talked to any of my people about me?"

"Girl, I heard all the stories. True or not, what's that got to do with me, or us?"

"I'm sorry I've judged you all these years. To me, you were that mean usher at church."

"That's not your fault. I needed to allow God to soften me up. He brought your father into my life to do that. It's hard to be judged by people who don't know you. I try not to do that to others."

*Been a while since I've been here...*Stephanie thought, sitting in the very church she was raised in. Being there always made her sad. It reminded her of her mother, who she'd never gotten along with. *I'd* *give anything if she were sitting beside me right now, frowning about something I did, said, wore, or my attitude in general.*

Instead, she was seated beside Brenda, who seemed delighted, sitting next to Lawrence, who was also bursting with pride. She wanted to take them out in the lobby and explain—I'm still *that,* Stephanie. As much as she tried to hang on to her old self, her father, stepmother, and it seems everybody else in her life was happy to let her die, except her two siblings.

"If you're going to be sitting in our church on Sunday, I'll be visiting elsewhere," her sister Margo said the day before. "Lightning might hit that place if you're in there."

"I was always taught church was the place for sinners," Stephanie said.

"Sinners capable of changing maybe. Not for people like you."

Stephanie closed her eyes, *Lord forgive me for the way I cursed out my sister yesterday, but she asked for it.*

She opened her eyes and enjoyed the service. Once the sermon was over, the pastor called for new converts. She was moved to make the public affirmation of what God had been speaking into her heart for months. She belonged to Him; He belonged to her. It was time she made sure the rest of her life lined up with that reality, regardless of what anyone else thought.

"What was that all about? You walking up to the altar with your false humility. You might have Dad fooled, but I see through you. He and Brenda better watch their valuables," Kevin, who'd slipped in at some point during the service, said to her afterward.

"As a symbol of my new life, I'm going to refrain from beating the hell out of you in the church sanctuary," Stephanie said, grinning so hard she felt like her teeth were grinding. "But don't push me, boy."

She rolled her eyes and turned, nearly running into Gia.

"Oh, hey..."

"Hey yourself. Congratulations, I'm happy for you."

"Thank you. That means a lot coming from you. I haven't forgotten about the loan."

"Girl, I told you then, it wasn't a loan. We're sisters now, and I can give you a gift when I want to. You look amazing, so from what I can see, it was a seed sown in good ground, as the pastor said."

Stephanie thanked her and started to move along but saw something in Gia's eyes.

"Can we talk sometime? I don't know what it is, but I feel like you and I can connect. I need a friend, a real friend."

Stephanie blinked. *Miss perfection wants me to be her friend?* "Of course, anytime, Gia, but for real, I have no answers. I need God more than I need anything. I wish I could tell you I have myself together, but I don't."

"Girl, listen to you," Gia said, stepping back. "You're so real, so honest. Even when you were the old Stephanie, you didn't apologize to nobody. I want to know how to be real; how to leave all the crap—"

"You're not buying her act, are you?" Kevin said, stepping between them. "Stephanie is getting in good with the old folks, so they can cut her off a little somethin'. I hear she's already gotten a house full of furniture. She knows there's more where that came from. Trust me, she will do what it takes, even if it means using God to get it. But then, you know a little about scheming yourself."

"I'll see you at the house. Brenda wants me to help out," Stephanie said, moving away from them as they stared each other down.

"That was an awesome step you took today. Any idea where you're going from here? It's best to be a part of a church; it helps us grow and be accountable," Brenda said as she sliced cucumbers for a tossed salad.

"Actually, I've been thinking about it for a long time. Today just seemed to be the right day to do the right thing," Stephanie said, admiring her own handiwork in frosting a cake.

"I'm happy for you. God is going to do wonders in your life."

"I miss my mother," Stephanie said, putting down the knife, "She wanted so much for me to be the person I'm becoming. We never got along. No offense Miss Brenda, you're a good woman, and you make my dad happy, but I wish my mom were here.

"That's understandable. I hope you and I can become friends. I always wanted more children, and you and your siblings have been such a blessing to my life in different ways."

Just then, the doorbell rang, and they heard Lawrence starting to greet the guests who were trickling in.

"You're moving into a new house, congratulations," Rhonda, Brenda's friend from church, said later, as they were all eating.

"Thank you. It's a little large for just me and Lawrence, so the plan is for my mother to move in also. We're still working on that."

"I'm coming," Corene, who'd been sitting nearby, said. "I already know how I'm going to arrange my furniture. I just need a little more time, that's all."

"Better hurry up," Kevin said. "There are squatters among us, who already have their sights on your space." He spoke loud enough, so Stephanie, who was busy attending the food table, could hear him.

"Screw you!" Stephanie yelled, and the guests turned her way. "Excuse me, everybody," she said, scowling at her brother.

Lawrence was in Kevin's face immediately. "I didn't invite you here to offend my guests. You've been at it since you walked through the door. If you can't contain yourself—"

"Alright, Dad," Kevin said, holding up his hands.

A moment later, the doorbell rang, and Reginald entered the house. Gia grinned and hurried to meet him.

"Everybody, this is Reginald."

"This is Reginald," Kevin mimicked, and watched as Gia took the bottle of wine he brought, and they kissed at the door. He stared the man down as Gia led him around the room and away from him. It was a small gathering, however, and their confrontation was inevitable.

"This is Kevin. Lawrence's son," Gia tried to sound natural and disinterested, but there was tension in her voice.

Kevin sneered and refused to shake the hand offered. Gia fidgeted while trying to guide Reginald away, but he stood firm, meeting Kevin's look with a stare of his own. The portrait of where he stood in Gia's life crystallized at that moment. He'd met another man caught in her net, but by the jittery way she was behaving, the feelings were mutual. He allowed himself to be led away and introduced to a few more people, before abruptly remembering somewhere he needed to be.

"One of my questions about you has been answered. There's someone you're deeply involved with, and I just met him. It was nice knowing you," Reginald said to her at the door and was gone before she had a chance to lie.

Kevin spied the couple's terse conversation, then piled his plate high with food, relishing his meal intensely.

Gia's bubbly persona became subdued, and she refused to look in Kevin's direction, though she hung around the rest of that afternoon, mostly sitting off to herself.

"What's this?" Chase said, throwing a letter on Gia's desk.

"It speaks for itself. I've resigned."

"Where are you going?"

"I'd prefer not to say. I thought you of all people would be happy."

"You think you're smart, don't you?"

"Huh?"

"Are you going to pretend you have nothing to do with the inquiry going on about my handling of departmental finances?"

"Nothing to do with me."

"Liar."

"They've given you paperwork, is my name anywhere?"

"They're citing anonymous sources; I have no doubt you're one of them. Now you're leaving so you won't have to face the music. But I'll find you. I'll tell your new employers all about you. I'm going to get you for this."

She sat frozen at her desk. Chase was speaking loudly and making no attempt to conceal the hostility. The flutter of activity around the office ceased.

"I want you out of here now. I don't accept your resignation. I'm terminating you immediately."

She frowned, and a laugh caught in her throat. "That letter is just your copy; HR already has one. I can leave whenever you say, but I will still receive my salary and bonuses for the next two weeks."

"No surprise, you've gone behind my back to HR. You've been making a habit of doing that, but this isn't over."

She shook her head and collected her belongings, anxious to depart that office. She'd never seen him so out of control, making threats out in the open where everyone could hear. He usually did his dirt in back rooms and under tables. Before she could leave, however, her desk phone rang. She'd been summoned to a meeting in Human Resources.

"We understand you've submitted your resignation today. Can I ask you if there are any reasons we should know of why we're losing you? I've looked at your record, and your performance has been exemplary." Ken Ross, the director of HR, said. "If you tell us you're leaving for a better opportunity, we support you wholeheartedly. However, if there is another situation, harassment from a senior staff member, for instance, we'd like the opportunity to address it. We won't tolerate that type of environment in our workplace."

"Chase and I have encountered some difficulties, and those problems ultimately led me to seek out a better opportunity. However, I'm not going to sit here and cry harassment. Whatever the problems we've had, I had a share in them."

"Then the information we've received from another source is true. There is some extra-curricular—"

"No, there *is* not. I will admit to past errors in judgment, of a personal nature, that have made it difficult for me to remain employed here.

Ken nodded. "I hear what you are and aren't saying. I'll ask one more time, and I have a legal representative here to witness your responses," he nodded to a young man who pressed a button on the console. "This conversation is now being recorded. Gia Collier, this is your opportunity, if you so desire, to make a harassment claim against this organization, Titan Brokerage. Please be advised your answer will bind or release this organization from any liability from future claims you might later decide to bring against us. We are willing to document and settle this claim without litigation." He nodded to the younger man who pressed a button again. "Off the record, there may be other complainants."

Hmm...somebody else has already threatened litigation; they're trying to take care of everything at one time. No wonder Chase is so pissed off; his career is dead. He'd better hold on to his wife...

"Ms. Collier,"

"You know what, Ken. I'm not comfortable continuing without consulting my own legal counsel. I'll request they provide you with a statement from me, and I'll refrain from answering at this time. I will tell you; I just had a threatening exchange with Chase about an hour ago, heard by my co-workers. I'm frankly more concerned with the present."

"Yes, we were advised about that. Which is why I called you before you left the building."

"Can we talk in private and without the recording?" Gia said.

Ken nodded at the young attorney who exited the room through a rear door. He pressed a button on the table, showing Gia that the recording had been stopped.

"There was a consensual relationship. It wasn't long and has been over for more than a year. I received no special privileges, promotions, or perks as a result. Anything I've achieved, I did so by hard work, nothing else. While it was unethical and unprofessional, when it started, we were both single. When I ended it, Chase wanted me gone. He made some threats, and we had some battles, but I thought it inappropriate to run to you; I felt I needed to take responsibility for my own actions."

Ken nodded.

"I found *ways...*" Gia paused and nodded slowly while looking intently at Ken. "to defend myself."

"Let me guess," Ken said. "A paper trail of expensed business trips to conferences never attended at posh resorts in premium locations. We know about those, but your name never turned up," he frowned then nodded, his gaze sharpening.

"Then I get a call from his wife about three months ago, accusing me of being his traveling partner on a recent trip. I told her I was not the one, then he's at my desk accusing me of telling his wife and reporting his misdeeds to you. He makes threats. I start looking for another job. I don't need that."

Ken sighed. "Alright, Ms. Collier. I understand the situation. You didn't run to us because you weren't guilt-free in the situation. You have a clear case of harassment, but when a past relationship is involved, it's your word against his. What I'm going to say now is strictly confidential. Chase is done. He'll be fired, but if our organization can protect its reputation, we'll keep his dirt under the carpet."

"However, if one of you young women, and there's a growing list, causes headlines, he's going to take the fall, not us. You'd better watch yourself; as you've indicated, he's not behaving rationally. We've received information about a case of domestic violence."

The interview ended with Ken offering Gia a modest salary increase to stay with the organization, which she declined. After more discussion, she went on record with a claim of harassment against Chase. Ken advised her that because he was her superior, he was held to a higher standard of conduct and that despite her bad choices, Gia was a victim. The legal process would need to play out, and she would be hearing from the firm's counsel.

They agreed that with the shake-up coming in her former department, she should leave immediately. As they parted. Ken wished her good luck and better choices in her new career.

Gia cleaned out her desk and, with a single box holding her belongings, asked the security guard to escort her to her car. She spoke to no one as she exited the lobby, ready to leave her past career, and mistakes behind.

28

"No, I was serious. I want us to get together. I need someone to talk to. I don't mean any harm, but my best girlfriend, Monique, is sweet but doesn't have an ounce of sense," Gia said while on the phone with Stephanie, a month after the family dinner.

Stephanie laughed. "And you think I do? Do I need to remind you how I walked up into your place and asked you for—"

"I gave it to you, didn't I? I haven't thought about it since. Look, girl, you were down and needed some money. Now's your time to pay me back. I need your ear. We're sisters now, you can give me that."

"What about Margo? She's the one with the husband, family, and perfect life."

"I'm not interested in perfection. Anyway, your sister is wound too tight for me, and if you think you're the user in your family, baby, you got it wrong. She's getting all she can out of Brenda Collier Foster, dumping her with the kids every weekend. I need to warn her, but Brenda will set her straight in due time."

"I don't believe it," Stephanie said.

"Don't let her fool you. Lawrence has softened her up, but my momma's still under there somewhere," Gia said, laughing.

"Back to the point—why do you want to talk to a loser like me?"

"First of all, you need to stop putting yourself down. I'll be honest, you were a loser, big time. But you've changed. It's all over you. Now come on, where are we going to meet? Dinner is on me."

Gia almost begged me to have dinner with her. If that ain't...She laughed to herself as she walked into the eatery. She and Gia were the same age and were both pretty in different ways. Gia was more model, slim with long legs, and a flawless complexion. Stephanie was also tall but more full-figured.

"That's another thing I envy about you. You make being pretty look so effortless," Gia said as Stephanie slid into the booth.

"What are you talking about?"

"How much money do you spend on your hair, nails, brows, and lashes?"

"None baby, cause I don't have the cash to spend. What you see was done at home or by God."

Gia smiled, then her expression froze as something caught her attention over Stephanie's shoulder.

"Something wrong?" Stephanie said, whipping her head around.

Gia shook her head. "Thought I saw somebody I don't want to see. That's all." It was the fourth time it had happened in the three weeks since she'd left her previous job. Chase's face would come into view, then disappear suddenly. She'd see only a head of dark hair styled like his on a man his build, leaving whatever building she was in. She'd started to follow him once, but found herself being led into a hidden alleyway, and retreated.

"That's not good," Stephanie said, studying her. "I guess you do need to talk."

The smile returned to Gia's face. "Don't mind me. I didn't bring you here to cry the blues on your shoulder. You know, when I saw you that day at church, I just thought you and I could click. There's a peace about you. I found myself interested in what's going on in your world."

"Well, where should I start? That night I came to your place?"

"Don't mention that again," Gia said, with a wave of her hand.

"No?" Stephanie said. "That was a sort of turning point for me—kind of like a new low. I was living with this guy named Laron and robbed him blind for about six months, gambling at the casino. Meanwhile, I was two-timing him with another guy, a gambler, who was busy robbing me while I was robbing him. Laron got wise and closed a bank account I was writing checks on. I ended up getting locked up for fraud, and Daddy had to bail me out."

"Girl, you're lying!" Gia said, hitting the table.

"You haven't heard; nobody in my family told you?"

"I don't think anyone knows but your dad, and he's not going to tell anybody, especially your *holier-than-God-himself* siblings."

Stephanie raised an eyebrow. "That's why you and my brother broke it off."

"We haven't started on me yet. Keep going."

"Had a gorgeous public defender who helped get the felony charges dropped down to a misdemeanor. I thought he liked me. Girl, he took his payment the old-fashioned way then dumped me."

"That bastard," Gia said, diving into a plate of linguine with clam sauce.

Stephanie waved her hand. "He served his purpose, and I've been with worse; trust me. I ended up moving into this dive rooming house and was too ashamed to tell Daddy where I lived. Then God started dealing with me."

"What was that like—I mean, what happened?"

Stephanie shrugged while munching on a breadstick. "I don't know—a thought here, a thought there. Then one day, this little old man comes pulling up to the curb where I was sitting watching my life go by and told me I need to spread the joy of the Lord—or something like that. Girl, I was blown away."

"Then what?"

"Stuff started happening. I've gotten two promotions on my job. I've found a new career as a Professional Image Consultant—"

"That's what I noticed about you. You know how to carry yourself."

"I've been working with some women's shelters, and I've applied for a city contract. What can I say? That day, when that old man approached me, I wanted so bad to be back in a casino. I haven't had that desire since."

"I guess God takes care of people who are looking for Him."

"Where'd you get the idea I was looking for God? Girl—I was looking for some cash. For whatever reason, God was looking for me."

Gia lifted her wine glass and started swirling the liquid. "I guess that's why I found myself envying you that day. Maybe envy isn't the right word, more like admiration. I wish God would look for me, then maybe I wouldn't make some of the decisions I make. Maybe I'd live a better life."

Stephanie leaned over the table and touched her hand. "He is looking for you. He's waiting for you to notice."

Gia leaned back in her chair, "Yeah, you think so?"

"I know so. Sometimes it takes the right person to tell you. Maybe I'm that person."

Gia thought about the chain of events that brought them there. Two girls who'd grown up together but had nothing to do with each other. Suddenly, their parents are married; she has a failed relationship with Stephanie's brother and now...*all things work together for the good of them that love the Lord...do I love Him?*

"Are you okay?" Stephanie said, seeing on Gia's face that she'd left the room.

Gia shook herself, "Huh, I'm fine. It's just that you have me thinking."

The two of them ate silently for some time, and Stephanie noticed Gia, usually so in control in every situation, was distracted.

She wanted to ask what happened between her and Kevin but decided to pick a lighter topic. "I hear you've started a new job. How's it going?"

"Thanksgiving is coming. Mom has moved in with Lawrence and me, so I thought it would be a good opportunity for family reconciliation," Brenda said to her brother Darwin, over the phone in early October. She was giving herself and her siblings plenty of time to clear their schedules so they could come for a long weekend. "We have plenty of room, and Daddy is also going to be here."

"Of course, he should be there," Darwin said. "How are we going to have a family Thanksgiving dinner, with him stuck in that place you've put him in?"

"I'm not going there today, Darwin," Brenda said, quietly taking a deep breath. "When you come, I'll take you to see his accommodations. When Marvin visits, he always has good things to say about the facility."

"I'll think about this Thanksgiving thing. I want to talk to my mother about it first. If this is just your way of showing off, the new house your husband has bought for you, I'm not interested."

Lord, family reconciliation is a nice idea; sometimes I wonder if it's worth it.

"Darwin, I promise you I have no other motive but reconciliation. It's been too long since we've been together with our parents, and honestly, daddy is declining. I'm not sure how much longer we'll have him."

He became silent on the other line, then Brenda heard him clearing his throat. "I don't mean to be critical, Brenda. I know you don't believe me, but knowing my dad is sick has been hard for me. I can't face it. I want my dad back. I want the Deacon to be back on the first row at church, doing his thing."

"I understand. You and Christine are the two youngest. She's seen him once since he's been sick. I'm begging her to make this trip, and so far, she's given me every excuse she can think of. I'm not trying to be a controlling witch. I'm trying to help us deal with a difficult situation. If daddy isn't healed, he's going to die, and once a person is gone, all that's left are memories and regrets. We've already lost so much of who he is to Alzheimer's. We need to be together now, more than ever."

Darwin was silent again, "I'll be there," he said, the words catching in his throat. He ended the call without saying goodbye.

Brenda knew he meant it, but she'd have to make several calls to get him to follow through. Christine was another story. She might have to fly to California and drag her sister back to town, but Brenda was prepared to do that if necessary. *No, on second thought, I'll send mom.*

"Sorry, Kevin. Due to budget cuts, I was told I'd have to cut one position. I reviewed everyone's performance, and though you've rebounded in the second half of the year, that first half dragged you down. You're the weak link; I'm sorry, but I've got to let you go.

"What happened to last hired. I have seniority."

"This is a performance-based business. Michaela is new, but she's kicked butt during the time she's been here. I can't justify keeping you and letting her go. It's a business decision. If I keep you, my superiors will question my commitment to meeting our goals."

"This isn't fair. I've busted my tail."

"The last six months, yes, you have, but Michaela's numbers are through the roof."

Kevin shook his head, "How long do I have?"

"You can leave now, and you'll receive six weeks' severance, or you can stay on until the end of the year. If you don't find something internally at that time, the severance pay will still be yours. We reserve the right to ask you to leave at any time we feel you're deliberately dragging your feet."

When Kevin stood, his face was flushed, but he held out a trembling hand to Zach. "Understood. I'll stick around and see what happens and use my vacation time to interview."

Zach nodded. "I know its hard, man. Keep your head up, as I said, this is strictly about numbers. If something opens up here or in another office, I'll let you know, and do whatever I can."

Kevin nodded. When he got back to his desk, everything around him was funeral quiet; the news had obviously leaked out. No one looked his way or said anything to him the rest of that morning. It seemed to him they were waiting to see if he was packing up to go. He wanted to. Walking out the door with six weeks of severance and an unemployment check seemed unwise to him, however. He'd hang around, as humiliating as it was, until he found another job or the New Year hit, whichever came first.

"I heard you've been cut. Sorry," Michaela said, standing at the entry of his cubicle later that day.

"Thanks," Kevin muttered, without looking at her. When it came to her, it was doubly embarrassing. He'd trained her, she'd refused to go out with him, and now she was taking his job.

What was I thinking; why didn't I see this coming? Kevin sat, staring into a glass of beer, at a bar, near his house. He didn't want to talk to anybody but didn't want to sit alone at home and drink. While he was out, he wouldn't get plastered, even though he wanted to.

"Rough day, huh?" he heard a woman's voice. When he looked up, he saw it was Grace, a girl he'd dated awhile back. All he could manage was a half-smile and a nod, as she slid into the chair beside him, uninvited. He was okay with it; Grace was adequate company for the mood he was in. She was a good listener and talked sparingly.

"Is it still that same girl?" Grace said, and Kevin winced, wondering if everybody knew how he'd fallen apart over Gia.

He shook his head, "Lost my job today."

"Oh no," Grace said. "What are you going to do?"

"Move on. They've given me until the end of the year."

"That's good, at least they didn't kick you out on your butt. You wouldn't believe how many people I know, had a job in the morning, and were walked out of the building with their belongings before noon."

Kevin nodded, "I guess I should be grateful for that."

"Any ideas what you're going to do?"

"Nope. There's no place else I've ever wanted to work. I got hired right after college, and I was comfortable; maybe too comfortable."

"Things happen for a reason," Grace said, lifting her drink for a toast.

Although Kevin didn't feel like it, he toasted her anyway.

They ended up leaving the bar together. She invited him back to her place, where she prepared dinner, and Kevin was reminded of what a good cook Grace was. When she threw a tantrum after he declined her offer to spend the night, he was reminded of why he'd stopped calling her.

29

Gia had been kept in the loop by her former co-workers. Chase had been fired, and he and the firm were being sued for sexual harassment. The lawsuit, while it was public record, did not make big headlines. She sat back and waited to see if she would be called as a witness, but so far, no one had contacted her. She was sure; however, Chase was following her.

He'd stopped making any effort to conceal himself and appeared everywhere she went. She never knew when she'd spot him, but he'd make sure she did. At the supermarket, whichever one she chose to go to, he'd turn up. Even when she changed her movements, he still found her.

He kept his distance but made sure she saw him. Sometimes he'd smile, smirk, wink, or blow a kiss. Anything to make her blood run cold, then he'd leave.

'He should know by now I have nothing to do with his problems. Why won't he leave me alone? She thought, while driving down the street, certain the car traveling behind her was his.

"What was he like before he was terminated?" Gia asked Shelly, his former secretary.

"He'd lost it. He sat in his office for hours, had the most terrible arguments with his wife, and did nothing. The brass left him alone; they were finished with him. They assigned me to Alan, who'd picked up on his duties. It was like, Chase didn't even know he'd stopped functioning. He came into the office and left without saying anything to anyone.

No one knew his schedule or cared. It was the weirdest thing I ever saw. Then one day, security intercepted him at the door, confiscated his keys, and escorted him back to his car. I was told to pack up his office, and a courier picked up the boxes that day. Alan moved into his office the next week, and it's as if Chase never existed."

"Wow."

"Nobody has heard or seen him since."

I have, Gia thought.

"I heard they're in the process of settling the lawsuits, and there were several." Gia's eyebrows raised as no one had contacted her—*just as well.* "The only two complainants I know of were Cindy Martel and Regina Logan, but I heard there were more. Chase was a busy boy. Now, it's business as usual, but we miss you. Your position is still open, are you thinking about coming back?"

"No. Things are good here, but keep me posted. I'll talk to you later," Gia said, hanging up.

What am I going to do? I guess I'm being stalked. What can I do about it?

She was terrified. It's one thing to deal with a rational person, but Chase was over the edge and had been for a while. He had no reason to follow her but seemed fixated on her anyway.

After a week went by, she started to relax, noticing Chase hadn't shown up for a few days. *Maybe he's thinking clearly now,* she told herself, hoping it was true. Later that same day, however, her office phone rang; the caller ID displayed 'Blocked.' When she picked up the receiver, she heard background noise, but no one spoke. "Hello, is someone there? Can I help you—hello?" The line then went dead. It happened twice more that day, while she was at her desk. When she checked her call log for that day, 'Blocked' had dialed her desk phone, ten other times. She was thankful she'd changed her cellphone number.

After work, she went to her mother's house to consult the only person she knew in law enforcement, her stepfather Lawrence.

"You say, he hasn't said anything to you or approached you, and you have no proof, he's the one making the phone calls?" Lawrence said, stirring a cup of coffee.

"I know it's him, but no, I have no proof," she said, seated across from him at the kitchen table.

Lawrence sighed heavily. "There've been no threats—"

"He threatened me months ago when we still worked together. I've since quit, and he was fired. His firing had nothing to do with me, and he must know that by now, but—"

"People like that don't care what the truth is. His life is in shambles, and he needs to blame somebody. Looks like you're it," Lawrence said

"What do I do?"

"Until he approaches you or makes a threat. I'm not sure there's anything you can do. What did he say when he threatened you? That may give you a clue as to his intentions."

"He just said he was going to get me. He was going to make me pay."

"Humph," Lawrence said, sipping his coffee. "He may be a bully who just wants to scare you for a while. If that's the case, he'll go away eventually."

"Eventually!" she said, throwing up her hands. "That could mean months."

Lawrence nodded.

"I can't live in fear that long."

"I understand, but I'm not sure what to tell you. You can file a complaint, a restraining order, but right now, it appears he's maintaining a legally acceptable distance. The phone thing is tricky, but I'm sure the police can prove he's the culprit, and tell him to stop, but he hasn't said anything to you. Unfortunately for you, he can play as many games as he wants until he tries to carry out one of his threats—"

"You mean, I have to be in danger, to get some help. There's no way for me to get help so I can stay safe?"

"Read the news. How many women have filed orders against abusive husbands, and nothing was done until it was too late?"

Gia slumped back in her chair, "I feel so powerless. I didn't do anything to deserve this, and I'm being terrorized. You're telling me my only hope is if I'm attacked, then I can get help. This is insane."

"Gia, what's wrong?" Brenda said, rushing into the room. She'd come into the house and heard Gia's last statement.

"Nothing Ma. I'm being harassed by my former boss, and there doesn't seem to be much I can do about it." Gia went on to explain to her mother how Chase was showing up at her familiar haunts but hadn't addressed her.

"Why don't you move in here, for a while, until he goes away? I can't stand the thought of you being by yourself."

"Thanks, I'll think about it."

"No, you won't think about it. Lawrence is going to take you home so you can get some things," Brenda said, nearly pulling Gia out of the chair. "I'll go upstairs and get the room ready."

"Momma—"

"Girl, this is for me, not you. I can't sleep knowing some crazy person is after you. If you won't come here, then Lawrence and I will move in with you. Which do you prefer?"

I knew it was a mistake to come here. Bossy Miss Brenda strikes again...

When Lawrence parked the car, in front of Gia's townhouse, he turned into a bodyguard. "What kind of car does he drive?" He said, looking up and down the street.

"Um, a silver Lexus SUV," she said, fishing for her keys.

"There's one over there, and someone is sitting in the driver's seat," Lawrence said.

"What!" Gia said. She always checked the street when she left the house and returned but had never seen Chase's vehicle.

"Over there, parked on that adjacent street," Lawrence said, pointing to an area she never would've looked, but there he was.

"Come on, let's go see what he wants," Lawrence said, driving around the block to approach his vehicle from behind.

"He's expecting you to show up in your car, so we'll catch him by surprise."

"I don't think this is a good idea, Lawrence. You're putting yourself in danger."

"I work in a prison. I think I can handle myself with this white-collar bully." Lawrence slowed his car as he drove past the silver SUV. "Is that him?"

Gia looked up, and the man sitting behind the wheel of the car was Chase. He was staring straight ahead, as if watching her driveway, bobbing his head like he was listening to music.

"That's him," she hissed.

Lawrence drove to the stop sign. "Is there a back entrance to your house, where he won't see you going in?"

Gia directed him to her back door.

"I'm going to have a chat with him, and I'll be back to get you," Lawrence said as she exited the car.

"Be careful-please."

Lawrence went up the street again, and this time he parked and walked to Chase's SUV, in the same no-nonsense gait he used as he walked through the rows of cell blocks. He stopped at the driver's side of the car and heard loud music. The other man's attention was focused on Gia's townhouse; he must have noticed the light had come on inside. Lawrence pounded on the windshield.

"Yeah?" Chase said, lowering the window.

"Good evening. My name is Officer Lawrence," he said, flashing his work badge quickly. "We've received a complaint from one of the neighbors about a man lurking in the neighborhood. Do you live around here?"

"I'm waiting for a friend," Chase said and started to raise the window.

Lawrence pounded on the window again, and Chase, glaring at him, lowered it. "You'll need to wait somewhere else. There are families in this neighborhood, and a man sitting in a car for extended periods causes alarm. Either get out of the car and find your friend or come back when they're home."

"Look, officer," Chase said, clenching his teeth.

"We can go find your friend if you like. Where do they live?"

Chase cursed at Lawrence, started his vehicle, and zoomed off.

Lawrence, having made a note of the license plate number, went back to Gia's place.

"He's gone for now, but Brenda's suggestion of your staying with us is a good one," Lawrence said as she climbed into the car. "Here's the plate number of his car. Everywhere you go, look around for it, and when you see it again: at work, the supermarket, wherever, call the cops and tell them you're being stalked. Give them the plate number and nothing else; let them do the rest. Eventually, he may follow you to our house. He's going to regret that day."

Gia threw her arms around Lawrence's neck and squeezed him tight. "Thank you so much. "

Lawrence chuckled, "Thank yourself. Too many young women would've tried to deal with this alone. You came and got help. We're going to get you through this."

30

"Who are you?" Dan Lovelace said to the woman who'd come waltzing into his office at the Shepherd's Heart Charity, asking where she could set up.

Stephanie checked her watch; she didn't have time to explain to another non-profit paper pusher who'd simply scoff at what she was there to do.

"I was referred by the county?" she said, nodding her head to jog his memory. His office had received a phone call as she'd been present when that call was made.

He nodded, but his expression was blank.

"I'm the employment image consultant."

"The what?" he said, half frowning, half smirking.

"I'm here to counsel clients seeking employment on how to project a professional appearance. My name is Stephanie Foster, and your office was contacted. I assure you."

Dan shrugged then went back to the paperwork on his desk. "Yeah, probably. Somebody's always calling about something. I have over a hundred residents in this shelter on any given day, I can't keep track of everything." He then spotted a telephone memo sitting on top of a pile of papers. "There you are Miss Foster. I have it right here." He turned to an open door on the other side of the room. "Jeanne, are you out there?"

"Why are you yelling?" An older woman said as she came briskly into the office.

"Sorry, but this is Miss Foster," he said, pointing. "She needs a free conference room, and will probably need help locating the clients she's here to see. Who knows where they've gotten to."

"Yes, I took the call, remember," Jean said, then turned to Stephanie. "I have everything set-up. You can follow me."

Dan looked up from his paperwork and, noticing Stephanie for the first time, smiled. She wore a gray-blue pantsuit with heels, had a great figure, and no wedding ring. "It was nice meeting you too, Miss Foster."

Stephanie rolled her eyes as she was in a hurry. She was getting paid for the assignment, but not much and could ill afford to be late to her paying job.

"You have a nice place, Brenda. Thanks for the invite. It's about time we got beyond our bickering and became a family again. Life is too short."

Brenda threw her arms around her brother Marvin, then his wife, Joann. "I'm so glad you're here. You don't realize how much you miss family until we're back together again."

"I must say, marriage has been a fountain of youth for you. I swear you look twenty years younger than the last time I saw you," Joann said. "There's your little sister descending the stairs," she pointed to Gia.

"Sometimes she acts like my sister, other times my baby, but most of the time it's like I have two mothers around here.

"I thought you had your own house?" Marvin said.

"She's staying with us for a while. She's been having some problems with a former co-worker," Brenda said.

"Momma, where are you?" Marvin called out to Corene, who was in the kitchen, snapping fresh green beans for Thanksgiving dinner.

She ran out to embrace her oldest son and his wife, then led them into the kitchen where Marvin senior sat at the table watching her every move. They'd collected him from the facility early that morning, and he hadn't oriented himself to the unfamiliar surroundings. His former house had been sold a few weeks prior. "Look, daddy, your oldest is here."

Marvin blinked at his son, then turned back to his wife.

It was the day before Thanksgiving, and Brenda was expecting her other two siblings with their families to arrive in town later that afternoon.

"He's not doing well, is he?" Marvin said to Brenda in a hushed tone, his brow creased.

Brenda shook her head. "The doctors have adjusted his meds as much as they can, and he's still declining. Keep praying because it's completely in God's hands at this point. I wasn't being a drama queen when I begged you guys to come home. We don't know if this will be our last chance to share the holiday together. The doctors aren't saying much, just that the 'disease is progressing as expected...'"

Marvin nodded, but Brenda could see his face tighten and the knot form in his throat. His voice broke as he spoke. "It's hard to see my pops like he is so frail and lifeless. That man had so much life and energy in him. Lawrence came up and patted him on the back at just the right time.

"Brother in law, why don't we settle down and play some cards or dominoes. Brenda tells me you're a bit of a hustler, but I think I can hang with you. If pool is your game, got a new table downstairs, just delivered last week."

"Please go shoot pool with him, Marvin. He's been dying for some real competition, as he puts it; beating me is too easy." Brenda left them so she could tend to meal preparations.

"How's it going, Mom?"

"They're just green beans, Brenda. I think I can manage. I don't know why you won't let me help with the big stuff. I'm still the better cook. Who do you think taught you?"

"I didn't say you can't help," Brenda said, checking on the 7up cake's baking in one of the two ovens. Her large gourmet kitchen was her favorite part of the new home and was perfect for preparing large meals for family gatherings. "I'm making sure you can relax and enjoy the family. You know, once you start working, you don't know how to stop. I'm letting you know you don't have to start. Gia and I will take care of everything."

Corene's laugh came out as a cackle, "You and who? That beauty queen of yours can't peel a potato."

"Yeah, but she'll pull out her charge cards and buy what she can't make," Brenda said. Their laughter exploded when Gia sauntered into the kitchen on cue.

"Ha Ha Ha, you two were laughing at me again," Gia said, accustomed to being the object of their domestic jokes. She'd been staying with them for over two weeks and had rarely ventured into the kitchen. If Brenda or Corene were too busy or tired to prepare a meal, Gia had it delivered. She possessed a collection of menus for every restaurant within a thirty-mile radius. "I'm headed to the airport. Uncle Darwin's flight gets in soon. Do you need me to stop at the store for anything on my way back?"

"We're fine. Just be ready to roll up your sleeves and ruin your manicure. We have some serious cooking to do tonight," Brenda said.

Gia stopped and displayed the multicolored sparkle of her fresh manicure. "I don't think so; this work of art cost me fifty bucks this morning. When I get back, we'll discuss what my contribution should be."

Her mother and grandmother erupted into another round of raucous laughter, as Gia kissed her grandfather's forehead and exited the kitchen, shaking her head.

"Nice to meet you, Lawrence. Sorry, I couldn't make the wedding," Darwin said.

"You're here now, and we're happy to see you," Lawrence said, shaking Darwin's hand warmly.

Nice guy, he'd have to be to put up with my sister.

When Brenda emerged from the kitchen trailing behind his mother, Darwin barely recognized her. Not only was she smiling at him, for a change, but she'd updated her look. For the first time in years, he realized she was an attractive woman; then she hugged him. His heart started pounding. *Daddy must be doing bad...*

"What's happened," he said, clutching Brenda's shoulders and stepping back.

"Relax boy," Brenda said, rolling her eyes. "I'm simply glad to see your sorry butt."

He exhaled, smiled then pulled her into a bear hug. "I'm glad to see you too."

Brenda greeted the rest of her brother's family. Darwin had brought his long-time girlfriend, Aliya, his three kids, all of whom were now young adults, and two grandkids.

Christine and her clan: husband, two college students, and her granddaughter arrived within that same hour. Brenda calculated they'd need food for at least thirty guests for the evening's meal, the next morning's breakfast, and Thanksgiving dinner.

Lawrence laughs at me for stocking that freezer, but it's going to come in handy this weekend, she thought.

For the most part, it was a joyful holiday. Brenda's siblings struggled, however, confronted with their father's condition. Christine handled it the worst and, on that first day, begged her husband to take her to the hotel before dinner, complaining of a headache.

Brenda knew her sister was running away; if she could've boarded a plane for home that night, she would have. It was difficult for everyone. Their father, though present, was like a ghost, and looked at them with the expression of a confused stranger. There were brief periods when he'd come to life, remembering names, places, and events, which were sometimes decades in the past.

"I love you, daddy," Darwin said, hugging and kissing his father's forehead, as they were sitting around the family room after dinner.

His father simply gazed back at him and nodded.

"Where'd you come from?" Kevin had slipped into the house un-noticed and had grabbed a plate of dinner. He was now sitting off to himself in the upstairs loft, staring at his laptop. Gia, who'd been on her way to her room, stumbled on him.

"I've been here for a while. You didn't think I was going to miss this meal, did you?"

"Is that all you came for?" His eyes dropped down to the computer screen.

"Really, what's been happening with you? I haven't heard from you in a while," she said, sliding down on the couch beside him. After her break up with Reginald, she'd stopped calling him.

"Been busy. How's the new job?"

"Fine."

"How did your undercover lover take you leaving, or did you two go together?"

"I don't appreciate that remark."

"So."

"Why are you so rude to me? Why bother talking to me if you're going to be that way?" She stood.

"Sorry," he covered his eyes with his hand just as she was about to walk away. "Sorry, sorry. I'm sorry. I've got things going on. I guess I'm taking them out on you."

"You're not the only one with things going on," she said, sitting down again. "My crazy ex-boss is stalking me. I've had to move in here."

"What?" He sat up straight. "You mean the one you were—"

She nodded.

"The police—"

"All he does is follow and call me. He hasn't approached or said anything. What am I supposed to tell the police?"

He shrugged.

"Anyway, Lawrence said, he'll step out of line at some point. Your dad is a mess. Says he hopes he's around when it happens, he'll make sure he won't go around intimidating women anymore."

"That's my dad. He means it too. I'm sorry to hear you're going through that. I'm sure it'll work out one way or the other."

They sat a few moments silently.

"I'm being let go from my job."

"What! You've been there for years."

"My boss says my overall numbers for the year show I'm the weak link. The problem is he's right. I didn't put in the effort I should have."

"If you need some help. I can get your resume out. I'm a believer in knowing people who know people who know people. That's the way you survive in the jungle."

He smiled, "Thanks. If I need to, I'll take you upon it. I've got until the new year."

"That's not long," she said, standing. "You may want to get a jump on things. Think about it." She then went to her room.

He continued sitting in the loft while the daylight faded. Instead of searching around for the light switch, he sat in the darkened room, the only light coming from his computer screen and under Gia's bedroom door.

The house was full of activity. From where he sat, he could hear kids in the family room directly below him playing video games. Brenda's and other women's voices were coming from the kitchen, their volumes drowning out the kids at times. He also heard a loud men's conversation coming from the downstairs game room. He decided to fold up his computer and head down to watch the pool game, so his dad wouldn't accuse him of being anti-social.

31

"There you are, Stephanie. I've been asking about you all day," Brenda said, seeing her step into the kitchen, amid the whirlwind of activity on the eve of Thanksgiving.

"Looks like you guys have everything under control. It smells heavenly in here." Stephanie leaned her elbows on the large island in the center of the room. She counted about five other women and a couple teen girls, chopping, stirring, rinsing, and cleaning. Brenda was barking orders like it was a large-scale construction site. "I need my hard hat and jackhammer, so I can do some damage up in here," she grinned.

"You don't want no part of this," Corene, who was stirring a pot on the stove, said. "Your step-mom is a hard taskmaster. I know what our slave ancestors felt like."

Just then, Gia strolled into the kitchen, her face plastered to her iPad screen. When she glanced up, she was met with a burst of laughter, and Brenda's folded arms.

"Whaaat?" she said, whining. "I said I was coming to help. I'm ready now." She then surveyed the scene and counted how many hands were already at work. "On second thought," she winked at Stephanie, "let's go hang out and leave these ladies to do their thing. I'm not one to get in the way of progress."

Stephanie gave Brenda a side glance.

"Go," Brenda said with a wave. "The two of you will trip over each other, trying to crack an egg. Just stay out of the way."

They heard cheers and jeers as they exited the kitchen; in two seconds flat Gia had coat, purse, and car keys in hand. "Whew! I'm glad you showed up. I've been avoiding that kitchen all day."

"Where are we going?" Stephanie said once they were outside. She had to almost jog to keep up.

"Hmm, that's a good question. I have been invited to a party or two," Gia said, climbing into the car.

"I didn't get dressed for any socializing." Stephanie slid into the passenger side, then noticed, Gia was only wearing jeans but with her mandatory stiletto-heeled boots.

"Don't sweat it, you always look the part." Gia gunned the engine of her sports car, then took a few minutes to look in her rearview mirror. She turned around and scanned both sides of the street, before backing out of the driveway.

"What are you looking for?" Stephanie said.

"It's who. I'm having a problem with a stalker. That's why I'm staying here right now. Mind if we stop over to my place. I never go there alone anymore."

"What's this stalker want?"

"I don't know. I used to work for him. He accused me of getting him fired, threatened me, and for the last month, he's been following me."

"That's scary."

"You're telling me. He won't say anything and maintains a legal distance. But wherever I go, I can count on him showing up at some time, weekdays, and weekends. I haven't noticed him here yet but wouldn't be surprised."

Gia drove to her townhouse and parked in the rear. When she and Stephanie got into the house, before turning on the lights, she scanned the street out front. A car was moving slowly down her street; she could see it was Chase. He'd followed her, or he'd been waiting.

"It's a holiday for God's sake. Don't you have somewhere to go?" Gia said, yelling at the window, while Stephanie watched her.

When she switched on the lights, she saw a piece of paper had been slid under the door. She picked it up and read the words written in red marker:

Your days of peace are over. No one can protect you from me.

Gia went back to the window and saw he had parked his SUV and was watching her house. Seeing her in the window, he smiled and waved.

"Bastard," Gia said, flinging the curtain shut.

"This is scary. How have you been living like this?"

"It's awful. Mainly because there's nothing I can do about it. At least he left this," Gia pointed to the note. "Something concrete I can give to the cops. Lawrence said it was just a matter of time before he'd stop playing it safe."

"What does he want—where did he come from?"

"He was my boss, and we used to—you know."

"Oh," Stephanie said.

"I broke it off, and he moved onto the wrong chick, who got him in trouble. He's been fired and sued. His wife dumped him, and now, as far as I can see, instead of admitting his mistakes and moving on with his life, he does this. Now I wish I would've sued him; bet he's not following those chicks who did."

"What a loser."

Gia sank down on her sofa. "You're telling me. I've asked around. No one has any idea where he is or what he's doing with himself. I've heard he's missed court dates having to do with his divorce.

Stephanie sat down on the couch beside her. "What are you going to do now?"

"The same thing I've been doing the past few weeks, every time I feel cornered. Pray, then call your dad to come and get me. Sorry about this, Stephanie. I thought he'd take the holiday off."

"Is he a big guy?"

Gia shook her head.

"Does he carry weapons that you know of? Is he a gun buff or anything like that?"

"Not when he was rational—what are you driving at?"

"He sounds like a punk to me. A punk who likes to scare girls."

"Yeah?"

"I think we should go over there and have a talk with him. Explain to him that you won't live in fear of him anymore. He can follow you wherever he wants to, but he will not control your life."

Gia shook her head firmly. "Steph, no, he's crazy—okay. I don't mess with crazy people."

"Sometimes you gotta show crazy people you're crazier. You also need to catch him when he's not expecting it."

Stephanie slid from the couch to her knees. "Come on. We're going to pray, and then we're going out there and tell that devil to go to hell."

Gia looked at her for a few minutes, but Stephanie had closed her eyes and started praying.

"Father, we know you haven't given us a spirit of fear...."

Gia listened to Stephanie's prayer, which sounds more like a declaration of war, and tried to echo her words and courage, but she was shaking with terror.

When Stephanie finished, she stood and grabbed her purse. "Is he still out there?"

Gia too scared to stand crawled to the window and peeked through it. "Yes."

Stephanie nodded then pulled a spray vial from her purse.

"How long will it take daddy to get here?"

"If he leaves right away, maybe ten minutes."

"Okay, call him. We'll wait five minutes, then we're going outside to have a talk?"

"What's that?" Gia pointed to the pink vial that looked like perfume Stephanie removed from her purse.

"Pepper spray girl. Do you have one?"

Gia shook her head, and Stephanie produced a second and tossed it to her. "I never leave home without it."

This chick is crazy. Gia thought while examining the slim vial in her hand. Suddenly she wasn't so scared anymore; Stephanie was showing her she didn't have to live her life a powerless victim of another person's dysfunction.

Gia stood next to the window and dialed Lawrence. When he answered, Stephanie, placed a finger to her lips and shook her head.

"He doesn't need to know; he'd just try to talk us out of it. You know how parents can be. They think it's their job to fix everything, but if you don't take this creep on yourself, he'll just keep finding ways to terrorize you when you're alone. Bullies rely on fear."

Gia nodded, agreeing with everything Stephanie said—well, her brain did anyway. Still, she was confused as to what they were supposed to do when they got to Chase's car. Stephanie's phrase 'we're gonna have a talk' was short on details.

"Ready?" Stephanie said, springing up from the couch and heading for the back door, leaving Gia behind.

Gia swallowed a lump in her throat and moved slowly. Stephanie stepped out the door, into the chilly night air, and waited for her.

"Girl, leave that suitcase in the house," she said, referring to Gia's oversized Coach bag. "We ain't taking a trip. Get your keys and weapon, and let's move."

Gia slunk back into the house and re-emerged seconds later.

"Which way?" Stephanie said, starting to walk toward the rear of the small backyard.

"Make a right, and another one past the dumpsters," Gia said.

Once they exited the fence and were out of the yard, they walked through the paved alleyway.

"Take off those shoes, they're making too much noise. What if we need to make a quick getaway, how are you gonna run in those?" She was referring to Gia's stiletto boots.

"My sneakers are in here." Gia walked to her car.

"Your shoes aren't much better," Gia said, noticing Stephanie's heels.

"If I need to run, all I have to do is kick these bad boys off. You can't do that with boots."

Gia nodded and rolled her eyes, trying to remember the last time she'd felt so hapless.

"Now what?" she said, tying her sneakers, noticing the November night was getting colder by the minute. "What are we supposed to accomplish by confronting a crazy person?"

"You say you know this guy, right?" Stephanie, who'd started walking toward the alley, said.

"Yeah, we used to fool around a little," Gia said, speeding up to keep pace.

"Then, you should be able to ask him a simple question like—what do you want." They were lowering their voices as they walked.

"What do I care what he wants?"

"You want him to stop, don't you? If he sees you cowering, hiding, looking for protection, moving out of your own house, for God's sake. You're just feeding the monster. You've got to call him out one way or the other." Stephanie stopped once they had a view of the street.

"Look, we're not going to start a fight. This is going to be a calm and rational conversation. We brought this," she produced the vial, "In case things get ugly." She then eased closer toward the street. "Do you see him?"

Gia heard her heart pounding as she walked past a clump of bushes and pointed. "He's there."

Stephanie noticed her trembling. "Look if you're not okay with this—"

"No. You're right. Everything you said was right—I think."

"The only reason we're doing this is we know we have a back-up. Daddy will be here any minute. Now take a deep breath."

Gia did as instructed.

"Let's go."

"Dad, you still haven't told me what's going on. Why are we headed to Gia's?" Kevin said while sitting in the passenger seat of Lawrence's SUV. "And why did you tell Brenda we're going to the store?"

"I didn't want her to worry. Gia's been having some issues with her old boss."

"She told me something about it."

"She just called, and he's parked outside of her place. She and Stephanie are inside. We'd better get over there quick, and I'll need your help. I know that hot-tempered daughter of mine."

"If Stephanie makes trouble, I'm not pulling her butt out of it."

"She can't help herself. She's not one to sit back and wait for things to happen."

Kevin cut his eyes at his father, then looked out the window grimacing. During their childhood, he was always finishing fights, Stephanie would start. She was always going to war with somebody. Once people realized she was crazy, however, they never started up with her again.

"There he is," Stephanie whispered to Gia. "Staring right at your window. He has no idea we're walking up behind him. Got your spray?"

Gia fumbled in her pocket and pulled out the vial.

"Hold it like this, but keep your hand in your pocket. We're not trying to attack unless the guy becomes unreasonable."

Gia nodded.

"Ready. Go first, and I'll follow. Walk up and act like you've run into him in the mall somewhere. Make nice."

"What!" Gia hissed.

"The element of surprise is on our side. Trust me. I'll be right here with you."

Gia glared at Stephanie as she debated returning to the house. Curiosity, about what would happen, overruled her fear, however. She took a deep breath, fluffed her hair, moistened her lips, and pasted on a smile. She then straightened her posture and began strutting to Chase's car.

"I knew you had it in you," Stephanie whispered with a giggle.

Chase's attention was still focused on the front of her house when she approached from behind and rapped on the windshield. His head nearly hit the roof of the car as he lowered the window and stared at her.

"Hi, Chase. Don't you think it's time for us to talk?"

He continued staring, noticed Stephanie standing behind her, then spoke. "You did your talking, and I told you you'd pay."

"Aren't you getting tired of this?"

"You need to worry about yourself, not me."

"Is that so?" She folded her arms and leaned back on her heels. "Just what is there for me to worry about, huh? Your little chicken games, following me all around town?"

Stephanie's eyes widened as she watched her. *Oh Lord, what have I done? What happened to that scared little girl I had to drag out here. Now she's trying to start the fight.* She tugged lightly on Gia's leather jacket but could tell her stepsister was feeling it. *Hope daddy gets here soon...*

"Look, witch," he said, thrusting his arm out of the window to point a finger in her face. "I told you—"

"And I'm telling you. Follow me wherever you want to. Have a ball doing it. But I will not spend another minute of my life worrying about it. You want to do something to me, well here I am. Take your best shot. I promise you you're going to have a fight on your hands."

"You have a lot of mouth since you've got your friend there to back you up. She's not going to be with you everywhere you go. Remember that while you're talking so tough. You don't tell me when I'm going to make good on my promises. I'll bide my time; I have plenty of it thanks to you."

"She's not going to be here, but you know what, God will."

He exploded in loud laughter, but Stephanie noticed there was no smile on his face.

"Keep praying to your God. You're going to need him after I'm through with you."

"Stephanie and Gia, what do you think you're doing!" Lawrence shouted from his car that had been creeping up the street.

"Let's go. We'll let Daddy deal with him," Stephanie said, trying to lead her away.

"No, I'm sick of this fool. Get out of the car, now!"

"Damn you," he growled, raising the window.

"You don't call the shots here. You asked for this, so get out of the car!" Gia screamed, pounding the glass, while he gunned the engine.

"Gia," Lawrence said, pushing past Stephanie. Chase sped off erratically, nearly colliding with a car at the curb.

The three of them, and Kevin, who'd strode into the scene after parking the SUV, stood on the sidewalk watching Chase's car race down the street.

That punk, Gia thought.

32

"What did you and Stephanie call yourselves doing?" Lawrence said.

Gia avoided his eyes and shivered, suddenly realizing how cold it was outside.

"You were about to jump all over the same guy you've been hiding out at our house to avoid."

"She sure was," Stephanie said, giggling.

Lawrence spun around, "It's not funny. I know you put her up to it."

"Daddy, please give me credit for some sense. We weren't going to jump the guy, at least that wasn't my original suggestion. I thought it best she catch him off guard and confront him."

"With what your good looks?"

"We had this," Gia said, producing the vial of pepper spray.

"Wonderful," Lawrence groaned. "You two are too dangerous to be on your own."

Kevin laughed so hard he had to sit down, as Lawrence, sighing and shaking his head, walked to his car.

"Ask Thelma and Louise if they're coming," he said to Kevin.

"Can you two be trusted to stay out of trouble for the rest of the evening?" He said, smiling at Gia, "You hang out with Steph, no telling where you'll end up."

"We'll be just fine," Gia said, walking toward the house. "Steph, come on, it's cold out here."

He looked on as the two women entered the house. Lawrence startled him with the car horn.

"Are you coming with me or staying with them?" He yelled.

"I don't think I'm invited," Kevin said, sliding into the driver's seat. "Since when are they, such bosom buddies?"

"What's happened?" Brenda said, confronting Lawrence and Kevin at the front door as they entered. Although it was late in the evening, the house was still full of guests, and the kitchen busy with activity.

"I looked around for you, and you were gone, Kevin too. With Gia's situation, I couldn't help wondering."

"I didn't want to worry you unnecessarily, but yes Gia called. The guy had apparently followed her from here to her house, or he was just staked out there."

"Oh, no. He probably knows where Gia's been staying."

"I don't think you have to worry about him anymore," Kevin said, snickering as he ducked into the kitchen.

"What's he talking about? What happened; what's so funny?"

Lawrence tried to wipe the smirk off his own face. "Those girls decided to take matters into their own hands. After calling me, they went outside, armed with pepper spray, and jumped in his face."

"What? That doesn't even sound like Gia."

"No? That's Stephanie all the way."

"My God; what happened?"

"I had to keep Gia off him, that's what happened. He backed down and ran away. I need a drink."

"What do you think is going to happen?" Brenda said as she trailed Lawrence, who'd grabbed a bottle of Cognac that was sitting on the usually empty bar in the dining room.

"He's either going to give up and go away, seeing she's not scared anymore, or he's going to come back more aggressively. In that case, she'll have enough grounds to alert the cops. She'll know soon enough."

"What got into those girls?"

Lawrence shrugged as he sat down with his drink. "I wouldn't have recommended it, but it was probably the right thing to do. She needed to smoke him out, or this thing will drag on for months.

Brenda sighed. "I suppose you're right, but what if—"

"Come on, Bren, you know what-ifs are God's territory."

"Thank you, Stephanie. I owe you, for real," Gia said, throwing her arms around her. "This whole thing had me in such a bad place. You helped me see things the way they really were. I was so scared I'd lost it a little."

Stephanie returned the embrace, then squeezed Gia's shoulder. They were seated in a booth at a local jazz club where a friend of Gia's was having a party. "Don't assume it's over. You're going to have to watch out for yourself even more for the next couple of weeks. He knows he can't keep up that cute stuff, following you and showing up wherever you are. You're not frightened, which will make him more dangerous, or he'll go away. Let's hope for the latter."

"If you could've seen that man a couple years ago," Gia said, shaking her head. "He had it all together. A successful career, great looks, a new wife who was loaded, and he wouldn't stop fooling around on her. I guess I had my part in that also."

"You were seeing him and—"

Gia covered her face and nodded. "I don't know what's wrong with me. I can't stick with one man unless he's married. What made it worse was I kept lying to Kevin. I'd disappear for weekends at a time."

"How'd he find out?"

"He was about to dump me because he knew something was up. We had a fight, and I bragged about it. He's never forgiven me."

"That's my brother. You gotta live up to his high moral standards, as if he really has any."

"All he wanted was for me to belong to him, to be honest, and faithful. I couldn't do it, Steph," Gia shook her head and drained her wine glass.

"Look, I've been around that block—hell, I built it. The reason why you couldn't settle in and do the 'right' thing; that thing that's expected of you is because something was missing. It wasn't supposed to work out. Don't beat yourself up because you weren't the perfect little woman to an imperfect man. If you could've been everything he wanted, he would've let *you* down. That's what we do to each other. I've lied, stolen, and cheated more men, then you can count, but I don't spend a whole lot of time beating myself up about it. There's only one who'll never let you down. Give you one guess. You take on that new DNA, and it changes everything."

"You have a way of making things so clear. I've been beating myself up, feeling like I messed up something that was shaky from the start."

Stephanie winked. "My brother has had a field day, pointing the finger at you, so he doesn't have to look at himself, and you fell right into it."

Gia nodded, then her expression turned serious. " I'm tired of pretending. This stalking thing terrified me; commitment and everything else scares me. I can't seem to move forward."

Stephanie squeezed her hand. "You know what the answer is."

As the music and the crowd grew louder, Gia longed to talk more. She was hungry for Stephanie to tell her the answers, give her the pieces of the puzzle missing from her life. Stephanie, however, had run into some old friends and was engaged in lively conversation. After all, they were at a party, not a counseling session.

She's right...I do know what the answer is.

The next morning Gia descended the stairs in her pajamas and came upon the army of busy cooks, preparing a large breakfast as well as whipping up more delicacies for the Thanksgiving dinner later that day. She was perfectly comfortable, pouring a cup of coffee while being a spectator. "Who's going to eat all this food?"

"Thanksgiving is only once a year, and there are a lot of men in this house today. You know all they do on Thanksgiving is eat, watch the game, sleep, and eat some more," her Aunt Christine said, from across the room.

Brenda smiled at her sister; happy she'd finally loosened up. Their father was seated in the corner of the room, watching everyone, mainly his wife.

"We're getting everything done now so we can make it to the Thanksgiving service today. Are you going to join us?" Brenda said to Gia, with her customary raised eyebrow.

"Maybe," Gia said, walking around her mother, then grabbing a clean plate from the dish rack. "If ya'll feed me properly—that is."

The women in the kitchen burst into laughter, but Gia, loading a plate of eggs, sausage, toast, and grits, was unperturbed.

The Thanksgiving service was brief but spirited and held more meaning for Gia than she expected. She saw herself in everything: every scripture, every song, even the sermon seemed to be about her. She felt no guilt, no fear, but love. Her life was a love story, and her lover had been waiting patiently for her all along. *All this time, I've been running the other direction. Thank you, God, for still loving me.* She remained in deep thought in her seat once the service was over.

"You alright, Gia?" her mother said, while the family made their way out of the church sanctuary.

"I'm fine," Gia said, sounding far away. "I just need a few minutes. I'll meet you at the car." She was unsure as to whether her mother understood that she was having a talk with Jesus—for the first time – heart to heart. She was unwilling to lose that moment to explain.

Brenda stood at the entry of the sanctuary watching Gia sitting alone, and still with her head bowed. *Lord, you are amazing!*

"Brenda and I would fight for hours, about nothing," Marvin Jr., said, delving into his plate piled high with candied yams and collard greens.

"Not true," Brenda said, from the other end of the table. "We found a reason even if we had to invent one."

"Remember that time..." Darwin chimed in, but Brenda was having difficulty following the animated conversation. She was seated beside their father, who required help to eat his meal. She insisted on doing so to allow her mother to enjoy the day. It had been years since the four siblings had been in one place, and for once, everyone was friendly.

"It's been a long time since I've been home," Christine said to Brenda while laying back in a recliner. "I've been avoiding it. Just didn't seem possible we could be a family anymore once daddy got sick."

"It's been hard, but you showed up at the right time. This is the first time in years we've been in the same room without arguing."

"What are your plans for tomorrow? Christine said, yawning.

"We need to take Daddy back to the facility. He's starting to get restless; his routine is all he lives for. I was hoping we could all go along to drop him off. I think it would be good for you to see his living arrangements. You'll have peace knowing he's well cared for. His illness is so hard to deal with."

"I don't know," Christine's mouth twisted. "Leaving my daddy in a nursing home is likely to give me nightmares, not peace."

"Remember," Brenda said, standing. "We're not young anymore, and we might need to be in a residential care facility one day. Do you think Daddy expected to get sick in his mid-seventies? If he had the choice, he would've gone to heaven first."

Christine bristled then glanced at her watch.

"Don't run off mad, Chris," Brenda said, sitting down again. "And forgive me for getting on my soapbox."

Christine nodded, then leaned her head back in the plush chair and closed her eyes. She stayed that way for some time, and Brenda left her alone.

What the rest didn't know was she and her mother had received Marvin's prognosis. There was a strong chance, this would be her father's last Thanksgiving.

33

"Daddy, this is nice. I like your room," Darwin said. Brenda could see tears welling in her brother's eyes.

"It's nice," Marvin Sr echoed, his relief at being back in familiar surroundings was evident. He'd become jovial and talkative as soon as he'd entered the facility, followed by his wife, children, and all the grand and great grands who'd come to town for the holiday.

Brenda made a mental note to contact her father's siblings, two sisters, and invite them to come for Christmas. They knew he was sick, but she wanted to make sure they had an opportunity to see him, still looking like himself. The disease was affecting his features.

"Mr. Marvin, you sure have a beautiful family," Eugenia, his favorite nursing assistant, said as she helped him get comfortable.

Marvin nodded though he was oblivious to the crowd around him. Eugenia, who took care of him most days, was the only person that mattered to him at that moment.

"Time to say, goodbye daddy," Brenda said, for the benefit of her siblings, all of whom were wrestling emotionally.

Christine threw her arms around her father's neck, then rushed out of the room, her husband trailing behind her. Marvin and Darwin said their goodbyes to their father together, each standing beside him, a hand on his shoulder. Then the grandkids took their turns.

Everyone's mood was subdued during the drive to a nearby restaurant where they had lunch. The festive holiday had ended.

Family members began departing town early the next morning, with a sense that the next time they'd get together could be a more somber occasion.

"You're late."

Stephanie glanced up from her laptop and saw Dan Lovelace, the mission director, standing in the doorway. "I wasn't aware I was on your clock. Am I in your way or something?" She frowned. "County services never said I needed to—"

"Calm down, Ms. Foster," he said, entering the room. "That was my weak attempt at humor."

"That's what you call a joke?" She screwed up her face and laid down the papers she'd been holding. He claimed to be joking, but there was no trace of humor in his expression.

"How have you been Ms. Foster, I've noticed you haven't been around for a while," he said, putting down his bag, and taking a seat at his desk.

"Fine," she said, watching him. He'd never once stopped to make small talk. In fact, he treated her as if she were a nuisance.

"I was a little worried you wouldn't be back. I had to check myself. I haven't been all that nice."

"Humph, you got that right," Stephanie said. "If it makes you feel any better, you're not the only one. Most of the people who run the shelters, treat me like what I do is a joke."

"Come on, Ms. Foster."

"Stephanie, please since you're being nice."

"Stephanie, I never meant to treat you that way; it's just when you do this type of work you can get worn out with people in general, no matter how beautiful they are."

Stephanie blinked twice and placed a hand to her chest. "Oh my, charming as well as," she made a gesture of leaning back to get a full view of him, "handsome. Why have I never noticed before?"

He grinned. "I think you've had enough fun at my expense. I was hoping for the opportunity to apologize for the way I've treated you. I hope you accept," he said, walking toward the door.

"Absolutely. Feel free to apologize to me *an-nee-time*," Stephanie said, pursing her lips; she could see him blushing as he turned and left the room. "Yessir—anytime," she smiled and repeated to herself.

"Keep your chin up, son, something will open up. The job market is tough, but people are being hired every day. You might have to take something to get you by but," Lawrence paused to lean over and take his pool shot.

"I know that, Dad," Kevin said. "I'll do what I need to do, but the phone isn't ringing at all. No bites, no nibbles, no prospects. It can't keep going this way."

Lawrence exhaled loudly. Of all his children, his son whined the most. "Have you prayed about this at all? There's nothing I can tell you if you're not willing to ask God. I have no answers."

"What am I supposed to say? God, I know you haven't heard from me in a while, matter of fact, the last time was that car wreck four years ago—the one you got me out of without a scratch."

"Good start, son. Now take your shot," he said, gesturing to the pool table.

"You're not listening."

"Yes, I am listening. Now take the shot."

Kevin leaned over the pool table grumbling, and after he took the shot, hitting the five ball into the corner pocket, he turned to his dad so he could brag. Lawrence, however, had put away his cue stick and left the room.

Gia had been praying throughout the day every day, for weeks. Having discovered there was always something to talk to God about when there was no one else she could confide in or trust. After spotting

Chase waiting in his car, across the street from her job, as she was leaving for the day, she began praying for him also.

As she made her way to her car in the employee parking lot, she halted before getting in. Her thoughts about him prevented her from burrowing into the safety of her automobile. He would only follow her; how safe would that be?

She took a breath, deposited her belongings onto the back seat then, walked to Chase's SUV.

Maybe it's not him, perhaps I'm just paranoid, she thought as she edged closer to the vehicle, but he turned and scowled as she approached. Their eyes locked. He glared at her as if he were paralyzed, hate-filled his eyes, while his hands gripped the steering wheel like he was going to rip it out. The only thing she read in his expression was murder. She motioned for him to lower the window. He did so while staring at her like he was ready to strangle her right there on the street. *What if he has a gun?*

"Not a good idea for you to come over here," he said through clenched teeth.

"Can we talk?"

"You thought I was gone, didn't you. Thought you were safe. I wanted you to think that, but you won't get rid of me. I'll be around every time you breathe."

"Okay, fine," Gia said, nodding, then taking a deep breath, feeling the fear leaving. "I just want you to know that whenever you see me, wherever you follow me, I'm not afraid of you. I'm praying for you every moment that God will give you the help and guidance you need."

"Do you think saying that crap is supposed to protect you?"

"As you can see, I don't care about me anymore. I care about you; about what's happened to you. You can be the man you were again, but this time you can be even better."

"Save the sermon."

"You had an incredible mind, and I learned so much from you. I want to see you become that man again."

"I'm ruined, because of you and bitches like you. I got nothing left but a little payback."

"That's not true," she said, aware that she was standing on a busy street. She felt crazy. "Do you mind if I pray for you, right now."

"Give me a break, all of a sudden you're Mother Teresa?"

She bowed her head slightly, "Father God, you know what your son needs, what he's searching for—" She was startled when he suddenly pulled off, causing her to stumble into the street. Fortunately, she landed behind a parked car and not in the lane of traffic.

"You did what? You approached that maniac; what if he had a gun? You're taking too many cues from Stephanie," Lawrence said when Gia recounted to him the episode with Chase that afternoon. They were at the dinner table, as Gia drove straight to their house after being helped off the ground by some passersby.

"Gia, how could you," Brenda chimed in. "He knocked you down; he could have run you over." She then set a plate of smothered turkey wings, macaroni and cheese, and green beans in front of her. Gia grabbed her fork.

"Take your mind off your plate for a minute. This has got to stop," Lawrence said, leaning across the table so she would look at him. "I know Stephanie meant well, and she gets away with that kind of stuff, but she's lived a tougher life. She thinks she knows how to handle herself. I'm not so sure but—"

"It has nothing to do with Stephanie this time, really. I was trusting the Lord. He wouldn't let me cower in fear in my car, while Chase follows me from place to place."

Lawrence stared at her, wanting to contradict, but her expressions of faith awakened him.

"I'm glad you're okay, baby. Do you think it's finally over?" Brenda said, offering Gia butter for her dinner roll.

34

"Hello, Mr. Lovelace, it's nice to see you outside of your office," Stephanie said to Dan as he walked up to her after church service. Running into him had been a pleasant surprise.

"Same here, but I thought we had an understanding," he said, folding his arms, his expression unsmiling. Stephanie frowned.

"My name is Dan." He burst into a grin.

She nodded and rolled her eyes while they stood in the aisle between the rows of pews. The other congregants were slowly making their way to the exits. "Yes, I remember your name. I didn't want to assume the informality away from the office. Your boo might be listening; wouldn't want her to get the wrong idea." She made a gesture of looking for his companion.

"That was subtle," he smirked.

She tipped her head to the side, smiled, and waited.

"There is no 'boo' here or anywhere else. I'm not in a relationship right now, and I've never been married.

She smiled, then turned to the friend she'd come to church with, who was conversing a few feet away. "I'll call you later, Girl." Then, linking arms with Dan and showing him all her teeth, she allowed him to escort her out of the building. "This is my first time visiting this church. Are you a member here?" She said as they strolled toward the parking lot.

Gia sat at her desk at work, tapping her pen on the blotter, feeling uneasy. It had been over a month since the episode with Chase. She hadn't seen or heard from him since, and while she was happy and relieved, she wondered what had happened to him. Hoping he'd come back to sanity and hadn't merely shifted his anger onto another target.

She closed her eyes and took a few moments, as she did every day, to pray for Chase and was happy for the peaceful atmosphere at work that allowed her those little breaks.

Scanning her computer screen reviewing the sales numbers for her division, she noticed her results were down for the fiscal year to date. It had been her tendency to spring into action and make everyone who worked for her miserable until the numbers improved. She'd built her career and reputation on being proactive and quick to respond. While also firing underperformers as necessary

That's not how she did things now. Neither numbers nor dollars seemed worth the commotion. She was learning that a good leader develops their people without threatening them. Yes, her numbers were down now, but the team she was bringing together had great potential. And unlike the numbers-driven environment of her previous employer, her current management supported her desire to build her team. She wasn't putting in the long hours, wasn't overly stressed, and wasn't pressuring herself or anyone else.

She leaned her head back, closed her eyes then took a deep breath before diving into the strategy to get the numbers closer to where they needed to be. Gazing out the window at the snow-covered landscape, she anticipated the day when her team would take the lead as the goal setters in their organization by their performance. *Before it's all over, they'll have to keep revising the numbers to keep pace with us,* she thought, a smile forming on her lips.

"The way I hear it, his family had filed a missing person report on him; he'd disappeared. Cops found him and closed the case. He wanted to stay missing. Then a little over a month ago, Chase showed up at his wife's door, and she let him stay; they're trying to work things out."

"I'm glad to hear it," Gia said to her former co-worker Melody while they were having lunch. "I'd run into him a couple times, and he was over the edge."

"I heard he'd been sending threatening correspondence and harassing phone calls, but nobody could prove it was him."

Gia lifted her glass of iced tea, "Let's make a toast to God who can bring us all back when we've gone over the edge, ' 'cause we've all been there.

Melody lifted her glass. "You got that right."

"You're a feisty woman with style."

"And?" Stephanie said to Dan as they were sharing another meal together, the third one that week. This time instead of a restaurant, they were having Chinese take-out in his office as they both had to work late that evening.

"You're a woman of God. What else do you want me to say? I like you because I do. I don't have any long-winded explanations. I'm not a wordy guy."

Stephanie shook her head and focused on her egg roll.

"Let me turn this conversation around, tell me why you like me—assuming you do, of course." She laughed.

"No, I'm serious you grill me every time I ask you out, but you have yet to turn me down. Why; are you simply curious as to my motivations?"

"That's a silly question."

"My point exactly."

"You're a man, you work every day, you're not bad to look at, and you're a Christian. Even if I weren't attracted to you, I'd have to do a double-take."

"Why, thank you," he said with a mock bow.

"Don't get me wrong. I know I'm cute."

"Do you really?" Dan raised an eyebrow.

" I also have my baggage and a whole lot of goblins in my closet liable to jump out and do a little dance at any moment."

"So, I have a past."

"Nothing like mine."

"I can imagine," he said, holding up his hand. "You've given me enough obvious hints to figure out the rest. I like the you, I see now. The woman who doesn't pretend she's been an angel all her life. Your honesty is refreshing, but you don't need to throw your past in my face. It doesn't change anything."

"Are you for real? My siblings are going to love you; they've made careers out of berating me about my life."

"Really?"

"Please don't turn therapist on me," she said, rolling her eyes while dousing her food with soy sauce.

"Can't help it; that's my profession. You need to get beyond what others think, but I suspect the real issue lies in what you think of you." He took the fork from her hand and gently pulled her to a seat next to him. "I pray that one day you'll see yourself the way I see you. The time you put in helping people when you could be somewhere doing for yourself."

"I do get paid," Stephanie said.

"You call that getting paid? You'd do better panhandling."

Stephanie laughed. "You make me sound so charitable and generous. I don't even like people that much; I simply like what I do. This is about me, not some grandiose desire I have to save the world."

"That's how God gets us to a place where we're helping people while we help ourselves. He gives us something we love doing. I didn't go to school for all the years I did to run a homeless shelter; believe me, I had other plans. But as an intern, while I was working on my masters, I saw so many of the people charged with caring for the weak, willing to give up and throw them away. This job was thrust upon me because I challenged assumptions. I believed we could take care of people's basic needs while treating them with dignity. It's been a rough ride, and reality has torn holes into many of my ideals, but we still manage to do amazing work with the resources we receive. I'm always challenged to do more." Suddenly he looked around as if he'd forgotten where he was. "I'm sorry," he smiled.

"No need to apologize."

"The point I was trying to make before I went into my sermon was, God is working in your life—accept it, embrace it, and stop trying to discount it."

Stephanie couldn't recall any of the cute, sharp retorts she was known for. The passion in his words made anything she thought to say seem silly and out of place. She felt herself doing what he'd suggested, accept that he liked and admired her as much as she did him, and the path God had placed before her, which seemed to make no sense.

"I'm speechless for the first time in my life."

He chuckled, then took her hand and kissed it. "Don't worry, if it lasts too long, I'll call a doctor."

35

Get ready, today might be the day, Kevin told himself that morning, as he had each morning the previous two weeks. His job was to have ended effective the first day of the new year, but it was now mid-January.

"Don't worry about that now, there'll be plenty of time after the holidays for you to pack up and leave," Zach told him on December 30th, when he started packing up his desk. No one had said a word since.

"I don't know what to tell you," Zach said on Friday when Kevin asked when his last day would be. He was in no hurry but was reluctant to get comfortable.

That morning, as Kevin feared, Zach was waiting at his cubicle as he walked in; a lump formed in his throat.

"Ease up, young man," Zach said, noticing Kevin's sagging countenance, "it's a new account I need you to start working on, not a funeral," he laughed and slapped him on the back.

"A new account, but I thought—"

"You didn't get my e-mail? You must've been gone for the day. I called corporate on Friday, and they've informed me the staff reduction plan has been canceled."

"You mean postponed," Kevin said, hanging up his coat and dropping into a chair.

"They used the word canceled, so I'm relaying to you what I was told. Seems a fat new contract was signed, and we can't get rid of anybody. There are some managers pretty ticked off about it; some good people got pushed out the door, and now they'll need to be replaced. Good thing you didn't bail, or I'd have been in the same boat."

Kevin leaned his elbows on his desk and squeezed his eyes closed.

"Boy, if I didn't know better, I'd swear those are tears," Zach said. "Welcome back and remember the emotion of this moment in a few months when the work is piled so high you won't be able to see your desk." He chuckled as he walked out.

"That's what the man said, dad. My lay-off has been canceled. Every time I think about it, I start laughing, then the tears start forming because I know this was God from start to finish.

"This deserves a celebration. Come over for dinner, I'll tell Brenda to make your favorite," Lawrence said, still laughing as they hung up.

Later that night, Brenda placed a bowl of shrimp jambalaya in front of Kevin and smiled. "Congratulations, I hear you have a lot to thank God for.

Epilogue

"Deacon Marvin loved the Lord. He stayed committed to his service; even in his illness, the work of God's house was on his mind..." the Pastor's voice rang clear that morning in the church sanctuary as he eulogized Marvin Sr, who'd died suddenly, on a bright June morning the week prior.

Brenda's tears flowed as she was going to miss her dad, but Alzheimer's had taken him from her long before.

"Daddy!" Christine wailed from the end of the pew to her right. "I want my Daddy!"

Her husband sat helplessly as the two white-uniformed church nurses worked on her, vigorously flapping the funeral home fans, and administering smelling salts. Brenda was grateful Lawrence, and her other siblings separated them. It wouldn't do for her to slap her sister, in front of the congregants, the pastor, and their father's casket. She shot Lawrence a side glance, which he returned, and she detected laughter in his eyes, while his expression remained solemn.

Despite Christine's hysterics, she appreciated the beauty with which her father's pastor delivered his remarks. *Nobody preaches a better funeral.* She believed this time he was especially eloquent and thanked God for that also.

The service was brief, but Brenda felt it was powerful, accurately reflecting her father's life of devotion to the Lord. He was a man of few words, and nobody but he knew the hours he'd spent serving in the church, ensuring it was clean and ready for service. He did it for God and didn't care who knew.

Stephanie and Dan sat near the rear of the church; his arm draped around her shoulders. It was a sad day for her family, but there were better days ahead. The following weekend, in another church, she and Dan were going to be married.

"He left behind a powerful legacy. That's what we should all live for," Dan said, whispering. "I'm sorry I never knew him." Stephanie smiled and nodded. She'd only met Marvin Senior a few times and was filled with admiration hearing the impact of his life.

"Are you okay?" Kevin said in Gia's ear, having moved to a seat behind her. He'd been sitting two rows back and could see her shoulders heaving as she sobbed silently. She shook her head, unable to answer.

His sister Margot, who sat beside her, was struggling to keep her four-year-old quiet. She slid over immediately so he could take the seat next to Gia.

Once next to her, Gia buried her face in his chest and allowed her tears to flow. As the female soloist belted out an A cappella rendition of His Eye Is on the Sparrow and multicolored sunlight flooded the sanctuary through the stained-glass windows, Kevin cradled her, stroking her back and resting his head on hers. Mindful of the occasion, he stifled the delight wanting to burst forth on his face, during the funeral.